A Requiem For The Dead

A REQUIEM FOR THE DEAD

A BENOIT AND DAYNE MYSTERY

WINTER AUSTIN

TULE
PUBLISHING

DEDICATION

To my parents, Chris and Brenda
For instilling in me the love of reading.
And an unquenchable thirst for murder and mayhem.

CHAPTER ONE

Day 1: Sunday, February 25, 4:32 a.m.

THE LEATHER SATCHEL slid past the edge of her shoulder and slipped off her arm, hitting the floor upside down. Files, papers, and an odd assortment of office paraphernalia scattered across the tile flooring.

"Shit."

Dr. Olivia Remington-Thorpe kicked the garage door shut and flung aside her pocketbook, keys, and coat. This was just the crap icing on the shit cake after the night she had. God, how she hated working the ER on a full moon in late February after Juniper, Iowa, had seen another snowstorm blow through and melt away. Between the cabin fever overtaking the younger generation with their attempts to pull off some stupid stunt they saw on social media and a sudden uptick in drug overdoses, she'd had enough. The lone saving grace to redeem this awful night? She hadn't been needed for an autopsy. Thank God for small mercies.

Squatting down, she surveyed the mess. Fatigue dragged on her shoulders. The tight muscles in her back and neck made for an unrelenting pounding in her head. She could barely hold her eyes open.

Screw it.

If Dominic didn't like it when he came home, then he

could damn well pick it up. It wasn't like her husband was going to be around any time soon. He'd turned scarcity into a fine art. Taking all the shifts opposite of her so as to not be in the house at the same time as she.

Her skin tightened as she grew flush. Dominic did this on purpose. For more than a year he'd used these types of passive aggressive tactics instead of speaking with her. Which was fine by her, since all they seemed to do when they were together was fight. If she didn't know any better, she'd swear he started the arguments in order to keep her at bay.

Olivia had noticed fractures in their marriage before the clashes—before she'd committed a grievous *faux pas*—and had brushed them off as mere nuisances of their professions, but it seemed the cracks were more than skin deep for Dominic. No one in their circle of friends knew about their strained relationship. They'd retained the facade of a happy marriage in front of prying eyes of those who could discover they were strangers living in the same house. No matter what she did to repair the damage, Dominic would retreat or cut her down. Divorce had been brought up, but neither of them seemed to want to get around to putting it into motion.

Olivia stepped over the chaos, leaving it behind to head upstairs to the master bedroom she had commandeered. As she shuffled along the hallway, she let her hair loose from its tie and scratched her scalp. Soaking in a hot Epsom salt bath sounded wonderful. Maybe a bit of lavender to ease the aches and pains and soothe the raging beast inside. Add a cup of chamomile tea and it would do her good. Probably help her go right to sleep.

A squeak from the kitchen brought her to a halt. Slowly,

she turned, listening. The faint click of bone china made her stiffen. Was Dominic home? How could he be? He should be in the ER. Olivia saw his vehicle in the doctors' parking lot before she left. She had, hadn't she? As tired as she was, it was probable she mistook someone else's SUV for his.

The soft sound of the refrigerator resealing made her scrunch her nose. There was no mistaking that noise for her wearied brain playing tricks on her. Someone was in the kitchen.

Maybe Dominic was home. Olivia consulted her watch: 4:41. Was he running late? Or did he have a delayed start at the ER, so he hadn't left yet? All possible.

Despite their animosity toward each other, Dominic—ever the gentleman—left the garage space for her use and put his car behind the house under the car port. When he parked there, she didn't see his vehicle because she pulled straight into the garage and entered the house through the connected doorway.

More sounds came from the kitchen, further piquing her interest. She abandoned her plan for a hot bath and redirected course for the swinging door dividing the hall from the kitchen. She pushed the door inward and peeked around the edge.

No one was there.

The lights mounted under the wall cabinets were on, the only illumination in the kitchen. A single teacup and saucer sat in the center of the island counter. Steam rose from the delicate china. Olivia stepped inside the kitchen and glanced around, but there was no sign of whomever made the tea and left it. She crept up to the counter and studied the teacup.

The tea had just begun to steep, the water not quite dark enough. She moved to the stove where the kettle sat and found it hot to the touch. Why hadn't she heard the whistle?

Olivia wrenched around at the scuffing noise behind her.

CHAPTER TWO

Sunday, February 25, 7:48 a.m.—3 Hours Missing

JUNIPER, IOWA, RANG in the new year with temperatures in the single digits and wind chills in the negatives. The follow-up was a snowfall every weekend for the next month. By February, the whole of the Midwest was over winter. But winter was far from over in Iowa. A few more snowfalls preceded a rash of days with unseasonably warm weather. Then another bout of snow to cover up the mud.

Deputy Detective Lila Dayne was not unaccustomed to large snowfalls and bitterly cold temps, having lived a goodly amount of her life in Chicago. However, the open fields and rural areas of Iowa rivaled the windiest, and chilliest, day Chicago could conjure up. Back in the day, none of this would faze her. Now, after surviving two assaults that should have killed her and several strenuous years as a law enforcement officer, she wasn't too keen on the cold.

With March a few days away, she was looking forward to spring and warmer temperatures. The full moon had not been a welcome sight last night. By the looks of the reports scattered across her desk from the night shift, it had been a doozie.

Everyone was suffering from a horrendous case of cabin fever, and Lila didn't blame them as she glared at the jiggling legs of the only other deputy in the office. The squeaking noise from his duty holster and chair joining the jangling of a loose zipper on his coat.

"Meyer, if you don't stop doing the jitterbug, I'll come over there and duct tape you to the chair."

Deputy Brent Meyer stilled his bobbing knees. "Sorry." He swatted the computer monitor. "Nothing wants to load."

"You trying to hamster wheel it won't make it work any faster."

He grumbled something.

"What?"

Meyer's face flushed red. "I said, I wish this county would get its ass in gear and get caught up with the times. These broadband speeds are stupid slow."

Lila stifled a yawn—too many early mornings and long days. "You bring that up with the local internet provider. Better yet, tell the county commissioners."

"That bunch of outdated hack jobs won't listen."

She grinned. In the last few years, Meyer had finally grown into himself and grew bolder in his verbal assessment of the county and world at large. Or he was feeling the drain because the department was running on fewer people and longer shifts. The added weight tended to make him grouchy as much as it did her.

For the last four months, Lila and Interim Sheriff Raphael Fontaine had been trading off supervisor duties while their fearless leader recovered from self-made complications after surgery. Eckardt County Sheriff's Department was not only missing its sheriff but two deputies as well. One was out after being seriously injured with a shattered leg and the other coping with the fallout from an arrest gone wrong. Those left were putting in the extra work to cover for their partners, but the stress was getting to them. A parade of attorneys, state investigators parading in and out following up on all the loose ends from October didn't help. And a nosey public, who claimed they were well-intentioned but were nothing more than busybodies looking for the juicy gossip to bolster their questionable status in the community.

Lila and Fontaine were still sorting out the mess left behind from the Halloween murders. Sheriff Elizabeth Benoit's risky behavior and emotional state during the investigation into those murders put the department in a precarious legal position. Lawyers from all sides were having a field day with this fiasco. Lila didn't know how much longer she could endure the pressure. Top-notch investigator she might be. Leader, she was not.

She stared at the organized desk across from hers. Her usual partner—and lover?—Kyle Lundquist had pulled night duty. His empty chair was a stark reminder she hadn't seen him in the last two days. She'd hoped to get into the office early enough today to at least check on him, but he'd either clocked out early or just didn't bother to stop in.

Since Halloween night, when he'd discovered the truth behind his older sister's death and learned why his younger sister was riddled with anxiety, Kyle had withdrawn from Lila, their already-strained relationship further complicated by his inability to allow her to help him. His absence continued to create an ever-widening wound to Lila's already-damaged soul.

The telltale rapid clink of metal dragged her from her

mulling. Meyer's damn leg was at it again.

"Meyer, I swear to God ..."

The dispatch line ringing to life saved the deputy from her wrath. He bolted from his seat and hurried over to answer the phone. Their usual day dispatcher was dealing with a nasty respiratory infection, and the deputies were handling the calls on their own to give their night dispatcher her time to sleep. God forbid she be the next to go down and leave them even more understaffed.

"Eckardt County Sheriff's Office," Meyer answered.

Letting him deal with the call, Lila rose from her chair and ambled over to the coffeepot. Adding more caffeine to her already-taxed system wasn't a good idea, but right now, she didn't give two shits.

"Ma'am, would you repeat yourself? I didn't quite catch that."

Lila stopped midway to the coffee station and turned back to Meyer. If he was missing out on what the caller was saying, chances were they were on a cell phone and the connection was breaking up.

He bobbed his head twice, still listening. "Ma'am, I understand, but ..."

Abandoning her quest for more jitters and her mug, Lila joined Meyer at the dispatcher's desk. He looked up at her, his eyes widening. Perspiration glistened on his forehead. Lila held out her hand asking for the handset. He shook his head.

"Yes, ma'am, we'll be there as soon as we can." He tucked the handset between his shoulder and head and searched for something on the dispatcher's desk. After finding a pad and pen, he scribbled down an address. "It's going to take some time. Please, keep the area clear of anyone else." He wrote down a name. "Yes, I'll be sure she gets the message."

Lila grabbed the pad from him. The address was on the far southeastern edge of Eckardt County, cornered by the Des Moines River and the Mississippi, with miles of wild timber, open fields of tangled grasses, and swamps. Not many people lived there, and those who did weren't keen on law enforcement. Resident Kathy Miller was unfamiliar to Lila.

Meyer hung up and stood. "I have no idea what is out there. Kathy isn't one to convey a lot of information over the phone."

"We'll leave now." Lila headed back to her desk and grabbed her coat. "Who's to get the message?"

"She wanted me to tell the sheriff to get there," he said as he slid his arms into his coat.

"Not happening." Lila punched a few buttons on the dispatcher phone to forward calls to her cell.

"Why I said I'd pass on the message." Meyer started for the hallway with Lila coming on his heels. "We should alert Fontaine."

"After we assess the situation," she said as they strode down the hall.

"Separate units?" he asked.

"Yes. In case we get another call, we need to respond."

Meyer pushed through the door. "You're the boss."

Not really, but whatever.

LILA ALLOWED MEYER to lead the way. They found Kathy Miller bundled in an overly large, faded red-and-black checked coat, standing on the side of the road. Meyer and then Lila parked behind an ancient livestock trailer hooked to an equally ancient pickup truck.

Lila was out of her unit first, her breath clouding up in the chilly morning air. She adjusted her duty belt and carefully picked her way down the still snow-drifted ditch.

Kathy Miller inched her way toward Lila. She wore tall black boots caked with mud and flecks of pine shavings. The tip of her nose was cherry red, and a wild mess of white-streaked brown curls poked out from under a bright orange stocking hat.

"Where's Sheriff Benoit?" she asked.

"Busy at the moment. I'm Deputy Dayne. What seems to be the problem?"

Kathy Miller glanced over Lila's shoulder as Meyer joined them. "You look just like your daddy, boy."

Lila didn't have to guess Meyer's reaction to such a statement. Since the day he'd started working in the department, he'd get the same remarks from people all over Eckardt County, and every time, he'd flush red but kept his comments to himself. He did look a little like his father, but that was as far as Meyer wanted the resemblance to go. The two had a strained relationship, of which Meyer barely cultivated. Pratt Meyer was a hard man to get along with.

"Ms. Miller, the problem?" Lila pressed, getting the woman's attention back to her.

"Might be best to show you. Follow me."

Kathy Miller led them through a field of pale-gold grasses, bent and intertwined with weeds. Patches of snow, hard and crusty from the consistent thawing and freezing, crunched under foot. Kathy Miller didn't say a word as she huffed and puffed her way over the third of a mile of snarled terrain.

"What were you doing back here?" Lila asked as she struggled through the grass.

"I live just up the road. My heifer got loose, and I had to track her down. Found her out here."

"Where's the cow now?"

Kathy pointed back toward their vehicles. "In the trailer."

Lila eyed the woman. She didn't need to ask how Kathy managed to wrangle the heifer into the trailer alone. Over the years of residing in Iowa, Lila had learned to appreciate the type of women who lived in Eckardt County. Kathy belonged to what Lila called the no-nonsense group, women who found ways to handle anything life threw at them from running farms alone or manning their own businesses. A class of woman Elizabeth Benoit belonged in.

"This way." Kathy set off to their right.

Another fifty or so yards they broke through the pockets of trees and tangled multiflora rose and emerged into another overgrown pasture.

Kathy stopped and pointed at the shadowed structure nestled between two towering oaks. "There. See it?"

"The shack?" Lila asked.

"It's not so much the shack as what's behind it."

Lila glanced at Meyer, then focused on Kathy. "What's behind it?"

Kathy just wiggled deeper into her coat and flicked her hand in the direction of the ominous shack. Apparently, this was as far as Kathy went.

"Is the place at least empty?" Lila asked.

"Ain't no one used it in years. I'm surprised it's still standing."

"Who's property is this?" Lila persisted.

"It ain't mine," Kathy remarked. She wagged her hand again then tucked it under her arm.

With a sigh, Lila waved Meyer forward and they both hiked through the crunchy pasture.

"Okay, homeboy, this ground has to belong to someone, and you're the residential know-it-all," Lila said as they trampled the stiff grass.

"It belonged to the Norwood family, but the estate is in probate," Meyer said. "The widow passed away three years ago, and her sole remaining relative was estranged; some long-distant cousin. No one can seem to find him, and the county has better things to do apparently than to get this place sold."

Like make Lila's life a living hell while the commissioners tried to find ways to make Sheriff Benoit pay for exposing more of their dirty secrets.

At the structure, Lila slowed her pace and cautiously rounded the aged and moss-covered building, squeezing between it and the oak.

She pulled up short. "My God."

Meyer came to stand at her right side. "Are those …"

"Bones."

Hundreds of bones. Scattered over an area of fifty or

more feet. It was like someone had opened a bunch of coffins and just tossed out the bodies. The skeletal remains near them still had portions of clothing attached.

"Is this a killer's dumping ground?" Meyer whispered.

A parade of spiders scurried down Lila's spine. She shivered violently at the idea that her new home had become a killer's area of focus. No. This wasn't right for a serial killer. She was as close to an expert on serial killers as one in law enforcement could come. This place was too disorganized for a serial killer. It looked too much like a—

"Battleground," she said.

"What?" Meyer asked.

"It looks like a battleground. Like they were killed here and just left as is."

"Who would do that? And how did we not hear about it sooner?"

"Don't know. Don't care at the moment." Lila licked her suddenly dry lips. "We need Des Moines for this." Des Moines being the Department of Criminal Investigations, the only place large enough and staffed with people more qualified to handle a crime scene of this caliber.

"You want to call them or me?"

She turned away from the makeshift graveyard. "I will. First, we need to secure this whole area and find out how far it goes."

Lila sensed deep in her gut there was a wide swath of carnage, and they had just spotted the tip of the iceberg.

CHAPTER THREE

Sunday, February 25, 9:23 a.m.—5 Hours Missing

S HERIFF ELIZABETH BENOIT was trapped. Stuck between the proverbial rock and a hard place. One rock, ex-husband Joel Fontaine. One hard place, Undersheriff Raphael "Rafe" Fontaine.

Two weeks ago, the brothers had secreted her out to the far reaches of the Fontaine family property and isolated her in a cozy little hunting cabin. Reason? Because she was a rebel. Apparently, she was trying to make her healing body relapse, again, and thus ruining her chances of continuing her responsibilities as sheriff. Also, because the brothers were fed up with trying to keep away people who wanted her back doing her job full-time before she should.

While Rafe continued to supervise the sheriff's department and uphold his duties, Joel stayed at the cabin to babysit Elizabeth.

Oh, those two had tried plying all manner of apologetic gifts and kiss-assery to appease their captive. Elizabeth was having none of it.

Fourteen days away from her home, her sister, and her people was fourteen days enough.

She stared at the brothers across the rough-hewn table with a mug of steaming cocoa nestled in between her intertwined hands. Rafe had returned from the night shift and was still wearing his uniform. Joel looked like he was about to prowl the woods to stalk prey of the four-legged kind.

Curled at her feet under the table, Bentley, Elizabeth's constant canine companion, snored away. The red border collie was in heaven clear out here in the middle of nowhere to have run of the timber and chase the recently awakened squirrels and rabbits.

"Boys."

Both men scowled at her chosen word. Oh, yes, she'd goad them 'til the cows came home.

"This little scheme to lock me away is over. I'm fully healed. Clean bill of health. It's time for me to get back to work."

Joel gave his brother a sly glance, then slumped back in his chair. "Ehh, yeah, no."

"I tend to agree." Rafe's deep gravelly voice was a stark contrast to his brother's whiskey-smooth one. "You came close to killing yourself with a hemorrhage, an infection, and had to have surgery again to repair the damage you did to yourself. Nah. You stay put."

She glared at the two. "At my last visit, Dominic said I was cleared for light duty."

"*If.*" Rafe pointed at the ceiling as he leaned closer to the table. "If you worked only two to three hours a day. You were doing no such thing."

"Whatever. You know as sheriff that's not enough time in a day to do the job."

Joel chuckled. "Maybe so." He shifted to hook a bulky arm over the chair's backrest. "There was the little matter of the follow-up to the Halloween murders. The murders you were explicitly told to stay out of and got involved in up to your pretty little head."

His last jab earned him a hard glare from his brother, which Joel ignored. When he looked at Elizabeth with her own perturbed glare, she felt a healthy dose of satisfaction at his peach-faced cringe. Over the years of working in and around a male-centered space, Elizabeth had perfected her soul-crushing stare of disgust when misogyny was uttered in her presence.

"How were we ever married?"

Joel gave her a shit-eating grin. The fact he was unfazed by her ire drove home one of the reasons they'd divorced.

"We're digressing here," Rafe interjected. "Give it a few more days, Ellie. Then—" His phone vibrated an incoming message. With a frown, he picked up the electronic device.

The cabin was positioned far from cell towers and reception for anything other than text messages was shoddy at best. This was a hunting lodge. Meant to be as far off the grid as they could allow.

Elizabeth lifted her mug and sipped the cooling cocoa, watching the concern play with Rafe's rugged features. She wished like hell life would stop mucking up her chances with him.

She felt her ex's piercing stare. She met his all-knowing gaze. A few years back, Joel had flat out told her to stop pussyfooting around and get with his brother. He'd given his blessing, knowing that whatever remained between them of their long-over marriage was gone. Elizabeth had never acted on her attraction. Neither had Rafe, too worried about what the rest of the world would think of the undersheriff and sheriff hooking up.

"Problems?" Joel asked, tearing his gaze from Elizabeth and focusing on his brother.

"Maybe." Rafe placed his phone face down on the table. There was a darkness flitting in his eyes.

Elizabeth knew that look. Something bad had happened in her county. "Rafe?"

He shook his head and stood, grabbing up his phone. "Joel, she's not to leave." He went to the cabin door.

Elizabeth stood. "Damn it, Rafe, I'm fine."

He took his coat down from the pegged board beside the door. "Ellie, for once"—he looked back at her as he slid into his Eckardt County Sheriff's Department coat—"sit this one out. I mean it." Leaving her with the warning, he exited the cabin.

She sank into her chair and gaped at the closed door. Absentmindedly, she picked up the mug and drank the cocoa.

"Why do you keep doing this to yourself?" Joel asked as he got up from the table and headed for the old-fashioned wood stove.

"I'll kindly remind you to keep any and all opinions to yourself."

He poured a cup of coffee from the stovetop percolator, then returned to stand next to her. "Before you go jumping down my throat, hear me out."

"I stopped hearing you out when every discussion with you turned into a full-out fight to prove you were right and I was wrong."

He resumed his seat across from her and placed his coffee

mug on the table between them. "We were married then. This isn't about right or wrong."

She gave him a side-eye. Something in her gaze must have given him the impression to go on, because on he went.

"Last time I was here, after I got shot, I reminded you of your desire for this job. And him. It's been almost four years and here we are. You're still living like a vestal virgin, and my brother is walking around with a serious case of blue balls."

Elizabeth groaned and pinched the bridge of her nose. "Must you talk to me like I'm one of the guys?"

"Never bothered you before."

She chuckled, dropping her hand to settle on Bentley's silky head propped on her lap. "I've been away from that life for a long while now. Like to think we have more refinement here in Iowa than crass army talk."

"Your deputies are mostly men, and you're telling me not a single one of them talks shop in the office?"

Elizabeth gave him a sly grin. "Just shows you how much respect my men have of me that they don't." She waved off this wayward line of conversation. "We're off topic. You have no room to talk about relationships, especially with your ex-wife. How much you want to bet the last time you were with any woman it was me?"

One of Joel's eyebrows lifted, and he made that "well" face.

She leaned forward, cupping her cooled cocoa mug. If she could steer this discussion off her and pin it on him, so be it. "Are you dating again?"

He shook his head. "Not really."

"It's one of *those* agreements, huh?" Those agreements

being him hooking up with another woman, hopefully his age, that wasn't into a long-term commitment either. More of a mutual sexual relationship of "I'll scratch yours if you scratch mine."

"Anyone I know?" she asked.

Joel frowned. "How did this turn into a conversation about me?"

"You brought up the blue balls."

"Now who's being crass?" He sighed and then he, too, leaned forward on the table. "Ellie, this dance you've been having with Rafe has gone on for years. You're in a high-stress job and nearly killed yourself. If that isn't a sign you need an outlet, then I don't know what is."

"It's not for a lack of trying on my part. He's the right-eous one. Why aren't you giving him this lecture?"

"I've tried."

"Then you know what I mean. So lay off. And don't pity me, either. For being the younger brother, Rafe is more responsible than you."

Joel's chair creaked as he repositioned his bulky frame. "Or lazy."

"He's far from that."

A comfortable silence fell between them. While Elizabeth finished her cocoa, Joel drank his coffee. After they'd divorced and she'd moved back to Juniper, they'd come to be more friends than divorcées. Fights between them were long over, and mutual respect had returned. Oh, they could argue like politicians from either side of the floor, but at the end of the day, they could leave the debate podium and share a beer or two. Elizabeth liked it.

"I've got some things need tending to back home," he said. Back being his home and livelihood in North Carolina as a Delta Force Selections officer.

"Rafe know this?"

"I'd expect him to know. I can't stay here forever and babysit you."

Elizabeth tilted her head. "Tell him you have to leave tomorrow. Maybe I can get out of this cozy little prison sooner and back to work."

"I mean, I could."

"But you won't."

Joel grinned. "Why would I not stick around to antagonize you a bit longer?"

Elizabeth was about to rebut when Bentley suddenly lifted her head and shuffled around to face the cabin door. She chuffed, then snorted in that agitated way dogs were apt to do when something bothered them.

The canine warning put Joel in motion, ever the operative. He jabbed a finger at Elizabeth, his silent message to stay put. She got the meaning loud and clear. He lifted the edge of his camo-printed shirt and drew a pistol from a hidden holster. He wasn't a guy to ever go through life unarmed.

Elizabeth itched to have her own sidearm, which Rafe had confiscated. She'd have to settle for her ex-husband's expertise in this area. One did not get to earn the secretive patch of The Unit if one wasn't an expert marksman.

Bentley cocked her head. Her dog's curious stance gave Elizabeth pause.

"Joel, I don't—"

Something thumped against the door, startling them. Bentley scooted backward until her rump was shoved up against Elizabeth's leg. Joel had raised his weapon level with his chest.

Every nerve in Elizabeth's body was on fire. She wanted to get up out of this chair and join Joel. But if she disobeyed him right now, there would be unfathomable repercussions, and she wasn't in the mood to fight.

The loud thump was followed by a series of muffled knocks, and then the door handle rattled. Joel was reaching for the handle when a strangled noise came from the other side.

"Ellie!"

She shot out of the chair. "Open it."

Joel yanked open the door and a form slumped inside. He hopped back, keeping his gun pointed at the newcomer.

"Dominic." Elizabeth broke rank and rushed to the fallen surgeon's side.

Seemingly assured the man was no threat, Joel stepped over his prone body and began sweeping the perimeter.

Elizabeth knelt beside Dominic and assessed. He was sans coat, and his usually immaculately pressed dress shirt was ripped and speckled brown and red. The black work slacks were streaked with mud, dead grass, and his shoes caked in the sticky clay soil of this area. His face was battered, eyes puffed and nose bleeding.

"My God, Dominic, what happened to you?"

He grappled to take hold of her hands. "Olivia."

"Elizabeth," Joel called from the yard.

She leaned out the door only to be yanked back by Dominic.

"Find her," he rasped.

"What?"

"Elizabeth!" The barked command held all the authority of a commanding officer.

She disentangled herself from Dominic's hold and scrambled outside. Joel was more than one hundred yards out and staring at something down the hill. As she hurried to join him, Bentley darted forward, low to the ground.

"What?" Elizabeth barked back. "There's an injured man in there."

Below them, the smoking wreckage of an unfamiliar Jeep sat crumpled against a pair of thick trees. There were no roads out here, just trails left by animals and paths made by human. The only way to get to this cabin was with all-terrain vehicles. While designed for this type of landscape, the Jeep was still too large. How it got here in the first place was a miracle in and of itself.

The dense stand of trees, the hill, and the thick walls of the cabin had prevented them from even hearing the Jeep crumple into the trunk.

"Is that his?" Joel asked.

"No. I've never seen that vehicle before."

"How did he know where to find you?" Joel demanded.

"I don't know," Elizabeth snapped.

She noticed the scars in the ground coming up the hill. Those would explain Dominic's soiled condition. The bruised face and blood were possibly from the accident.

"I'm checking the wreckage out." Joel started for the hill. "Tend to the doc."

"Then what?"

He gave her a hard look. "Then we get the hell out of here and find out what's going on."

Once he headed downhill, Elizabeth hot-footed it back to the cabin. Dominic had pulled himself inside, smearing blood, and lay on the floor with Bentley standing guard over him. Whatever answers Elizabeth hoped to get out of him would not come yet, as Dominic had passed out.

After making sure he still had a pulse and was breathing, she paid closer attention to his injuries. The facial wounds were not from a vehicle collision with trees. The blood had congealed and dried, meaning time had passed between receiving them and his arrival here.

Feeling more embarrassed than she should, Elizabeth lifted Dominic's shirt. Beneath was more bruising. She winced at a particularly large dark spot on his rib cage. With a tender touch, she felt the area, noting the give where a solid rib should be. This was not good.

Joel stomped inside, his weapon back in the holster. "He was the only one in the Jeep. There's a lot of blood on the driver's side."

Elizabeth looked up at him. "He's passed out." She sat back on her heels. "Someone worked him over bad. I think he's got broken ribs, and he's probably suffering from a concussion."

"Those don't explain all the blood." Joel crouched next to Dominic and rolled his limp body up on his side. "He's got a wound on his back."

"What are we going to do?"

Joel scrubbed his face. "Rafe left the four-seater." The

four-seater being the larger of the ATVs the brothers owned. "We'll get him to the hospital."

"Before you dragged me outside, he said something about finding Olivia." Elizabeth rolled up onto her feet. "You're certain there was no one else in there?"

He stood. "He was the only one. No other signs of a passenger." He pulled out his cell phone and checked it. "I've got no reception. I can't even send a text."

"Then we go."

"Gather what we need and put out the fire. I'll pull the ATV around and see if I can get him in it." Joel disappeared out the door.

Elizabeth took a shuddering breath and looked at her dog. Bentley hadn't moved from Dominic's side. Elizabeth's stomach cramped in that way she'd come to recognize as a warning to her of danger brewing in her county. A sign she never ignored.

CHAPTER FOUR

LILA TURNED AT the sound of someone's approach. Fontaine broke through the edge of the field. He looked like he needed five days of sleep.

"I'm here," he grumbled. "What was all-fired important it couldn't be explained over the phone?"

Lila eyed him. Her short stature really grated sometimes when she had to face off against the likes of Undersheriff Rafe Fontaine, whose six foot whatever the hell inches towered over her.

"First, I was lucky to even get a text out to you." She tipped her head. "Behind here."

Lila led the way around the shack. She pointed at the boneyard. "Second, tell me you want this plastered all over the airwaves."

"Sweet mother of God," he muttered, his head swiveling as he took in the site. "Why isn't the tape up?"

"Because we need to get the full layout. I think this goes back farther. DCI is on their way."

"Where's Dr. Remington-Thorpe?"

Lila hooked her hands on her duty belt. "No one can reach her. Meyer tried the hospital, and they seem to be having the same problem. And Dr. Thorpe is missing."

Fontaine's face scrunched. "Did you send Meyer to their

house?"

"I sent Lundquist to check it out before coming here." Lila shifted her weight. "Meyer is walking this to see how far out it goes."

"How long have they been here?" he asked, his voice more raspy than usual.

They. Human beings. People who were left here unbeknown to all. They would have families wondering what happened to them. Missing persons reports filed from God knows where or how far back. In all her years in law enforcement—even with the infamous I-80 serial killer on her dossier—Lila had never been involved with an investigation of this magnitude.

"A forensic anthropologist is going to have to tell us that. I can't even begin to guess." Lila took a shuddering breath.

Fontaine looked at her pointedly. She noticed the tight lines along his jaw. Before he spoke, she knew exactly what he was going to say.

"You sure you should be—"

She gestured for him to shut his mouth. "It's not a serial killer. I'll be fine."

Since her throwdown with the I-80 killer when she lost the one man who meant more to her than she thought possible, the sheriff and deputies of Eckardt County had been watching her closely. With good reason. Lila's first brutal encounter with the killer had left her with deep scars and an opioid addiction. She was close to five years sober and still seeing the head doc if the need arose, but otherwise, she was fine.

"You don't know that," Fontaine said. His meaning

could go either way.

"I'm by no means an expert in all fields of investigation." She met his frosty blue gaze. "Serial killers I do know. This is disorganized. Frenzied." She nodded at the nearest set of bones with large strips of cloth still attached. "I'd bet my right kidney we'll find bullets."

"You don't have a spare kidney to bet," he deadpanned.

"Did you just make a joke?" Lila smirked. "I thought it wasn't possible."

He brushed off her humor and faced the shack. "Have the two of you been in there?"

"Not yet." She sighed. "I'm debating whether to leave it for DCI or have Lundquist process it."

Fontaine made a rumbling noise low in his throat. "I want you and Lundquist in there first."

Yards away, Meyer emerged from the thickest part of the woods. "I found something!"

With Lila leading the way, she and Fontaine swung wide of the scattered remains taking a path Meyer already forged in his search. Once they joined him, he took them into the timber another twenty or so yards and stopped.

They stood on the edge of a slope. Erosion had created a steep drop with no clear path down, allowing plateaus of shale and limestone to jut out. Daring trees clung by their roots to the side of the incline, curving upward and giving the illusion from a distance there was more ground.

Meyer pointed down. Lila and Fontaine peeked over the edge. Two hundred feet below was a narrow, rocky shore butting a wide stream. Lila followed the water's easterly path to where it curved around a bend and disappeared.

"What's beyond that bend?" she asked.

"The juncture of the Des Moines River and the Missis-sippi," Fontaine answered.

She brought her attention back to the dark object jutting out of the streambed. A blackened hulk scarred by fire left rusting on the stream's edge.

"Well, we can narrow down the timeframe to after the flooding two summers ago. Or that thing would have been washed away," Lila said.

From this height, the rusted shell appeared to be some-thing like a large SUV. If Lila had to guess without being up close, she'd say it was one of those huge Suburbans the livestock families in the community tended to drive.

"There has to be more," Fontaine uttered.

"What?" She looked at him.

"More vehicles." He turned back to the makeshift grave-yard. "There are too many skeletal remains for a single vehicle."

"We can't be sure how many remains are actually there," she pointed out. "Scavengers have disturbed the site, proba-bly carrying off more limbs and parts to the far reaches of this county. We'll be lucky if we can find a fully intact skeleton."

"She's right," Meyer added. "From what I could tell, the scene is contained to the area behind the shack. I didn't find anything other than this burned-out car down there."

"We'll let DCI confirm the perimeters of the site before making any assumptions," Fontaine said and headed back the way they came.

Lila and Meyer remained where they stood, watching the

undersheriff stalk away.

"You got any reception on your phone?" Meyer asked.

She dug out her cell and checked. Three tiny dots showed where there should have been a 5G or LTE, or at least an SOS. "I've got nothing."

"You'd think by now Lundquist would be at the doc's place and we'd have an update," Meyer said.

Exactly. If he couldn't get through by cell phone, surely, he would have hailed them via radio. She cued her mic. "Lundquist, report?"

Seconds crawled, no response. She hailed him again, this time getting a line of static.

"Maybe we're too far from the cars?" Meyer suggested.

Maybe. Or maybe Kyle forgot his radio in his unit. Or … worse.

Don't go there, Lila. There could be legitimate logical reasons he's not hearing your summons.

"Flag this," she said. "I'll see what's going on."

She left Meyer to his duties. Hiking through the tall grasses and weeds as fast as she could without appearing to be panicked was a chore, but she managed. She passed Fontaine, who was staring at the skeletal remains near the shack. He didn't even look at her.

When she reached the wire fence, she tried the radio again. "Lundquist, report."

More static.

What was going on? Their radios had never gone out of commission, even in the most remote areas of the county.

She checked her phone again. It now had the SOS signal, but it wouldn't do her any good, only redirecting her call back to her. *Get closer to the cars.* When she'd texted Fontaine earlier, the phone had enough of a signal to send while they were right next to the cars. Come to think of it, the radio worked fine when she sent Lundquist to the Remington-Thorpe house.

A few years ago, the sheriff had weaseled the county commissioners out of funds to supply mobile data terminals capable of hooking up to a satellite and generating their own Wi-Fi networks when cell reception was down. For such a backward-thinking populace, it was a big deal, but Sheriff Benoit pulled it off. It had saved their hides on more than a few occasions to have those MDTs in their units.

Lila reached her car and tried her radio while checking her phone's connectivity. "Lundquist, update?"

The radio crackled this time. Her phone had upgraded to a weak Wi-Fi signal. Lila glanced up and down the road. Kathy Miller had long returned home—Meyer having taken her statement, which was minimal at best, and let her go. She probably had a landline from which she made her initial call to the department.

Fontaine emerged from around a tiny grove of crabapple trees jutting into the field.

"We have a problem," she called out.

He picked up his pace to get closer. "How so?"

"I can't reach Lundquist."

"Try again," he said as he came around the front side of her vehicle.

Resisting the urge to roll her eyes at him, she hit the mic again. "Lundquist, for the love of God, answer."

The radio squawked back when she released the button.

The connections were working now. Kyle's delay in responding drove her anxiety into a frenzy. Fontaine's piercing stare didn't help matters.

He was about to speak when their radios clicked and an out-of-breath Kyle came over the waves.

"Son of a bitch, Lila. Why aren't you answering?"

"I have been trying you for the last ten minutes," she rebutted.

"Whatever. We need a unit here. Something happened to Olivia and Dominic. There's blood, and the front hall has been trashed."

Lila's stomach plummeted. She and Fontaine blinked at each other.

Before she could respond to Lundquist, Fontaine's phone rang, startling them both. He dug out the shrilling object from his vest.

"Joel, what the hell?"

Lila watched his face as it morphed into a granite slate. "I'm on my way."

"What?" she demanded as he shoved his phone back into his vest.

"My brother has Dominic. He's been wounded."

The radio broke through. "Damn it, Lila, answer me."

Fontaine's steely gaze held Lila's. "I need to go." He broke eye contact and marched toward his Charger.

"I can't leave Meyer here alone." Not ever. Not since the day she'd walked into a gas station for a restroom break and came out to find the rookie deputy shot and bleeding to death.

Fontaine waved her off. "Do whatever you want. Shit has

hit the fan. We don't have time to argue. Tell Lundquist I'll meet him."

"Where's the sheriff?!" Lila yelled after.

"With my stupid brother." He ended the conversation by getting into the souped-up Charger and slamming the door.

Lila slapped the side of her car.

"Lila!"

She cued the mic. "Fontaine is coming to you." She watched the undersheriff peel out and leave in a dust cloud.

"When?" Lundquist demanded.

"I don't know. Just seal off the house and wait for him."

A moment passed before the radio clicked. "Why can't you come?"

Lila stared across the open field in the direction of the place where humans had unexplainably lost their lives and were discarded like trash. "Because I have a larger crime scene to process."

CHAPTER FIVE

H ER HEAD THROBBED, but on the pain scale it was a mere irritation in comparison to the debilitating agony in her arm. The pain pulsating through her pulled Olivia out of unconsciousness. Between the bouts of searing heat, she noticed she was lying on something soft. After her mind cleared of whatever drug had knocked her out, she became aware of her surroundings.

She was on a bed, staring at a white-painted ceiling. Somehow, she was still in her scrubs. Good. Eucalyptus, pungent and eye-watering, permeated the air. There was a hint of something woodsy, could be tea tree. A torrent of coughs stoked the fire in her arm. It was then she realized her left arm, heavy and cumbersome, was strapped to her torso. Olivia struggled onto her right elbow and blinked at the neon-yellow wrap encompassing a plaster cast backdropped by her wrinkled scrubs.

"Wha—"

"I thought it best to have your arm set and put in a cast."

She jolted at the deep voice.

He sat on a chair, feet from the bed, bald head tilted, his predatory stare capturing hers and holding. Horatio Johnson had always been a man to dress the part, his taste in the finer things having never gone out of style. Thug. Criminal.

Gangster. None of those applied to Horatio. He prided himself on being a businessman. What that business entailed was entirely up to the moment.

"Where am I?" Olivia's voice was as dry and brittle as she felt.

He held out his hands like a placating politician. "Somewhere safe."

"I'm never safe when it comes to you. It's why I left you."

"No," he barked. "You left me because you got over being the rebel daughter."

"You killed people!"

Horatio's eyes glittered. "Only those who deserved it."

The callous way he uttered those words brought back those old emotions in Olivia. The deadness inside like gasping for air in a cold, blackened coffin.

His hard stare receded as he reached inside his gray blazer and withdrew a bottle. He shook it, rattling the pills inside. "You still allergic to morphine?"

"You don't just outgrow an allergy to narcotics."

A brilliant smile lit up his features. "I thought so." He popped the cap and shook out a white pill. "Percocet?"

"I'd rather not."

He nodded at her casted arm as he slid the pill bottle inside the blazer. "No amount of ibuprofen is going to cut the pain. My guy had to reset it, and it sounded bad."

"It wouldn't have been broken if your *man* hadn't thrown me around like a rag doll."

"I apologize for Adrian. He can get overzealous." Horatio stood, and as he came closer to the bed, he picked up a glass of water sitting beside a clear bottle with pink pills Olivia hadn't seen. "I think a little itching far outweighs the torture of a broken bone. But just in case, there's Benadryl."

"Speaking from experience." It was more statement than question—she knew Horatio's long, bloody history.

Olivia glared at the oval tablet settled in the deep crevices of his palm. She shook from pain and trying to keep herself upright on her good arm. Sweat beaded along her hairline. If she took the Percocet, she'd be at his mercy. If she didn't, she'd turn delirious, which would put her at even greater risk. At least he had the foresight to get antihistamines if the need arose, which invariably it would.

With clumsy movements, which ended up with her taking Horatio's assistance, she moved to sit on the edge of the bed. She clawed the tablet from his hand and tossed it back with a shot of water. The cool liquid hit her throat, and her brain triggered the need for rehydration. She gulped the entire contents. After she licked the last drop from the rim, Horatio took the glass and resumed his seat.

They sat in silence.

Olivia scrutinized the room, taking in the cleanliness and modern, open appeal. It was more than just a bedroom, it looked like an apartment, similar to what one would find over a garage or in an attic. Furniture was sparse with the full-sized bed, the plush armchair Horatio sat in, and a small round table for two. Behind Horatio, against the wall, was a basic kitchen with a college-dorm refrigerator and a sink. Two cabinets hung above the sink and on each side were a minuscule amount of counterspace, of which one was taken up by what looked like a countertop oven.

"Planning on keeping me here forever?" Olivia asked, her attention drawn back to him.

"I haven't decided."

"This is kidnapping. If you took me across state lines, it's a federal offense."

Horatio's grin mirrored that of a hyena. "I'm well aware of those facts, Liv."

"Don't call me that. You lost that privilege a long time ago." She leaned forward, careful to keep her balance and not pitch over the side of the bed. "I was abducted from my home, against my will, and told my husband had aligned himself with the likes of you. You of all people." She sneered at him. "What is going on?"

His arm jutted out, pulling back the cuff of his blazer and shirt, and he studied his watch, then dropped his arm and stood. "All in due time." He moved to the table where his coat lay. "I have business to attend to. In the meantime, rest." He turned as he shrugged into his coat. "I took it upon myself to allow you one pleasure."

Olivia followed his pointed look to a large mover's box placed at the head of the bed on the floor. "What is that?"

"Reading material. I'm sure you'll find it fascinating, as it caters to your morbid obsessions. It is why you became a medical examiner, right?"

"Horatio, I'm begging you, don't do this."

He sighed. "You've got to understand, Liv, if Dominic had not allowed himself to be drawn into his mess ... I kept my end of the agreement and have continued to do so."

He was many things, but when it came to Olivia, Horatio was still a man very much in love. She could also claim he was a man scorned.

"Don't overdo it, Liv." With that, he departed through the single door to the place. The bastard would press the issue of her nickname because he could.

Olivia heard the distinct click of locks. The keyholes were on the inside, designed to keep her trapped. A prison. She shuddered. Blinking away the moisture building in her eyes, she gingerly rose from the bed. On shaking legs, she shuffled to the lone pane of windows opposite the door.

The beveled glass looked old, seated inside bands of metal, probably lead-based. Olivia braced a hand near the frame and searched the wood for a way to open the windows but found nothing. Her attention turned to the scene through the glass, and she let out a strangled cry.

There were tops of trees as far as her eye could see, many of them old and scraggly. A few smatterings of rooftops broke through the monotony of trees. She was in the middle of nowhere. Not a town nor a city. The uniformity of the area spoke of planning. Where this building's exact location in the scheme of things was mystery. It had a rural, somewhat residential look to it.

Far below, a yard ringed by a sagging wire fence sealed in the old building from its neighbors, whether they be two-legged or four. Thick patches of snow still pockmarked the yard. To the right, she could make out the wooden staircase leading down to the ground. She didn't see where the steps ended or the edge of the building.

The Percocet was kicking in, and bouts of wooziness were flittering through her head. Olivia rested her forehead against the cool glass and closed her eyes, drawing in calming breaths. If she panicked, she wouldn't figure a way out of this. So long as her injured arm hurt, Horatio would make sure she was taking the pills and keep her unbalanced.

She lifted her head from the glass and turned. The large mover's box beckoned. Curious, she shambled back to the bed. After dragging the box around one-handed, she sat with it between her legs. She plunged her hand between the center of the crisscrossed flaps and pried them open.

Seated in neat formation, just as they would have been inside a filing cabinet, were office folders. Some thick with information, others thin, all labeled with an alphabetical-numerical code. A systematic code typically used by law enforcement and forensic techs—one she was all too familiar with. Olivia, after waiting for her head to stop feeling like it would float away, drew out one particularly fat folder and laid it across her lap. Before the others slumped against each other, she spotted more at the bottom, but maybe that was a trick of her mind. She'd get to it later.

Using her casted arm as a brace for the folder, she flipped it open. Autopsy reports. She frowned as she lifted the pages and found beneath the reports case records. Below those, photos of taped-off scenes where piles of bones lay exposed to the elements.

Olivia tucked the top pages under the back of the folder and carefully studied—best she could since her eyes were becoming increasingly unfocused—each photo. Bleached, and in some cases weathered, bones were scattered among browned and crinkled tree leaves and dormant grasses. She looked through a few more photos before rolling back the top pages, leafing through them until she found a police report.

This peculiarly situated boneyard was on an island in the middle of the Mississippi. It had been discovered by some curious fishermen when they decided to explore the island. Due to the quantity of skeletal remains left there, the FBI and a team of forensic anthropologists had been brought in. Many of the bodies were missing many of the bones, and a few of them were without skulls.

Olivia's attention began to waver, and her eyelids grew heavy. Shaking free of the Percocet's pull was going to be difficult. Thankfully, the agony in her arm was gone. She closed the file and set it on the floor beside the box. She'd study it further once she was clear-headed.

She withdrew a few more files, finding a couple of reports with nothing more than a scribbled sticky note or folders with several police and forensic reports. The urge to use the restroom forced her to pause.

After a few trials and errors, she found the door sheltering a modest bathroom. Everything about using the facilities was made awkward with the cast and her drug-induced high, yet somehow, she managed. Upon returning to the bed and the box of files, she decided she needed to sleep off the drug's effects.

Gingerly, she laid down and pulled a blanket over herself. When and if Horatio returned, she was going to tell him to give her different painkillers, because there was no way she'd take another round of Percocet. She tucked the extra pillows under her injured arm and closed her eyes.

As she waited for the lull of sleep to take her, her sluggish brain mulled over the files Horatio had left her. He had an ulterior motive. One thing was certain—the files linked back to whatever he claimed Dominic had gotten himself into. And Olivia was expected to uncover the truth on her own.

CHAPTER SIX

ONCE THEY MADE it back to the Fontaine homestead, Elizabeth and Joel managed to load the still unconscious Dominic in Joel's truck. As he drove them to the hospital, Elizabeth sat in the back with Dominic's head in her lap. Bentley stared at them from the front passenger seat.

Over his Bluetooth, Joel finally contacted his brother.

"Where you at?" Rafe demanded upon connection.

"Nearly to town limits," Joel barked back. "He's lost a lot of blood."

Rafe's long pause worried Elizabeth. He knew something they didn't.

"Rafe," she called out. It was all she had to say.

"Olivia is missing."

The news was like taking a blow to the back of the head. Once Elizabeth got her erratic emotions back in order, she met Joel's worried gaze in the rearview mirror.

"ER is prepped for him," Rafe went on. "The other deputies are working on the other matters."

Elizabeth scowled. "What other matters?"

"Joel, I'm having a Juniper police officer meet you at the hospital. I've got to get out to the Thorpe place."

"Rafe, what do you mean by other matters?" Elizabeth snapped. Her inquiry was met with dead silence. "He hung up on me."

"Don't go seeking trouble where it's not needed right now. He's got it in hand," Joel said.

She shoved her ex's admonishment away. She looked down at Dominic's battered face.

"What happened?" she whispered.

They were met at the ER bay by a trio of nurses. With assistance from Joel, they got Dominic on a stretcher, then rushed him into a room.

Elizabeth commanded Bentley to stay in the truck and followed the crew inside. She avoided the room where the nurses had taken Dominic, instead heading straight for the admittance desk.

The nurse on duty behind the desk gaped. "Sheriff, what are you doing here?"

"Came with Dr. Thorpe." Elizabeth leaned on the desktop and stared into the woman's eyes. "Was he scheduled for ER duty today?"

"Yes."

"Did he ever report in?"

A noise behind the nurse made her turn. Elizabeth glanced in the same direction. A stern-faced nurse loomed in the doorway separating the admittance area from small offices in the back.

"Sheriff," she said, "join me."

Elizabeth pushed off the counter, ambled around the station desk, and followed the charge nurse into a cramped room. Before closing the door, the nurse checked the hall. Then the two women stared at each other.

"What is it?" Elizabeth prompted.

"Keeping those younger nurses from gossiping on a regular basis is bad enough. I don't need them throwing around more wild speculations."

"So, you're telling me you've got answers to my questions."

The woman sighed and moved to sit down at a small desk area set into the wall. "I don't know that everything I can tell you is one-hundred-percent accurate, but when I've worked most ER shifts with Dr. Thorpe and Dr. Remington-Thorpe for the last two years, I picked up on some things."

"Like?"

"For one, they weren't speaking to each other anymore. There was a time when one or the other would stay longer after rotation change. Not true in the last year or so. Like tonight, Dr. Remington-Thorpe was out of here fifteen minutes early."

"Did Dr. Thorpe come in?" Elizabeth asked.

"Not that I saw. He's scheduled for the day shift. By the looks of things, he never checked in."

Which meant he'd gone somewhere else, wherever he'd gotten that Jeep, got beaten up, and shot or stabbed. By what he'd been wearing, Elizabeth assumed he planned to be at the hospital. Something had rerouted him. And that something might have Olivia?

Elizabeth leaned against the door. She felt grimy from Dominic's blood and the mud staining her clothing. She was more than a hair teed-off she hadn't paid closer attention to Olivia and Dominic.

"Were there any other signs things were not good between the two doctors?" she pressed on.

The charge nurse rocked back in her seat. "Not that they broadcasted you know, like public fights, yelling, or bad mouthing each other to the staff, none of that went on. It was more subtle, passive aggressive things."

Knowing the two as well as she thought she did, Elizabeth could see it. Olivia internalized a lot and never talked about herself or her problems. Dominic was just as bad about it as his wife. Elizabeth had brushed it off as the two being only a handful of Blacks in the community and still navigating the waters of working in a rural area. Come to think of it, though, Elizabeth knew so little about either one's past lives before moving to Iowa. She was certain Olivia had mentioned growing up in the suburbs of Chicago. Where, she didn't recall Olivia ever saying.

"But I did notice something odd with Dr. Thorpe," the charge nurse continued. "For the last three months on the days he had day shift, like today, he'd always arrive late. After we had a heart attack patient come in, and he wasn't here right away, I pressed him about it. He gave me the snide remark it wasn't my business as a nurse. Kinda threw me. He's never talked down to me or any nurse like that before."

"Did he ever leave earlier than scheduled if Dr. Remington-Thorpe was on the opposite duty?"

The nurse shook her head. "She always did night shift when she was rotated in for ER because she had her practice." She scrunched her features and leaned forward in her chair. "There was one time Dr. Thorpe arrived in soiled scrubs."

"Soiled how?"

"Blood. I think I saw some dirt." She tipped back and her face morphed into one of contemplation. "Come to think of it, the blood stains were splattered all over his top."

"Like he'd been in surgery?"

It took her a moment to think, then the woman nodded her head. "Yeah, like he had done surgery."

A rap on the door made Elizabeth shift. The charge nurse got up and opened it to reveal the desk nurse.

"Doctor is asking after you," she said, her gaze flicking to Elizabeth.

"After who?" the charge nurse insisted.

"Both of you, actually." She backed away from the doorway.

The charge nurse gestured for Elizabeth to go first. Together they exited the admittance station and turned down the hall toward the trauma room where they had taken Dominic.

Joel poked his head out of the waiting area when Elizabeth passed, giving her a most inquisitive expression. She waved him off, and he slinked back inside the room.

"Sheriff Benoit, I wasn't expecting you here," the doctor—one she hadn't met—said when he stepped out of the trauma room. He held out his hand. "I work in pediatrics."

That would explain why she had not met him.

"You got the unlucky short straw to come down here and fill in," she said.

"Yes." He looked back into the room. "I'm calling for a life flight up to Iowa City. We don't have anyone capable of handling his injuries. He was the only surgeon, and with Dr. Remington-Thorpe AWOL, there's nothing anyone here can do. We could call in someone from Burlington or Ottumwa, but they're strapped for doctors and surgeons as it is."

"Is Dr. Thorpe stable?"

"For now. It looks like someone took a sharp blade to him. It's close to his kidney." The pediatric doctor rubbed a hand over his face and blew air. "He's a mess."

"Okay, then we wait for the helicopter to get here," Elizabeth said.

"Does he have any family anywhere?" the doctor asked.

The charge nurse shrugged and suggested, "Maybe there's something in his personnel file."

"Please check," Elizabeth said.

The other woman headed back to her office.

"If there's nothing in the file, then I'll handle any authorizations needed, since his only known next of kin is missing," Elizabeth said.

Out of the corner of her eye she noticed movement. She looked down the hall as one of Juniper's finest strode toward them.

"Sheriff," he said.

"Officer Ross, I'm to assume you're the one tagged for security detail?" she asked.

James Ross had joined Juniper police about a year after Elizabeth had been elected sheriff. She didn't know much about the man. He wasn't from Eckardt County or Iowa as far as she learned. Ed, the Juniper police chief, seemed okay with adding an outsider to his ranks after the success of Elizabeth's hire of Deputy Detective Lila Dayne, herself an outsider.

Ross was younger than Elizabeth. He carried himself

with a swagger reminiscent of those who had long been in or around law enforcement.

"Yes, ma'am. Chief said it was Doc Thorpe. Somethin' happened to him?"

"Something, yes. A life flight is on its way, and we're getting things squared. Just keep an eye on things."

"Anything in particular I need to watch for?" Ross asked.

Elizabeth was about to tell him, but something in the way he narrowed his gaze made her redirect her thoughts. Gossiping nurses were one thing. Gossiping law enforcement was an entirely different animal.

"Just keep your eyes peeled for anything out of the ordinary."

She beckoned the doctor to follow her, and they wandered the hall toward the nurses' station. "Keep a lid on this as much as you can. Whoever tried to kill him is going to be looking for him."

The man nodded, and Elizabeth headed to the waiting room.

Joel turned from the TV. "So?"

She pressed a finger to her lips and sat down in a chair far from the doorway. After doing his own reconnaissance, Joel sat next to her, his back straight, his head tilted as if to listen for someone's approach.

"Text Rafe. Tell him as soon as Dominic is airlifted to Iowa City, I'm coming," she said quietly.

Joel reached into his coat. He withdrew a cell phone. Her cell phone.

Once he passed it to her, he stood. "Text him yourself, Sheriff." He winked, then wandered over to the doorway.

A sly grin on her lips, Elizabeth sent her message and settled farther into the chair, waiting for the blowback. Like it or not, she was back on the clock.

CHAPTER SEVEN

"SOME OF THESE bones haven't been here long," the Tyvek-wearing forensic anthropologist said as he stood, holding a squat, round bone.

He had introduced himself as Dr. Steven Pembrook. He didn't cross Lila as the scholarly or geek type as she'd pictured all anthropologists to be. Pembrook looked more like a guy who should be commanding the board of a corporation or a university president. She had noted the slight lilt to his voice but couldn't place the accent. The moment he'd arrived he'd been eager to get to work uncovering the bones.

"There's less staining on the underside," Pembrook continued. "They haven't been sitting in the soil very long."

"If you were to hazard a guess, what constitutes as not a very long time?" Lila asked.

"A few weeks to a few months."

"It's been snowing a lot in the last few months. If that body was placed on the snow, it just now reached the ground." Lila pointed at the bone he held. "That's clean of all tissue and material."

"Yet it contains quite a lot of chew marks. These bodies were left for animals to scavenge." He looked over the gravesite. "I doubt there's an intact skeleton among them."

"I was afraid of that."

Pembrook jutted his chin at the shack. "Has anyone gone in there?"

"Not yet." Lila looked at the weathered building. "It's on my list of things to do."

"Might be a good idea to do now."

"In other words, stop lurking over my shoulder, Deputy," Lila remarked.

He lowered himself next to the haphazard pile of bones he'd been examining. "Precise deduction, Watson."

A real cut-up this one was. Lila left him to his work and went to find another less occupied person able to assist her. She spotted Meyer hovering next to a female tech holding a large digital camera. He was in deep conversation with the woman—no point in pulling him away. Rounding the tree bracketing the shack, she caught movement across the field. She shielded her eyes from the brilliant midmorning sun and watched the man tromping through the field.

Deputy Kyle Lundquist was sans uniform and wearing civvies under a tan Carhartt coat. The normally well-kept beard had gone rogue, giving him more of the Viking aura of his native ancestry. On drawing closer, Lila could make out the deep lines carved into the corners of his eyes and in the furrowed brow. While his stride was purposeful, she could spot the moments he veered just a bit off course. He needed sleep.

He drew up in front of her.

"What are you doing here?" she asked.

"Fontaine kicked me out and took over the Remington-Thorpe house." Lundquist's cool gaze studied the activity going on behind her. "The sheriff is on her way there."

This news was surprising. "Fontaine is allowing it?"

His gaze slid back to her. "He wasn't given a choice. What's going on?"

Due to the limited reception, she hadn't explained any of this when she roused him from bed to go to the doctors' house.

Shifting to look back at the actions of the DCI techs and the anthropologist, she hooked her hands on her hips. "We have a mess of skeletal remains scattered all over." She pointed to the distant ledge where earth met water. "Over yonder is the burned-out husk of a vehicle left at the bottom of a huge drop to the river."

"Find any tracks?" he asked.

Shaking her head, she turned back to Lundquist. "Leads me to believe it was driven out here while there was snow on the ground."

He made a low noise in his throat. "Snow would have drifted bad back here with all that wind we had. It would have caused it to get stuck."

"If you want to wander around to find some clue as to how it got there, be my guest." Lila humped. "We have absolutely no idea what all"—she circled her hand—"this really is."

His light-brown eyebrows furrowed deep into his forehead, the effect making him look more ancient barbarian than modern-day man. "What do you think it is?"

Normally, in situations like these, she and Lundquist would methodically process the whole scene, he collecting evidence and tagging what he could test on his own, she doing a walk through and photographing everything. They were Eckardt County Sheriff Department's first line of crime techs. Lundquist knew she liked to gauge a scene without any suggestions or comments from anyone else. This was beyond anything Lila wanted to deal with alone, hence the slew of criminal investigators from Des Moines.

"I don't have a clue. I'm letting the forensic anthropologist, Dr. Pembrook, work that out." She moved toward the shack. "I was going to check this over. Now that you're here, we can do it more efficiently."

"Let me get my kit."

"Don't bother," she said, stopping him before he left. "I asked one of the DCI techs to leave me a box."

There was a twitch of irritation on his face, giving Lila an overwhelming need to explain away her actions.

"I didn't think you were coming out here," she blurted.

Kyle scratched the side of his face and shrugged, motions he'd adopted in the last few months anytime she did or said something out of character. Which were occurring a lot lately.

The worrisome plague of self-doubt and the perception she was being pushed away festered. Brushing off his behavior, she circled around him and headed for the evidence collection kit placed next to the shack door. As she ripped into a bag of latex-free gloves, Kyle joined her. Without a word, she slapped a pair into his hand.

Lila welcomed the cool feel of the nitrile gloves. Loaded with evidence bags and a flashlight, she opened the rickety shack door.

The musky odor of disuse and decaying wood enveloped her as she stepped inside. Both clicked on their flashlights and swept the beams over the interior.

The entire place wasn't much bigger than her kitchen and dining room combined. Tight quarters barely left room for the frame of a double-stacked bunk bed, a small broken table, and two chairs. An ancient woodstove sat in a corner, the stovepipe having fallen out of the wall years ago with an abandoned bird's nest filling the hole. Moss covered most surfaces, while leaves and dirt scattered across the floor. Derelict cobwebs draped corners and the lone dust-coated window beside the stove. Above a rusted sink hung a single cabinet, the door dangling haphazardly by one hinge.

It looked undisturbed. Indifferent to what lay just outside its walls.

"I don't think we're going to find any clues in here," Lundquist said in a low voice.

"We have to try."

Lila moved to the bunk bed, while Lundquist took the opposite side of the cramped quarters. As they worked— inching closer to the unspoken center point at the sink—Lila noticed a certain odor. She paused in her rummaging in a crumbling wood pile, straightened, and went still. She took a carefully drawn-in sniff, catching the scent. It was familiar, one she had become overly acquainted with two summers back.

Damp clay dirt.

The ground was still frozen. The riverbank too far away. What would cause the smell inside the shack? Where was it coming from?

She rotated away from the woodpile and let her nose guide her. Her focus sharpened. Lila picked up the inaudible chatter of the crew, along with the click and clack of tools and equipment outside. The smell was coming from the center of the shack.

Lundquist stopped his examination of the stove and directed his flashlight at her feet. "What is it?"

Lila held up a finger to shush him. She inched closer to the table and stopped. It was definitely stronger here.

"Lila?" Lundquist persisted.

"Do you smell it?" she asked.

"Smell what?"

"If I tell you, then I've triggered your brain to seek it out." She wafted the air in front of her face. "Come over here."

He scowled but did as she asked, then sniffed, his nostrils flaring. Perplexed, he took a more drawn-in breath. "Damp earth." He frowned. "The ground is frozen."

When he shifted closer to the toppled table, his size-fourteen boot thunked against the floorboards. A hollow echo came from below.

"What was that?" Lila squatted beside the table and set her hand on the floor. The debris lying about didn't move or rustle when she touched it. She fingered it, finding it more man-made material than natural. "It's fake."

She straightened. "Hit the floor again."

He did, harder than before. The hollow sound was more pronounced. "A trap door? In a hunting shack?"

"Maybe it was the cellar?" she provided.

Lundquist gave her a droll look.

"So maybe not."

Without telling him, they both moved away the table

and the chairs. Lila felt around until she located the edge of the cover and rolled it back. Dust flew into the air. Coughing, they waved it away.

Beneath the toes of their boots was a four-foot by six-foot door. Just large enough for a full-grown man to get through.

"Wanna do the honors?" Lila asked.

Grunting, Lundquist reached down and grasped the leather handle. He gave a hefty tug and the door came up on silent hinges. "Oiled."

Once he'd laid it back on the floor, they directed their flashlights into the hole. Well-maintained steps led down to a large pit, the walls along the steps were shored up by plywood sheets.

Lila met Lundquist's stern gaze. "Wanna see where it goes?"

"Get Meyer."

THEIR TRIO STOOD in the mouth of a tunnel, shining their flashlights into the murky depths. Lila was the only one able to somewhat stand straight. Lundquist's and Meyer's towering frames forced them to bend at the waist or squat to fit inside.

"How far do you think it goes?" Meyer asked.

"We're about to find out." Lila tacked a bright red marker flag at the edge of the plywood wall. "Mark the walls every hundred yards or so, that way we don't get lost if there are extra tunnels."

"Because you know there's going to be extra ones," Lundquist said drolly.

"Aren't you just a party pooper," she muttered and squeezed between him and the wall.

As their bodies squished together, he sucked in a sharp breath. Lila didn't have to think hard on what he was imagining or feeling. They hadn't been together in a long while, months in fact, and she was certain he craved her as much as she did him. Good thing Meyer was here to keep everything in perspective.

She slipped into the tunnel and looked over her shoulder. "Let's go."

The progress along the narrow corridor was slow and methodical. The pathway was mostly loose rock, covering the dirt and any traces of human movements through the tunnel. Every hundred yards Lila would stab a marker flag into the dirt walls, the plywood having ended back where the stairs met earth. Neither man spoke, but the sound of their breathing let Lila know they were still with her.

After placing the sixth flag, she stopped at a severe bend. She leaned into the rounded edge of the dirt wall and aimed her flashlight down the darkened shaft.

"It's not as wide," she warned them.

Lundquist poked his head around the corner. "I'm not going to fit through there." He looked back at Meyer. "Neither are you."

Lila stiffened. "I'm not going alone."

Twice, she'd survived a serial killer's attempts to end her life. Even dug her way out of a hole in the ground to escape his clutches. One would think Lila suffered from a form of claustrophobia brought on by the trauma, but she didn't. She did, however, have a healthy case of self-preservation. Going it alone the rest of the way with no one to watch her back didn't settle right with her.

"If you want to see where this leads, you're gonna have to. You're the only one small enough to squeeze through there," he told her.

She clamped down on her lip and stared into the abyss. Oh, this was going to sting on so many levels. Taking a deep breath of musty earth helped her find her center. She grabbed Lundquist's flashlight.

"I need more light," she said and plunged forward.

As she went along, Lila didn't bother to study the tunnel for evidence or clues. What was the point when she was more focused on not getting stuck? A quick check over her shoulder revealed she could no longer see Meyer's flashlight. Farther along, she paused, finding herself at a spot where the walls closed in.

She patted the walls, discovering it wasn't dirt but rock. If she tried wiggling through, even sideways, with her duty vest on, she would get stuck. Wouldn't the guys just love that. In these cramped conditions, she wouldn't be able to get out of her vest.

There had to be another way. Lila crouched down, finding the rock parted, and there was a wider gap at the bottom. As she passed the light up the left facing rock, a dark spot caught her eye. She held the beam steady and studied the mar on the gray surface. It was hard to tell if it was man-made or natural. She didn't have time to dwell on it.

With her phone, she snapped a few photos, zooming in

on the smudge for the last few, then tucked her cell into a vest pocket. On closer inspection, she decided the gap at the bottom was wide enough for her to crawl through. She felt the rock's underside until her hand found empty space on the opposite side. It wouldn't be a long crawl.

Lila got down on all fours and wormed her way through the opening, wincing as rock shards bit into her elbows and knees. Army crawling to the other side, she stopped once her rear passed under the boulders and sank to the ground, breathing hard.

"Shit," she muttered.

After catching her breath, she shimmed her legs under her and scrambled into a hunkered down position. The tunnel's ceiling was lower along here, and all rock.

A whooshing sound reached her ears. She held her breath and listened. It sounded like water.

She gathered herself for the awkward duck crawl and moved forward. The sound got louder the farther she went. At another large boulder she was forced to wriggle past, she discovered the tunnel widened, and it was getting brighter. The pebbles lining the pathway were now increasing in size. Soon enough, Lila was able to stand and move from stone to stone. Daylight became more prevalent, allowing her to shut off the flashlights.

Eventually, she was no longer in a tunnel but a cave. Lila gaped at the shimmering walls and expanse after the tight squeeze she'd endured. She studied the closest wall, noting the odd marks and indentations in the rock. It didn't look like this was natural. She looked about. Was this man-made? If yes, when?

The limestone and shale formed a path to a somewhat flat plateau Lila was able to walk on unhindered. The music of water dancing over rock drew her away from the tunnel. With her attention focused on finding an opening, she missed the sudden dip in the rock and slipped, falling on her backside. Pain rocketed through her body as flesh met stone.

"Son of a bitch."

She rolled to her side, breathing through the waves of agony. When it subsided enough for her to function, she scrambled to her feet. The slight decline was deceiving when a person was paying attention. It was the first step in a downward slope of what definitely looked man-made, but not recently. The steps were smoothed by age and water erosion. She followed them to a place where the cave met riverbed.

Lila stepped through an arched opening large enough to fit an ATV. Chirping and trilling birds welcomed her to their home. The shallow stream bubbled and frothed over rocks; a scrawny tree limb bobbed and floated along the water's center. She looked left. The rocky streambed narrowed, melding with the inclining embankment. Passage that way might be possible, but only on foot.

To Lila's right sat the charred remains of the SUV. She looked up and spotted the strange twisted and angled trees she had seen looking down. "Well, this is where it goes."

CHAPTER EIGHT

B Y ALL OUTWARD appearances, the Thorpe home looked fine. It was the destruction in the front hallway that turned Elizabeth's blood cold.

The sight before her screamed of a struggle. Broken wood furniture littered the floor at her feet. Down a ways, office files and other assorted supplies were scattered about. A huge dent in the wall where someone or something had collided with it, hard. On one of the files, Elizabeth saw a few spots of dried blood.

"You both didn't need to come," Rafe said, looking pointedly at his brother.

Elizabeth looked from her undersheriff to her ex-husband then back. "Since he was my only means for a ride, he came."

Rafe narrowed his eyes. "You stay put." He pointed at the garage entry where Joel stood.

Joel went stiff, clicking his heels together, and gave his younger brother a sharp, clean salute. "Sir, yes, sir."

The two and their antagonistic behavior were comical on good days, but a real pain in the ass in times like these. Elizabeth let it be. They could hash out their brotherly "love" on their own time.

"What have you found so far?" she pressed Rafe.

"I haven't gone over the entire house," he answered. "Most of the chaos is contained to the front hall."

She squatted next to a well-used and tattered day planner. The stamped wording had long ago lost its metallic coloring, leaving behind tiny flecks in the deeply pressed ridges, and the black paper was bleached in spots. Elizabeth was about to ask for a latex-free glove when Rafe handed her one.

"Is there any indication Dominic was here?" she asked, slipping on the glove.

He shook his head "Whatever happened, I think Olivia was alone and she put up a fight."

"To no avail." Elizabeth opened the day planner and flipped through the first few pages. "Where's Lundquist and Dayne? They should be going over this house with a fine-toothed comb."

"They're elsewhere."

She rose from her crouched position. "Elsewhere where? Doing what?"

Rafe stared at her, his gaze hardening. Here it came. The infamous Fontaine mule-headedness. He was turning away when Joel's chuckle made him stop.

"Bro, don't," he warned.

"Stay out of this," Rafe snapped.

"Knock it off." Elizabeth stepped between the two, blocking their showdown at high noon. "You owe me an update, *Deputy*. Something else is going on besides our missing medical examiner and critically injured surgeon. So out with it."

There was a momentary flash of anger on Rafe's face, but

he schooled himself. Hooking his thumbs behind his vest, he shifted into a relaxed stance. "We got a call-out to the old Norwood property near Kathy Miller's place. Dayne and Meyer found a boneyard."

"Eh … a what?"

"A boneyard. Large site with lots of scattered human remains. DCI and a forensic anthropologist are out there helping process it."

Elizabeth blinked at Rafe, her brain trying to register what he'd just said. A boneyard. In her county. Under her watch. How and when did this happen?

Oh, she knew how it happened. Eckardt had long been a breeding ground for homicides and serious criminal activity. With each case Elizabeth and her team closed and every criminal enterprise shut down, a new and more serious incident would arise. In the last six months, between her bouts with medical emergencies and the revelation of her sister's own foray into the criminal underworld, Elizabeth felt the tightly gripped reins begin to slip from her hands.

"A killer's dumping ground?" she blurted.

Rafe shook his head. "Dayne is dead certain it's not a serial killer's burial plot. She doesn't see the indicators."

"Then what is it?" Elizabeth demanded.

"We don't know. It's why the big guns were brought in for this. Dayne hypothesized maybe it was a place where people were shot."

"A killing field," Joel interrupted.

"Maybe." Rafe shrugged. "I don't see it. Dayne didn't sound like she believed it."

Elizabeth's mind raced with a thousand thoughts and

questions. How did Olivia's apparent abduction and Dominic's critical injuries coincide with this boneyard? Why were they just now being made aware of it? Was it coincidental these two events happened at the same time and yet had nothing to do with each other? Why was Dayne throwing out theories? It didn't sound like her.

Elizabeth's most critical thought—was she ready for something this serious?

"Stop trying to overanalyze it, Ellie," Rafe chided.

"I'm not."

"You are. Your face is getting that weird pensive look. Stuff like this happens, and there's nothing you can do to stop it." He took hold of her hand and squeezed it. "Let the team of experts do their job. If anyone will figure it out, it'll be Dayne."

He was right, of course. He was always right. Deputy Detective Lila Dayne had never failed to do the impossible. Because of her dogged determination and intuition, she'd brought down an elusive serial killer then slammed the book shut on a cold case that had haunted Elizabeth for more than two decades. If there was anyone she trusted more than the two men next to her, it was Lila Dayne.

"Don't forget," Joel cut in. "There's the Jeep the good doctor was driving left at the hunting cabin."

Elizabeth winced. "Crap. We need to get back there and process it."

"Jeep?" Rafe frowned. "Dominic never drove a Jeep."

"Precisely. He was driving someone else's vehicle from God knows where. We've got to backtrack the vehicle's path and see if we can find where he was stabbed," Elizabeth said.

Rafe growled. "Dammit. We've got too many crime scenes spread out all over the county and not enough people."

Elizabeth frowned, catching on to one missing person. "Where's Deputy Young?"

The grimace he gave her was not promising. For the last four months, Elizabeth had played hell getting him to update her on the goings-on in the department, especially with Deputy Corey Young's progress after her encounters with a grief-stricken madwoman in a barn loft.

"About that," Rafe started.

"Let me stop you right there. If she's not ready to come back, then she's not ready. But is she at least getting help?"

He shrugged. "I can't seem to get through to her. No one else in the department has had any luck either."

"Not even Dayne?"

"She's got her own demons to deal with."

He wasn't wrong there. Dayne had been through the fires of hell and somehow came out on the better side of it. Dayne had also been in the barn loft with Young, she'd seen the same things—she just hadn't been the unwilling participant in another woman's death as Young had been.

"I'll go see her," Elizabeth promised.

"Not today you will. Before we leave this house, we're going through it for evidence to see what happened to Olivia," Rafe said. "Then we're locking it down and going to the cabin and the Jeep."

"What about me?" Joel piped up.

"You're going back home to North Carolina."

THE THORPE HOUSE gave up very few clues other than what they found in the front hallway. Olivia's and Dominic's cars were missing, along with Olivia's phone. It looked as if their security system had been wiped; Rafe downloaded what he could of the videos just in case. They documented everything else on their cell phones with photos and dictation.

A lone teacup sat in the middle of the island counter. The tea itself looked untouched and had long gone cold. Elizabeth fiddled with the dangling string and label, drenched from sitting in the liquid. Olivia loved tea, preferring to drink it over coffee. It was a quirk that had baffled Elizabeth when she first met her.

When was the last time they had a coffee-tea date and just gabbed? Months? Maybe a year? Or was it longer?

Looking back at the doorway dividing the hall from the kitchen, Elizabeth reconstructed the potential scenario taking Olivia from this house. She had come home from her shift, alone. Many times, when Elizabeth would visit, she noted Olivia had placed her leather satchel and purse on the hallway table. If the attack took place out there, it would explain how the bags ended up on the floor and the table they sat on broken.

Elizabeth returned to the single cup. Had Olivia come in here to make a cup? Had she heard a noise in the house to make her abandon it and gone into the hall to investigate?

Or had the abductor come into the kitchen and flushed Olivia out into the hall?

Rafe stepped into the room, empty evidence bags in his

hands. "We should take the cup and the tea bag."

"Do you have a container for the liquid? I'm sure Lundquist will want it to test just in case. If not him, DCI will."

Once they'd bagged and tagged everything deemed important, including the blood-speckled file and the broken furniture, Elizabeth and Rafe left for the cabin while Joel headed back to the main Fontaine residence to do as his brother asked.

Now, Rafe stared straight ahead as he navigated the backroads behind his family's long-established property lines.

The silence in the Charger was ominous. Elizabeth dared not broach any subject with him, choosing to watch the late-February landscape roll past. Hard to imagine that in less than a month, this whole county would be sporting green everything if the weather played nice.

From the back seat, Bentley climbed onto the center console and settled her head on Elizabeth's shoulder. She reached up and sank her fingers into the dog's silky coat and massaged her head and ears.

Rafe's rough-hewn voice broke through the silence. "What do you know about Olivia's and Dominic's lives before they moved here?"

Elizabeth lifted her head from the headrest and looked at him. "Not much. I thought Olivia mentioned to me one time she was from the Chicago area, but don't quote me on that. Best I know about Dominic was he finished his residency in Iowa City and they both moved here shortly thereafter."

"Did Olivia do her residency at U of I, too?"

"Yes, I think."

Rafe mulled over her answers, his twitching facial muscles her only indication he was thinking hard. She let him be. Whatever was going through his head, he needed no interruptions from her.

Instead, Elizabeth did her own contemplations while she kept her focus on the scenery and her hand massaging her dog's head. She wanted to study the old day planner closer. Its age and the smudged ink on the first few pages spoke of its value to Olivia. Before the Fontaine brotherly interruption, Elizabeth had landed on a list of contacts with addresses and phone numbers. If someone was going to dumpster dive into Olivia's history, Elizabeth was going to be the only one.

Rafe left the gravel road for a dirt one. His progress down the narrow lane with the decades' worth of ruts was slow. Bentley scrabbled away from Elizabeth's touch, preparing to hop out as soon as Rafe parked.

The side-by-side came into view right where Joel and Elizabeth left it. Rafe parked the Charger in front of the ATV, and they exited the car. While he went to the trunk to get out the evidence kit, Elizabeth dug around in the glove compartment and found her sidearm. She smiled. He thought he'd been clever, keeping her weapon always in his reach and supposedly out of her sight. But she knew him better than he thought.

When he came around the backside of the car, she was clipping the holster to her belt. With a shake of his head, he kept on walking to the ATV. Bentley hopped into the back seat and settled in for the ride through the open fields and timbered areas.

The drive to the cabin was a five- to ten-minute ride depending on obstacles. It took Rafe less than that, driving faster than he probably should have.

He parked the ATV next to the cabin entrance, and they hiked over to the hill. Bentley stayed glued to Elizabeth's side. They crested the hill and looked down at the pair of trees where the Jeep had ended up.

"Where is it?" Rafe asked.

Elizabeth gaped at the empty space. It was gone. Vanished into thin air. Frantically, she looked about, but there was no sign of it.

"Ellie?"

"It was right there." She jabbed a finger at the point where the Jeep had crashed. "How do you haul a disabled vehicle out of here in"—she checked her watch—"four hours? That's how. They had four hours."

Abandoning any hope he'd have the answers, she hurried down the incline to the trees, Bentley hot on her heels. Someone might be able to make the Jeep disappear, but they couldn't make their prints vanish. Behind her, she heard the jingle of Rafe's duty belt as he followed her.

Near the trees, she pulled up and checked the ground. Bingo!

"Those look like track marks from a bucket loader," Rafe said as he squatted. "They made sure to go over every inch back and forth to cover up footprints and tire tread."

"Damn it!"

He rose. "We can still follow them. See where they went and how they got in and out of here."

"Think they could still be nearby?"

His gaze slid to her. "You haven't requaled with your weapon."

A sly smile slipped into place, and she winked at him. "I requaled with one of the best shooters."

Rafe rolled his eyes. "My brother is going to be the death of me. I shouldn't have let him anywhere near you."

"Too late now." Elizabeth took off, following the heavily marred path. "We're going to find out how Dominic managed to get a Jeep down here, and where it was taken to keep us out of it."

THE TRAIL ENDED at a well-traveled gravel road. Elizabeth and Rafe exited the ATV and carefully scoured the area for any signs as to which way the confiscators had taken the wrecked Jeep. She spotted the place where a truck and a trailer had been parked alongside the road, the tire marks indented into the soft ground on the shoulder. But what direction the vehicles had gone was anybody's guess. They could have done any number of scenarios.

"I've got nothing," Rafe said.

Elizabeth shaded her eyes looking west, watching the sun begin its downward crawl across the sky. She checked her watch, just past four p.m., then went back to shielding her eyes from the late winter sun. This road. This direction. She knew where it led.

Dropping her hand, she turned to Rafe. "Are you thinking what I'm thinking?"

He came to stand beside her, staring westward. "When

was the last time you spoke to him?"

"Not since Halloween."

"Last I heard he wasn't staying there anymore."

She looked up at Rafe. "Where would he have gone? He'd sustained near life-threatening injuries."

Rafe glanced at her. "Not life-threatening enough, apparently. He was up to his old tricks a few weeks after your second surgery."

She focused on her dog trotting along the road, her nose to the ground. "Doesn't tell me where he's staying."

"Knowing him, it could be any number of residences. He still has friends in low places. One thing's for sure, he hasn't been seen at The Watering Hole."

Kelley Sheehan not lording over all at the most popular bar in town? That was a surprise.

"We could still drive out there and see if he's home," Rafe suggested.

"This late in the day, I'd rather not take my chances. He's probably got the place booby-trapped. He made a lot of enemies with his last stunt."

Rafe blew out a heavy breath. "And he keeps making more. He's avoided contact with the county attorney and the state as much as he can. When they do manage to corner him, he refuses to answer their questions on his activities leading up to Halloween and the deaths."

Elizabeth narrowed her eyes. She was all too aware of this revelation about disgraced ex-sheriff, Kelley Sheehan. Her sister, Marnie, kept her appraised when she could. Marnie had been pulled into the machinations of Sheehan's self-centered—albeit well-meaning—plot to bring down a slew of sick, perverted twats who had been instrumental in the death of two of Elizabeth's friends more than twenty-five years ago.

"What do you want to do?" Rafe asked.

Sighing, Elizabeth looked back at the setting sun. "We were thwarted from seeing what that Jeep could have held. Let's see what a new day brings us." She met his gaze. "In the meantime, I want to see this graveyard of bones. I need an update from my lead detective."

Rafe checked his watch. "They'll probably be wrapping up what they've done today. I don't see the DCI team working in the dark. The area is too remote." He pulled out his cell phone and held it aloft. "No reception out here. It's spotty at best where they're at."

"All the more reason to drive out there." Elizabeth whistled for Bentley. "I want to grab the rest of my things from the cabin, and we're going. I'll sleep in my own bed tonight."

He eyed her warily. "Like you're even bothering to go home."

She gave him a one-sided shrug. "We're in the thick of a new set of cases. You're probably right."

CHAPTER NINE

RATTLING LOCKS AND clicks pulled Olivia from her research. Shadows' creeping fingers were invading the small apartment, touching the edges of the files and reports scattered across the floor around her. Her blurry eyes took a moment to focus, then the door opened. In swept Horatio, along with the scintillating aroma of food heavy on spices, garlic, and tomato. Looming behind him was his right-hand man. Adrian, was it?

Olivia bit back a smile at the strips of white stabilizing tape over the dark man's nose. He might have broken her arm, but she got her licks in good.

While Adrian ensured the door was firmly locked, Horatio carried two large, insulated bags to the infantile counters around the sink.

"You must be starving," he said by way of greeting.

"Good evening to you, too. What is the official time?" Olivia pressed.

He paused in removing the containers from the bags and glanced back at her. "Time is irrelevant."

"Bullshit."

His brilliant grin prodded at the embers burning hot inside of her. Horatio returned to his task. "I see the box enticed you. Anything interesting you'd like to share?"

Slowly, methodically, Olivia worked around her sling-encased arm and got up from the floor. She noted the gleam in Adrian's eyes as he watched her struggle. Oh, yes, he'd never lend an offer of assistance.

"You drag me from my home with a veiled threat that my husband is up to no good, and you're breaking a decades-long agreement to keep me from something. Then have your *man* rough me up, lock me away, and leave me with nothing to do but read old files."

Horatio faced her during her mini tirade.

"I want answers," she said.

"Don't we all." He went back to serving up what looked like a rice dish.

Olivia's stomach growled at the mouthwatering smell. She hadn't eaten since the protein bar she'd devoured during the middle of her overnight shift. The pain of her broken bone and the small amount of Percocet in her system had squelched any need for food. But the drug had worn off, the pain had ebbed to the point she could ignore it, and now her body was crying out for sustenance. Against her will, she inched closer to Horatio. From the corner of her eye, she caught Adrian's subtle movement to follow her progress.

"Like I can do anything to him," she snapped, pointing at her casted arm.

"It's fine, Adrian." Horatio rotated, holding up a bowl. "You ever been to New Orleans?"

She stared at the heaping, jumbled, red mess in the white ceramic dish. Saliva pooled in her mouth. She swallowed it and met Horatio's amused gaze. "I have not."

"Hmm, then you're in for a treat. Adrian here is from

New Orleans, and he's a damn fine cook, too."

"What is it?"

"Jambalaya." Horatio offered it like a sacrifice. "You'll like it."

Olivia eyed the bowl, then looked directly into Horatio's eyes. While she studied him, searching for any signs of trickery, he seemed to be studying her in return. Gone were the youthful lines and smoothness of a man just coming into his prime—in his place was an older man, a more refined man with deep lines webbing from the corners of his eyes. He was two years older than her but looked nearly a decade more now. When they'd first hooked up, he had inherited an empire of bars, clubs, and an assorted mess of "businesses" at the too-young age of nineteen. His father and older brother were killed in a mysterious car accident.

Olivia, chafing at the seemingly unattainable expectations and restrictions her upper Northside family had put on her, had slipped easily into Horatio's arms, falling hard under his tender ministrations. Eight months crept past before her parents figured out what she was doing; two weeks later she was living with Horatio. The blowback had left an ocean-sized rift between her and her family. One she'd never dared to mend.

To this day, Olivia and her parents were not on speaking terms.

By kidnapping her from her home, Horatio reminded her why she hated him. Why she made him swear to leave her alone.

Horatio lowered the bowl and set it back on the counter. "You must be in need of more pain meds?" He reached inside his coat.

"Don't." Her head swam after the brief bout of exertion. "No more of that. Just over the counter."

He frowned. "I don't know 'bout that. You don't look like you're handling it too good."

"I'm not in the mood to argue. You put me through all of this and left a box of case files for a reason. I can't focus if I'm doped up. A mix of ibuprofen and acetaminophen is all I need."

After a moment's scrutiny, Horatio gestured at Adrian. The big man came beside his boss and held out a bag he withdrew from his coat pocket. Horatio indicated he wanted Adrian to give it to Olivia. Given the deepening of the perpetual scowl, Adrian was none too pleased with having to do this. He thrust the bag in Olivia's vicinity.

With a sly smile, she took the white pharmacy bag and shook it. Pill bottles rattled inside.

"Should be sufficient to carry you through while you're here," Horatio said, then once more picked up the bowl of jambalaya. "You'll want to eat first." He motioned for her to move to the small table.

Resigned to the demands of her stomach, Olivia headed to the table and sat, setting the bag beside her. Horatio placed the bowl and a spoon before her, then returned to the counter to pull out an array of beverages.

As she ate, he brought her a large bottle of water.

"You're not eating," she said between spoonfuls.

"This is for you."

Olivia paused in her eating and set the spoon down. "Horatio, let's be honest here. What is going on?"

He tilted his head, staring at her with that all-knowing look of a man who knew her too well, or he thought he knew her. Theirs had been an odd relationship. One people whispered about behind backs and scorned in her face. But she had been a headstrong, immature woman back then and thought she knew better. How wrong she'd been.

"If I'm honest," he started, "and let's face it, you know I am." He leaned forward. "I don't know what's going on. What I do know is, your man is an idiot and got himself caught up in something, putting you both in danger. Then he dragged me into it."

Olivia pressed her back into the chair, gnawing on her lip. What could Dominic have possibly aligned himself with to compel Horatio to such measures as forcefully kidnapping her?

Horatio nodded at the strewn mess of reports and files. "This took me a while to pull together. Me and my boys can't make heads or tails of it. But I knew you would." He sat back in his chair. "You were the sharp one. I always admired that about you."

"Those are case files. Autopsy reports. Forensic analysis. How did you manage to get all of it?"

He flashed his brilliant grin. "Pays to know the right people in the right places."

"Greasing the palms of easily bribed cops and lab assistants?"

"If it gets you what you want, why not?"

She pressed fingers against her forehead, feeling the ache in her head strengthen. She'd spent the better part of the afternoon trying to read without her reading glasses, and the strain on her eyes had manifested into a full-blown migraine. Horatio and his word tap dance were not making matters better.

"We can discuss these subjects tomorrow," he said. "Eat, hydrate, rest." He touched her knee. "Take the edge off the pain."

She glared at him. "I'm your prisoner. Not a favored guest."

His hand slipped away. He regarded her down the length of his broad nose. The lift and angle of his chin giving off an air of superiority.

"There was a time—not so long ago—you would have looked at me in a different light."

Olivia narrowed her gaze more. "That time is long over. I know you for what you really are and am no longer drawn to your power."

Horatio stared at her a moment more, then rose from the seat. With a motion to Adrian, the two men left, wordlessly. At the door, Horatio looked back at Olivia. The darkness filling his eyes gave her a momentary stab of trepidation. A slight dip of his chin was all she received before he swept out of the apartment. The telltale click and clack of the locks engaging were her reminder she was stuck here.

She counted down the seconds until she was certain he and his man were gone, then gave into the full body shivers. Closing her eyes, she drew in a shuddering breath, then released it slowly. Horatio was not a man to trifle with, and each verbal joust between them would only increase his drift toward violence. As he continued to remind her, their shared history was the single laurel branch protecting her from him.

From here on out, she had to keep her tongue in check and placate him as best she could in order to get out of this unscathed.

Olivia gazed at the jambalaya. He was right, she needed to keep up her strength and give her body all the fuel it needed to heal and to sort through the tangled mess those reports and files provided. The sooner she figured out what was going on and what her husband had gotten himself into, the sooner she could devise an escape plan.

CHAPTER TEN

LEFT ALONE, LILA studied the scene spread before her. Her trained eyes took in the shapes and forms, the way the vestiges of light played with the shadows and structures. The stillness of the evening woods broken by the low hum of a generator powering three spotlights Lila had turned on to better see this macabre graveyard.

DCI and the forensic teams had packed up what they didn't want left behind and called it a day before the sun completely set. She had sent Meyer and Kyle on their ways. Despite this huge mess and the need for more work, they still had duties as deputies to perform. With Fontaine and the sheriff out of pocket, it was left to Lila to dole out the orders. Frankly, she needed the time to herself to absorb this whole day and process it.

Finding the tunnel and the cave gave a whole new element to this exposed boneyard. A puzzle piece she struggled to place in the right sequence. Right along with the burned shell of a vehicle.

The crime techs had found no signs of bullets or that guns were used on any of the victims. Which ruled out Lila's theory this had been a shootout and the losers left behind to rot. A few of the remains had traces of tissue, but it was so degraded, forensics was not holding out any hope the finds would produce any significant test results.

Lila kept reminding herself this was day one. They were not done here. More clues would reveal themselves as the teams continued to comb and dig their way over this whole area. Time was of the essence, but it was also on their side.

She left her post and began to carefully pick a path around the outer edge of the spotlight's reach, keeping her focus trained on the scattered piles of bones.

The normally bone-deep chill had returned, turning her breath to a cloud. She hunkered deeper into her coat, burying her hands in the pockets.

What need would someone, or someones, have to leave bodies here for the predators and scavengers to raid? She paused, taking in the backside of the shack, shadowed by the looming trees it sat between. Who knew about this place to be able to leave remains behind undetected?

Kathy Miller would need to be questioned again. A job Lila reserved for herself.

Resuming her slow trek around the boneyard, Lila scrutinized the bones and scraps of clothing lying about. Why would someone—who obviously had spent a good deal of time out here if the sheer amount of remains was any indication—leave behind such telltale indicators of who the victims were? Perhaps they didn't care. Or they were confident enough to think that there wasn't any markers on the clothing to tie back to them or the victims themselves. No DNA. No trace evidence. Nothing to point fingers at the perpetrator of this crime. Whatever crime this was.

Dr. Pembrook, the forensic anthropologist, had stated the styles of the clothing ranged between male and female.

Which threw out any thought this was the work of a serial killer. Something Lila still stood firm on this not being.

Stopping again, this time, directly across from the point where she'd begun, she squinted past the lights and spotted movement coming from the other side. She reached for her sidearm, pausing when the figure stepped into the pool of light.

"I heard my point woman on this case was still here."

Lila dropped her hand away from her pistol grip. "I heard my sheriff took back the reins and is running her department again."

Sheriff Benoit tilted her head just so and hooked her hands on her hips. "Why don't you give me the four-one-one?"

After joining her boss, Lila stood facing the boneyard. Neither woman spoke, giving a silent requiem for the dead.

"How many?" Benoit asked after a sufficient amount of time had passed.

"We don't know. Dr. Pembrook, the forensic anthropologist, doesn't hold out hope of finding an intact skeleton. He's certain we're looking at multiple remains, but no way to narrow down a firm number."

Benoit continued to stare at the scene. The planes of her face had sharpened in the last few months, showing the repercussions of her self-inflicted injuries and time to heal from them.

"You have any thoughts on whether this is connected with the disappearance of our medical examiner and the attack on her husband?" she asked.

Lila shifted to face her sheriff. "If there is one, I can't

seem to find it. It doesn't mean I'm not ruling out the possibility of a correlation leading to a causation."

Benoit half turned her head to look at Lila, studied her a moment, then went back to looking at the scene. "The single piece of evidence tying to Dominic's injuries has been stolen."

Lila blinked at the sheriff. "Come again?"

"Fontaine and I returned to where he'd crashed a Jeep. It was gone. We saw plenty of evidence someone had used track-type machinery to get it out of there and cover up any other incriminating prints, but the trail led back to a dead end."

"So you came out here to see how it fits into all of this?" Lila asked.

Benoit didn't speak right away, simply crossed her arms at her chest and leaned more of her weight back onto her left leg. She craned her neck, tipping her head just right for the darkness to cover her face. The shade made her look more hardened than Lila remembered. This was not the same overly rational and heavily compassionate woman who had hired Lila all those years back. The events of the past October and thereafter had altered something inside the sheriff.

During the Halloween incident, Lila had struggled to keep the sheriff in her lane. Was she about to encounter the same MO this time around? Again, friends were involved somehow. When it came to family and friends, Sheriff Elizabeth Benoit forgot herself and turned into a loose cannon.

Benoit resumed her previous posture, bringing her face back into the light. The darkness was gone, but the sensations lingered. "While disturbing, none of this"—she flicked a hand at the spotlighted scene—"makes any sense to me. How does what happened to Dominic figure into this? And why is Olivia missing?"

"She's for sure missing?" Lila asked.

"Yes. We have a BOLO out for her and Dominic's vehicles—neither were at the house. I gave Lundquist a box of evidence to process, because it damn well looks like someone took her forcibly." Benoit tucked her hands into her coat pockets. "And I have no idea where to start looking for her."

"What do we know of her and Dominic's pasts?"

"Only that they both did their residency in Iowa City and then moved here. Olivia never talked about her life before Iowa. Dominic was tightlipped about himself, period."

The timing of Dominic's injuries, Olivia's abduction, and the discovery of this boneyard was seriously circumspect. A niggling sensation in the corner of her mind warned Lila this was all connected. If so, the sheriff would be the last person able to separate her personal connection to the persons of interest, suspect or not. It would be a repeat of the Halloween murders all over again.

"There's more," Lila remarked.

Her bluntness brought the sheriff around. "Explain."

"Better yet, I'll show you."

Lila led the way into the shack. Before the teams had left, she, Meyer, and Lundquist had set up a series of lights inside the shack and down into the tunnel. Upon stepping inside the structure, Lila hit the switch on the first lamp, triggering the electrical system connected to the already running generator. The shack's interior glowed. A bubble of light haloed from the tunnel entrance.

"What is all of this?" Benoit asked as she circled the opened trap door.

"Don't rightly know. We didn't get a chance to update Fontaine." Lila met Benoit's piercing gaze. "So, here's your update. The tunnel leads through a winding and narrow path toward a tributary several hundred yards past the boneyard. The path opens into a cave."

"Am I to assume you were the one to go through it?" Benoit looked pointedly at Lila's filthy uniform.

"I was the only one small enough to get through, yes."

"What did you find in the cave?"

Lila circumvented the trap door, staring down into its bowels. "Nothing extraordinary. Tomorrow, I'm having Meyer rig up a camera on a robot to record the path and document anything of interest." She reached into her vest and withdrew her phone. She pulled up the photos she'd taken of the underside of the rock she had wiggled under. "I did find something out of place in there." She handed over her phone to the sheriff. "Thoughts?"

Benoit studied the image, adjusting the zoom and backing it off. "Could be anything." She handed Lila her phone. "But you think it's a significant find."

"I want a swab test done on it to confirm or rule out my initial ideas before I jump to any conclusions." She returned her phone to its pocket on her vest. "I'm most likely going to be the one to go back in since I'm the only one with the body size to move around in there."

Benoit moved to the mouth of the tunnel and squatted

before the steps. The lights behind her and below lit up the sheriff's body. She stayed there, her arms resting on her thighs, as she stared into the gaping hole.

Lila noticed the twitches in the sheriff's face. The narrowing of her eyes. Benoit was coming up with an idea.

"What do you think this all means, Deputy Detective?" Her gaze lifted from the tunnel and met Lila's.

"My honest opinion?"

"Be as brutal as you want."

Lila let the statement hang in the air between them. She had mulled over the particulars all day, adding in the pieces as they had been discovered. The single most thought always came forefront when she latched onto any conclusion. It was a scary one. A conclusion to turn her blood cold.

"My brutal, honest opinion. We have a pit of vipers in our county. The likes of which we have not encountered before."

Benoit let out a long hiss of breath. She pushed off the floor and stood to her full height. "This could become a federal ordeal."

"It could. If it comes to that, I know a few people."

"Let's see how long we can keep this in house. The last thing I need is a media madhouse if this gets out nationally."

Lila nodded. "We do need to consider having constant security around here. We're too short-staffed to handle it on our own."

"I'll call in a few favors. I know some trustworthy guys who'd give their left nut to do some work."

A smile tickled the corners of Lila's mouth at her boss's remark. "You've been hanging around your ex lately."

"Old habits die hard." Benoit jutted her chin at the shack door. "That the only way in, other than this tunnel?"

"Yep. We can seal it off tonight. I've got a way to lock the trap door in case someone comes through the tunnel."

"Get it done. Fontaine is on his way to Iowa City to get an in-person update on Dr. Thorpe. I'm heading to the department."

"Pulling an all-nighter?" Lila asked.

"That's the plan, yes. You should go home and get some rest. This week is shaping up to be a doozy."

"Yes, ma'am." Lila moved to do just that. "Sheriff."

"Yeah?"

"It's good having you back in the saddle again."

Benoit chuckled. "You've been spending too much time around the locals. Your Chicago is fading."

"I don't see that as a bad thing."

LILA GOT SNUBBED the moment she walked into her little bungalow and toed off her boots. Her pet Siamese fighting betta darted into his Easter Island statue to hide when she tossed her Eckardt County Sheriff Department coat onto the sofa.

"Love you, too, Gerry two-point-oh."

She paused long enough to inspect his bubble nest. Her first betta fish, Gerry number one, had passed a month back. Luckily, Lila had noticed the signs and knew her fish was in his twilight days. After a bit of searching, she found the perfect replacement betta. She kept the two males separate until Gerry One died. Gerry Two had taken over the fish tank with relish, but he was even more uppity than Gerry One.

Gerry Two had begun a bubble nest. A promising sign he was getting comfortable in his new home with a human owner.

Lila noticed there was still bits of food from his morning feeding, so she left him be.

A shiver took hold of her. She bumped up the temp on the thermostat, kicking on the furnace. She headed for the kitchen, unbuttoning her uniform top. A hot shower followed up by a long soak in the Jacuzzi with the jets on sounded wonderful.

She freed the last button, then there was a knock on the door. Whoever was out there better have a good excuse for bothering her. Unbothered that she wasn't presentable—she did have on a tank under the shirt—she stalked back to the front door and peeked through the sidelite.

Lila braced herself and pried open the door.

Decked out in his uniform and a black ball cap with deputy embroidered in bold white reflective lettering across the front, Kyle shoved his hands into his deputy jacket.

She'd seen him in uniform hundreds of times—removed it from him just as many—and even to this day he still made her chest tighten at the sight.

He did his own perusal of her partially undressed state, glanced out at the street, then back to her. "Can I come in?"

Wondering why he'd even ask, she stepped aside and gestured for him to enter. Once he passed her, she swung the door shut. "You didn't have to ask."

He shrugged and focused on the fish tank. "That's not Gerry."

"It's Gerry Two. Original guy died last month."

"And you couldn't think to tell me?"

"He's a fish. It's not like you had any emotional attachment to him."

"Would have been nice to know."

Rolling her eyes, Lila moved to the kitchen. "Why are you here?" She slipped out of the dirty shirt and chucked it toward the laundry cabinet.

When he didn't answer, she faced him. He'd removed his ball cap and was crushing it. He refused to look at her. That niggling voice in the back of her mind began to speak louder, and it wasn't telling her good tidings.

Lundquist finally lifted his gaze. The war waging in those blue-green depths confirmed what the voice was shouting now.

"Are you breaking it off with me?" she blurted.

His face contorted as if she'd slapped him. After a few seconds, he rearranged his features and shook his head. Without a word, he flicked his ball cap onto the only armchair she owned and entered the kitchen.

When he got closer, Lila held up a hand; it collided with his chest. "Whatever excuses you're about to tell me, just save it. I don't want to hear them."

"I'm not making any excuses." He took her hand in his and dragged it down. "Is that what you thought I came here for?"

"For months now, you haven't given me any reason to think otherwise. Every day since you found out what killed your sister, you've been distant. You made sure we were always on opposite shifts, never giving me a chance to spend any time with you."

"With the sheriff out, I thought that was what you would want. It made more sense having me work the night shift with Fontaine and leaving you on the day shift with Meyer, so we always had someone with more experience available."

She freed her hand and backed a step. "Yet you never asked me if I wanted that arrangement."

"I didn't think it would have been such a big deal."

"Exactly. You didn't think. Even when we had down time, you made yourself as scarce as possible. You haven't set foot in this house until tonight."

Two-handed, he rubbed his face, then with a growl, jerked his hands down to his sides. "I had Freya to deal with, not to mention all the shit going on up here." He circled his head. "I wasn't about to unload on you after what you've been through."

She gave him a slight push. "I could have handled it. For God's sake, if anyone would know what you had to process through it was me."

He managed to snag her wagging arms and stilled her frantic movements. "Lila, you're not my therapist. Fixing my problems with sex would have only cheapened things between us."

Staring up at him, she saw a different light in his eyes. How had she misread him? Yes, he'd been distant. He hadn't spoken to her other than to review work-related situations or the occasional text messages to check in with her. Nothing more, nothing less. Standing here with him so close to her, she felt the slow drain of her resources.

She'd been holding herself together with thin sutures.

The strides she'd taken in the last few years were unraveling inside of her. She'd come to think of Kyle as more than just a fellow deputy and fellow investigator. Before his world had imploded at the revelations of his eldest sister's death, Lila was dancing with the idea of being in love with him. After his abrupt absence, she'd reconsidered her emotions. Had she lied to herself?

Now what?

If what he was saying, and what she was reading into what he was telling her, he was considering her feelings and her trauma. Damn it, he was too good for her.

"I would never try to be your therapist." She wrangled herself out of his hold. "I would be someone who understood."

"Even after what you witnessed Halloween night?"

"Believe me, I've seen worse than what those women did." She waved away his attempt to distract. "This isn't a great time to be talking about any of this. You're on duty, and I have to shower. What did you come here for?"

Kyle tilted his head and his blue-green gaze bore into her. Lila resisted the urge to squirm under the scrutiny. He moved toward her, she countered backward. They kept up the slow dance until he crowded her into the wall dividing her kitchen from the back rooms.

Under normal circumstances, she wouldn't allow anyone to put her in such a position. With Kyle it was different. They'd been through more than a few situations where they had to rely on each other. Not to mention the countless times she'd bared her body and her soul to him. He had memorized each and every scar marring her flesh. This man had done the impossible when it came to getting under her skin and nesting there.

"I realized today," he said in a low rumble, "when you looked at me with wariness in your eyes, that I had been wrong to stay away from you."

"So, you came here to kiss and make up?"

"Is that what you want?"

She focused on the open gap of his uniform exposing his throat, trying to quell the warm tingles washing through her. "You're on the clock," she croaked.

"I'm on break."

Lila looked at him sharply. "I'm not about to be your badge bunny."

He lowered his mouth to hers, hesitating a hairsbreadth away. "You're nowhere close to that."

"Nine to ten you get a callout."

"Then we better hurry up."

CHAPTER ELEVEN

J OEL'S TRUCK WAS parked in her drive.

Elizabeth pulled her Interceptor in beside his large vehicle and cut the engine. Bentley, standing on the center
console, gave a low woof.

"Yeah, I thought he was going home, too." Elizabeth
scratched Bentley's head. "Well, let's get this over with."

She exited the SUV and opened the back door for Bentley and grabbed her gear. As she trudged up the sidewalk, the
front door opened, and Joel stepped out. Bentley skidded to
a halt at his feet and chirped at him. He lowered himself
down to the collie's level and gave her a generous head rub.
When Elizabeth reached the porch, he rose to his full height.

"You look like hell," he commented.

"Funny, I don't feel like it." She adjusted her duffel bag
strap higher on her shoulder. "Aren't you supposed to be on
the road back to North Carolina?"

Joel propped the door wide, allowing Bentley to scuttle
inside. He gestured for Elizabeth to follow.

Once inside, she let the bag drop to the floor. The small
dining room table she kept for aesthetic purposes was graced
with a single table service and a lit candle. Bentley raced
straight for her food bowl and chowed down. Elizabeth's
stomach growled at the aroma of beef simmered in lush

gravy.

"Pot roast?" she asked Joel as he circumvented her for the kitchen.

"And mashed potatoes smothered in gravy along with green beans and bacon, just how you like it."

"Are you buttering me up for something?"

"Sit down. You need to eat."

Wary, she did as he ordered. His penchant for cooking a hearty meal always came right before he dropped a bomb. Not that Elizabeth minded half the time. Joel was a top-notch cook, better than her on any given day. A blessing his mother had bestowed upon both Fontaine sons and one Elizabeth and Marnie's own mother failed miserably at.

Elizabeth listened to him move around in her kitchen and her dog noisily crunch on her kibble instead of trying to read her ex-husband's mind. It was nice to come home to a meal. When she was going full bore as sheriff, there had been no time for hot meals that didn't come out of a greasy bag or Styrofoam container. The candle. Now that was circumspect. He must have a doozy of an admission or confession if he was using romantic lighting.

Joel rounded the towering room divider carrying a loaded plate with a fat slice of bread dangling on the side.

She eyed the plate he laid with a bit more flourish than necessary. "Since when did you learn how to bake bread?"

"I didn't." He sat down in the chair opposite her. "I bribed a certain baker extraordinaire to do it for me."

"Aside from the Amish community, the only other person capable of this feat is Freya Lundquist."

Joel grinned.

Elizabeth groaned. "You didn't."

"I did. And she was perfectly fine with me."

How she contained the shock, Elizabeth didn't know. Freya had long suffered from crippling anxiety brought on by the death of her eldest sister. Halloween night revealed the circumstances that brought Freya to her unnerving fear of men other than her father and brother.

"She was okay talking and interacting with you?"

"Even without her brother there. She's come a long way."

"Amazing," Elizabeth muttered.

"Eat," Joel prodded.

Giving him the stink eye, she picked up her fork and dug in. The pot roast melted in her mouth. God, whatever he did to make this roast so blasted tender was a mystery.

Bentley barked at the back door. Joel waved for Elizabeth to continue and went to let the border collie out for an evening bathroom break. When he returned, she laid the fork on the mashed potato mound.

"I've applied enough food to soften me up." She blew out the candle. "Why are you still here?"

Joel drew in a breath and lifted his shoulders. Even when he wasn't in uniform, he had to be erect and professional. "I've officially retired. My DD214 came through yesterday."

She stared at him, letting what he'd said soak in. He'd retired? Joel? The man who said he'd stay in the army until he either died or they kicked him out, whichever came first. He never wanted anything else in his life. His undying devotion to his Delta Force unit at times had been a point of contention between them, one of the driving factors in

Elizabeth eventually seeking a divorce. The last few years he'd been a Selection trainer, preparing the next generation of Delta Force operators. Seemed that was no longer the case.

"What do Nico and Craig think?" she asked, referring to two of his long-standing teammates and best friends.

"They're in the process of retiring, too." Joel sighed. "Today's army isn't the same one I enlisted with all those years ago. It was time to scrub out and move on."

"I suppose you haven't bothered to tell Rafe?"

Joel massaged his scarred and callused hands. "Figured you should be the first to know. Well ..." he tilted his head coyly, "the second one to know."

Elizabeth harkened back to their conversation earlier in the day. "The infamous other lady knew before me?"

"She was the force behind talking me into retiring."

Elizabeth pushed her plate aside and rested her arms over the knotted place mat. "How was this woman able to do what I never could?"

Joel gave her his notorious one-hundred-yard stare, the one where she'd have to metaphorically pick up a shovel and start digging if she wanted any details.

"I'm moving back to Iowa," he finally dropped the proverbial bomb.

Elizabeth slammed her back into the chair's whicker backing. "What?"

"Obviously, I can't stay out at the farm until I talked with Rafe first."

"Obviously," Elizabeth parroted sarcastically. "Am I to insinuate you plan to stay here?"

"I could stay at the cabin, but it'd make it highly inconvenient."

"Inconvenient?" She did not like where this was leading. Waving her hands about like a crazed conductor brought him to a halt. "Okay, let's stop right there."

Bentley's sharp bark at the back door hit the pause on anything Elizabeth was about to say.

With a vexing grin, Joel pushed to his feet and went to let in the dog. The collie raced into the house, did a manic circle around the table, then scurried over to her bed, and flopped down. While she lay there, panting, Joel returned to his seat across from Elizabeth.

"You were saying?" he prompted.

"So, you're just going to gloss over the tidbit about another woman managing to get you to retire from the army and you're going to leave her in North Carolina to move back to Iowa?"

Joel twined his fingers and placed his locked hands on top of his head as he slouched in the chair, stretching out his long legs. "No, she's planning to join me."

"What makes you think she'd be okay with you staying at your ex-wife's house?"

"She was fine with me staying with you while you were put in timeout the last few weeks."

Elizabeth shook her head. "Joel, what are you doing? You never wanted to live out your life in Iowa. It's why you took the first train ticket out of town and dragged me with you."

"Things change. I got older. I realized I had seen enough of the world and war."

"What are you going to do? You hated farming, and Rafe

sold off all the land anyway. All you've ever done is soldier-ing."

He brought his hands down and sat forward, laying his hands, palms down, on the place mat. His baby blues pinned her, making Elizabeth wish she had left the candle lit. She hated how he could hold her gaze and then spew whatever whiskey-honeyed words he wanted, and she'd cave.

"About that," he started.

Elizabeth closed her eyes and centered herself for the fall-out. She snapped open her eyes and locked onto him. "About what?"

"You're short manpower. You've got a lot of things going on at once, and if you're going back into the office, you need fresh blood."

"Are you implying I need to bring you into the sheriff's department?"

"I'm implying exactly that. Make me a deputy, Ellie."

"I can't do that."

"You can. It's perfectly acceptable."

"Joel, you haven't lived in Iowa for the last twenty-six years, and a few visits here and there don't constitute as a resident. There's no way anyone in Eckardt will allow me to deputize you. And besides, you have to fulfill this whole slew of requirements first."

"Already done."

"Excuse me?"

He started tapping the tabletop. "All the required paper-work, e-vals, and the like have been transferred from the base and turned into the Iowa Law Enforcement Academy. They took one look at my record and rubber-stamped my approval for employment just today."

Flabbergasted didn't quite cover how Elizabeth felt about all of this. "Joel, are you out of your ever-loving mind? You do realize, if I agree to this—and that's a huge if—you'll be the lowest ranking deputy in my department, under your younger brother at that. Oh, God, Rafe is going to blow a gasket when he finds out what you did."

"Ellie, I'm well aware of my standing in the hierarchy of your department, and I'm perfectly fine with it. You can't deny you need the help. With one deputy out on medical leave, of which there's no guarantee he's going to ever be able to come back, another on a mental hiatus, and the ones left standing have been pulling triple duty for the last five months, you are in dire need of new meat."

"Law enforcement is completely different from what you were doing in the Unit."

Joel folded his arms over his chest and rocked forward. "Just what exactly is it you think Delta operatives really do?"

Elizabeth bit her tongue and looked away.

His chuckle made her cheeks burn hot. "That's what I figured. Your perpetually inquisitive brain never would let you wonder about our operations without knowing full well what we did."

She snapped her gaze back to him. "Fine, what you did can be defined as *policing*. But it still doesn't resolve the problem of someone like you who's had full command of squads and trainees ever being able to follow orders. Especially from me."

"So certain I would get fed up with being under your thumb."

"I don't run my department like a dictator. You and I both know you always bristled under my demands when we were married."

"We're not married anymore, and I'm better trained than to act the fool if a woman is in command."

"I'm not just any woman, Joel."

"No, you're not." He sighed, letting his arms fall to his lap. "Just let me help for now. I can do the dirty work, graveyard shifts, prisoner transport, whatever you like. Give me until after you figure out where Olivia went and/or solve the case of this mysterious boneyard. If it's not working, I'll take my ass somewhere else."

Elizabeth mulled over his proposal. He wasn't wrong. She needed the extra help. And he was more than qualified to handle the duties. Problem was more on her end. Would she be able to handle both Fontaine brothers under her command?

"Swear?" she asked.

"Cross my heart, hope to die. I'll even let you stick the needle in my eye."

Elizabeth pinched her lips to keep the smile at bay. "Fine. But you can't stay here. You pack up your happy ass and go back to your brother's place, and you tell him exactly what you just told me."

"Spoilsport."

Staring at her ex-husband, Elizabeth felt the overwhelming need for a drink of something harder than the glass of tea set before her. She stood. Elizabeth called Bentley, who looked between her two humans, and then hopped up and trotted over to her true owner.

"I'm going to Marnie's."

Joel winked. "Don't be out too late."

CHAPTER TWELVE

Marnie's place was a bar called The Watering Hole and was within walking distance from Elizabeth's house. She and Bentley strolled into a low-buzzing atmosphere. The retro jukebox was pushing out Marnie's typical anti-establishment tunes from the 1960s with some '90s grunge thrown in for kicks. Despite her natural inclination against all things religion, Marnie wasn't usually open on Sundays out of respect for their rural areas' long history of religious order.

Lately, she'd open The Watering Hole's doors for a few hours in the evening, booting out anyone who showed up by eleven p.m. Elizabeth entered at 9:28 p.m.

Perched on an exposed support beam, her black tail flicking like a metronome, Luna, Marnie's cat, watched. Her golden-eye focus mostly on Bentley, who was keeping herself glued to Elizabeth's side.

The only paying patrons were two men sitting at the bar, half-empty beer glasses in hand, chatting away with the Goth woman behind the bar. Marnie looked at the doorway when Elizabeth stepped inside. Elizabeth broke her sister's steady gaze, and Marnie glanced over at a raised platform near the back of bar. Elizabeth followed her sister's pointed look and stopped midway when she spotted the single man seated up there.

Seemingly absorbed in his bourbon and a mess of papers in front of him, Kelley Sheehan sat like the king he considered himself. He hadn't noticed Elizabeth enter as far as she could tell.

However, the two men at the bar did notice and lightning fast they polished off their beers. One tossed a few bills on the bar, they both bid Marnie a good night, then vamoosed.

"Sheriff," they muttered as they passed.

"Gentlemen," she answered, watching them hurry out the door.

Frowning, she resumed her trek and straddled one of the still-warm stools. "They didn't need to bolt like I'd sic their wives on them."

Marnie sniffed. "That's not what got them to hightail it."

After she'd been abducted and endured torture at the hands of a woman she'd once called friend, Marnie had lost some of her flamboyant styles. She'd returned her hair to its normal shade of dark auburn, keeping a single skunk stripe instead of the Cruella de Vil style she'd had for years. Elizabeth noticed a new dragon tattoo covering the nasty scar on her sister's forearm, left behind from a vicious knife wound. There were probably plans for more or she already had them done to cover the other mutilations inflicted on her body.

"Where have you been?" Marnie asked reaching behind her to snatch a bottle of Johnnie Walker off the mirrored wall.

"Forced into a sabbatical out in the middle of nowhere."

Elizabeth took the whiskey tumbler Marnie passed over.

Marnie poured herself some whiskey. "I had a suspicion Rafe would have to do something underhanded to get you to actually listen."

"He didn't have to bring his big brother into the equation." Elizbeth held up her glass and tilted it to her sister. "Bottoms up."

The two shot their drinks and smacked down the glasses against the bar top.

Marnie leaned on her elbows. "Joel's in town?"

Flicking her glass closer to her sister, Elizabeth gestured for her to pour another round. Once she had her next shot, Elizabeth threw it back, not bothering to wait on Marnie this time.

"That bad, huh?" Marnie took her time with her whiskey.

"I'm not going to dump on you about it. How are things going for you?"

Marnie lifted one shoulder and took Elizabeth's empty glass. "At least I'm not sitting in prison."

At the mention of this, Elizabeth looked to the man still sitting on his throne. "After what he did, how can you let him back in here?"

"He's part owner."

"Seriously, what is he holding over you that you'd let him be a financial partner?"

"I'm not getting into it with you tonight. You're obviously hot about something with Joel, among other things." Marnie handed over a longneck. "Nurse this and not my past."

Elizabeth scowled at her sister but took the beer. She decided to pursue a safer topic. "How's Ben doing?"

Deputy Ben Fitzgerald was the last remaining holdover from the old guard who decided Elizabeth's turn as sheriff was worth sticking around for. Until he got ambushed by a couple of deranged women in an attempt to rescue Marnie.

"He has his good days and his bad." Marnie set the beer glasses in a soapy bath.

"Has he talked about what he plans to do once he's fully healed?"

Marnie glanced up from washing the glasses, then rinsed away the bubbles. "Ben's not much of a talker."

Seemed Marnie had taken a few lessons from her secretive husband. It took getting his leg shattered and Marnie being kidnapped for Elizabeth to find out the two had eloped. The real surprise came when she learned Ben had made her his medical surrogate.

The jukebox went quiet. In the absence of music, a loud clack from the back drew Elizabeth's attention. Sheehan stared at her as he pulled his hand from the bourbon bottle and took hold of his glass.

She slipped off the stool. "I'm gonna have a chat."

Marnie looked at her sharply. "Don't you dare start anything."

Elizabeth took a swig of the beer and winked at her sister, then sauntered up to the platform, joining Sheehan on his throne.

"May I?" she asked.

A slick smile made his craggy features darken. "You may."

The chair in front of her slid out. She swung around it and sat. Crossing her leg and hooking her arm holding over the back, she settled in.

"I'd heard tell you reemerged today," he said, his gravelly voice sounding more tired than in the past.

Marnie wasn't alone in bearing the scars of a knife blade. Sheehan had been given more than his fair share, most of which were inflicted on his torso, which he kept covered. It seemed his encounter with the crazed killer woman had drained some of the pep out of the old coot.

"Indeed, I have."

Elizabeth eyed him, giving him a window of opportunity to tell her he'd heard about today's events. Since she'd won the election and ousted him, Sheehan somehow still managed to keep his thumb on the goings-on in the sheriff's department and involve himself in all the big murder investigations. Until recently.

Elizabeth had long suspected Ben was still feeding Sheehan information. With Ben absent from the office, the ex-sheriff was out of the loop. It still disturbed Elizabeth that Marnie and Ben had involved themselves with Sheehan in one of his worst cooked-up schemes of this century.

When he didn't say anything further, Elizabeth took a long drag on the beer.

Sheehan tipped his glass back and swallowed the last of his bourbon. He placed the glass next to his papers, then shuffled them together. "What brings the great Sheriff Benoit out of hiding?"

"I wasn't hiding." She pointed the bottle at him. "Not like you've been. The DA has informed my undersheriff that you've been avoiding them like the plague."

"My lawyer is handling all of that nonsense."

"You have a lawyer? Who?"

Sheehan capped the bourbon. "None of your business. What do you want, Elizabeth, besides to annoy me?"

Elizabeth readjusted her position to lean closer to him, dangling the beer between her knees. "When was the last time you were out at your property?"

Wariness gleamed in his whiskey-colored eyes. The sly old snake was testing the air for danger. "What does that have to do with anything?"

She had to tread carefully. He'd either go to ground or start intervening in her ongoing investigations. For the last few years, whenever a major case came through the Eckardt County Sheriff's Department, Sheehan managed to attach himself either by providing cryptic messages or running his own investigation in the background. He was like a computer virus you could never find and eradicate.

"Just curious," she said. "You've made it a point to be scarce since you were released from the hospital."

"I don't see how it's any concern of yours to keep track of my whereabouts."

"You lost the right to anonymity when you dragged my sister into your schemes and got her jammed up."

Sheehan leaned toward her. "Your sister is of her own free mind."

Elizabeth held his stare. They had been doing this song and dance far longer than her brief term as sheriff of the county, and she was more than capable of making him back down.

His chair creaked as he sat back. His narrowed gaze holding steady on Elizabeth. "I don't have to answer you, but since you *asked* so nicely, I was there all day. It's where I live."

"A normal, average day for you?"

"Elizabeth, what are you driving at?"

She gave him a patronizing smile and stood. "Not a damn thing, Kelley. Enjoy the rest of your night."

As she returned to the bar, she downed more of the beer. Marnie glared at her as she stepped up to the gleaming wood.

"I told you not to start anything," she snarled.

Elizabeth smacked the nearly empty bottle on the top. "I didn't start a thing." She snapped her fingers and Bentley scrabbled out of her hiding spot behind the bar. "You really should reconsider who you keep company with, sister dearest."

Marnie jabbed a black-painted finger at Elizabeth's face. "You need to get off your high horse and go screw yourself. For someone who came off a relaxing sabbatical, you're being a real bitch."

Elizabeth departed with a middle finger salute to her sister. Bitch she might be, but after the last few hellish months, she was done being the levelheaded one. She was tired of shit being dredged up and exploding in her face. It was a constant theme of her career as sheriff.

When she took office, she vowed she'd clean up this county. She wanted to be the opposite of Sheehan and his predecessor, to be the strict, understanding sheriff who got things done. What had that gotten her? A whole lot of nothing but more trouble than she bargained for.

The Elizabeth Benoit of four years ago was done. She would enjoy swearing in her ex-husband tomorrow. Once he had the gold star pinned to his chest, she was going to let him do what he had always done best.

Elizabeth was unleashing the dogs of war.

CHAPTER THIRTEEN

Day 2, Monday, February 26—24 Hours Missing

UNABLE TO SLEEP because of the pain in her arm, Olivia worked through the night. When she'd stashed away the food Horatio had left her, she found a few pairs of reading glasses in the bag. She was popping ibuprofen like Skittles to keep the hurt at bay, along with copious amounts of black tea. Olivia had never liked coffee but was seriously reconsidering her aversion.

By four a.m., she'd created an organized timeline and evidence tree, using all four walls of the apartment and the floor. The whole macabre panoramic view was for her benefit alone. She'd filled half a legal pad with her notes and observations. As far as she was concerned, it was a whole lot of gibberish and nonsense.

Only one common denominator in every case stuck out. All the boneyards were found in isolated areas along the Mississippi River. None of the remains at these sites maintained any tissue samples. A seemingly impossible circumstance when one considered when the most recent or freshest bones were discovered.

Most baffling of all, there was little to no mention of this phenomena recorded in any of the reports. None of the agencies involved with the different burial sites had done more than document what they found, brought in a forensic team, and after a certain passage of time summarily called the cases cold, shoving them off to one disinterested investigator after another. The most recent—and the only case still considered open—she found was from three years ago. On the Illinois side of the Mississippi River, it was the singular scene closest to Eckardt County, even at eighty miles or more downriver. The boneyard there was situated on the river shoreline, not an island as some of the previous locations.

Olivia wanted to talk with every person involved with the prior investigations. Despite how detailed detectives and crime scene techs were in their reports, some things were better learned in conversation.

She sat on the bed, carefully massaging the muscles above the cast and mulling over her options. So long as Horatio kept her locked away, cut off from the outside world, she wouldn't be able to contact any of the departments about any of these cases and speak with the human beings involved. Unless she managed to sweet-talk him into letting her make a few calls.

She let out a derisive snort. Horatio was no fool. If there was a chance Olivia could alert someone to her predicament, he'd never allow it.

In between bouts of mind fog and throbbing pain, Olivia was left to wonder what happened to her husband. In an attempt to derail her brain from the aches, she would try to recall each of her conversations with Horatio. The way he spoke about Dominic and the equation to danger worried her. What was so dangerous it would drive Horatio to kidnap her from her home and her husband?

These case files and reports she was forced to go over held a link to Dominic's involvement. It was something bad—so bad he resorted to asking for help from Horatio, a man he only knew of by name.

Why?

Cross-legged on the bed, Olivia pressed her back into the wall and let her head rest there. She let her mind wander back to when she'd first met Dominic. They had been med students then. Young, overtasked, and apprehensive about their futures. Olivia was adjusting to a life without Horatio in it and Dominic seemed like a good way to reset herself.

Dominic didn't like to talk about his life before med school. Made it clear he had no family and those who had been involved with his childhood were no longer around. He was suave, caring, and more in line with Olivia's career path. By their second year together, she was in love. By year three, they were married.

Three months into their wedded bliss, a wedding gift arrived. From Horatio. Olivia had to explain who he was to her husband. At the time, Dominic didn't seem disturbed by the gesture or Olivia's past with a common Chicago thug. Or maybe she'd been in denial.

Whatever the case, Dominic never brought up Horatio or Olivia's past. Then they moved to Iowa. Life revolved around residency and securing jobs. Not once did Olivia ever think about second-guessing her husband.

Her weakened and overtasked eyes burned. Olivia rubbed at them. She should sleep. The rest would quiet her overcrowded brain.

First, another bathroom break.

In the small bathroom, she contemplated the shower stall, debating whether she should bother to attempt it. There were no plastic bags or anything to cover the cast, not that she'd seen anyway. She could always hold it over her head and try to keep the water off.

The thought of doing that and fatigue dragged further on her body. No, it was pointless.

A nap might help her change her mind.

Finished, she cleaned up, gave her face a washcloth bath, and shuffled back out into the main room. She eased onto the bed and lay flat on her back, shoving pillows under her casted arm to elevate it. Tilting her arm relieved some of the discomfort. Closing her eyes, she let her mind go blank.

It didn't last long. Her brain ran away with one thought after another, starting with the jam-packed week of patient appointments she wouldn't be there to handle.

No one in the office knew what happened to her, the patients would have to be shuffled around, her nurses and assistants were excellent with their knowledge of patients and who to schedule with which backup doctors. But what about the week after that? And the week following? She had no idea how long Horatio planned to keep her here. She had no clue what he intended to do with her after she gave him the answers he sought.

What about Dominic? If he was mixed up in something bad, had it finally caught up to him? It would certainly explain why Horatio swooped in and made her vanish. So, where was Dominic? Did he know she was gone? If he hadn't been harmed or detained, was he looking for her? Had he alerted the sheriff's department?

Was anyone looking for her? Olivia had lost track of where Elizabeth had gone weeks ago. She'd figured Rafe had something to do with Elizabeth going off grid, but she was left out of the loop. If Elizabeth wasn't around, had Lila figured out Olivia was missing?

Olivia groaned. Her head hurt. Her arm was killing her. And she couldn't make her brain shut up.

No more. Turn it off. Quiet down.

She drew in a deep breath and released it slowly. Did it again three more times until she was able to let her mind go blank.

The bones were located in isolated areas. Left under thick cover, but exposed nonetheless. Why weren't they buried?

Some of the locations were islands in the middle of the river. The soil reports ranged from sandy and wet or rocky and a few layers of dirt. Exposure also meant allowing predatory animals to get at the bodies. It didn't seem as if the suspects were wanting to waste the time to shovel and bury. If she dwelled on their motive hard enough, it made sense when she considered the sheer amount of human remains found at each sight. Digging a large hole would draw attention.

So how did the bodies decompose so quickly? Yes, wild animals would scavenge the sites, carrying off vital tissue and bones to identify someone. But the bones left behind had been relatively clean. The forensic anthropologist on one of the cases had noted there were no signs of large teeth markings or chips in the bones, which would have been made by the larger animals. Some of the older bones showed indications of gnawing rodents, a habit of small mammals to maintain rapidly growing teeth.

Olivia ran through a list of possible reasons for the flesh to be removed from the bones at a rapid pace. Chemical components, outside of naturally occurring ones, were not found present at any of the sites. The bones left behind showed no signs of manual indicators, like blades, to aid in the removal of tissue.

For the love of God, Olivia, stop this and go to sleep.

She could figure this out after she got some rest.

Again, she went through her ritual to quiet her mind. Exhaustion managed to drag her into the warm comfort of oblivion.

Flesh-eating insects.

Olivia snapped open her eyes and gasped. "That's it."

She struggled into a seated position, then sluggishly hopped up. Wasn't there something in her notes she had notated about a forensic entomologist being consulted? She grabbed up the legal pad, slid on a pair of reading glasses, and furiously scanned her horribly sloppy handwriting.

There! On the fourth page. Dr. A. S. Pollard from the University of Tennessee had been the one to note the finding at a location on the Arkansas/Mississippi border.

She had starred the location site and the note about three insect corpses settled inside a rib cage. Olivia stepped over the line of photos laid out on the floor and headed for the wall next to the front door where she had hung the location's reports and photos.

She peered through the lens with blurry eyes, until she found the photo of a close-up on a rib cage. There, nestled among tree debris and green grasses, were the carcasses of a flesh-eating insect, the dermestid beetle.

Were there any other sites who called in a forensic ento-mologist? Olivia rounded the room, skimming the reports and comparing to her notes, finding only one other place that reported an entomologist on site, who believed there were dermestid beetles involved but couldn't prove it.

It made sense if there was no sign of the beetle. They typically didn't hang around after consuming their meal, unless they were given a consistent food source. Tempera-tures would have to be ideal as well, along with darkened conditions. Most of the boneyards were in dense wooded areas, using the tree coverage to hide their activity from prying eyes from above. This was how the culprits—because there had to be more than one person—were doing this quickly and without detection.

Olivia stepped back and removed her glasses.

These beetles did not just show up in mass swarms. Somebody was bringing them in. Someone with access to a sheer number of beetles, possibly reproducing them on a regular basis. Who had that kind of access? And with a legit reason?

She placed an earpiece in her mouth and bit down on the hard plastic. This she could work with. These nuggets were worth mining these reports all over again. Like it or not, Horatio was going to have to allow her to make calls. Or he was about to find himself running all her investigative errands.

While he was at it, she was going to force him to update her on Dominic. If he refused, she would withhold her findings.

Olivia learned a lot from the man back in the day. Number one among them was how to push his buttons. Two could play this game.

CHAPTER FOURTEEN

LILA GAVE GERRY Two some fish flakes before she left her house. She swallowed the snort-chuckle when she recalled the indignation on Kyle's face when he found out she hadn't told him about Gerry One dying. Who knew a man could get so attached to a fish.

You loved some fish, too.

She had—the four special koi she'd raised while living in Chicago that had perished the night she almost lost her life. Their deaths were catalyst in her reasons for never getting koi again. The bettas were acceptable substitutes.

She locked up and headed for her car. After rounding the edge of the yew bush she let overgrow, she hesitated.

Leaning against the passenger side with two to-go cups in hand was Corey Young, in full uniform, sans her usual ball cap. Her long braid draped over her shoulder, blending into the dark-brown deputy's coat.

Lila fondled her car keys as she drew closer to Young. She noted the other woman's personal vehicle was parked behind hers. "Hey?"

"Hey." Young held out the second cup. "Freya sends her regards."

Taking the cup, Lila nodded her thanks. They didn't speak, just stared at each other.

"So?" Lila asked.

"So," Young said at the same time.

Their awkward stare down continued. Before the events of Halloween, Lila hadn't spent a lot of time with Young. The two women were opposites in many ways, but somehow, they finally got around to an easygoing working relationship. Then they both ended up in a predicament leading to the unintentional death of a suspect. The horrors Lila and Young witnessed in the defunct barn loft still left a bitter taste in Lila's mouth.

The staring wasn't getting them anywhere. By her appearance here in uniform, it seemed Young was wanting to get back into it. Lila had no qualms with it. Get back into she would.

Lila jiggled her keys. "Hop in."

Once they were both settled, Lila cranked the heat to combat the frigid air in the car. She ran the wipers to expose a spot in the frost on the windshield and sipped the coffee. The moment she had enough visibility through the frost, she left her parking spot and rounded the cul-de-sac drive. Beside her, Young stayed quiet, taking drinks from her cup and staring out the defrosted passenger side window. Lila wasn't used to having a partner in the car with her while she drove. Looked like today she'd have to make an exception.

After passing the street leading to the courthouse where the sheriff's department was housed, Lila decided to break the silence. "Sheriff know you're back on duty?"

Young stared straight ahead. "Not yet."

"When you plan on telling her?"

Young lifted a shoulder. "Soon."

Lila resumed her full attention to the road laid out before them, trying hard not to dissect Young's reasons for delaying her talk with the sheriff. Admittedly, Lila didn't blame Young for not facing Benoit right now. For months, through being grilled by one attorney after another on what went down, Lila had been trying to come to terms with how badly the events leading up to the Halloween murders had gone. It had been disjointed and crazy with no thought behind any of the investigation steps whatsoever. All of it led back to Sheriff Benoit and her personal vendetta.

Lila felt the buzzards circling, pecking at her well-ordered life. She had followed protocol, had done her damnedest to keep Benoit out of the investigation, and was still trying to keep the dirtier details out of the wrong hands. Yet, somehow, she, Lila, was made to feel guilty for not presenting her boss for the firing squad. If she weren't careful, she'd crack under the strain.

How most of them made it out of that Halloween fiasco unscathed was a miracle, but others had paid a price.

Lila glanced at Young. She appeared to be made of tougher material than Lila initially thought, but time would tell.

Lila placed her cup in the holder and used both hands to guide the car toward the edge of town for her planned first visit.

"Where we going?" Young asked.

"We've had some ... *things* happen in the last twenty-four hours. I've got to interview a lady who lives out of town."

Lila's answer made Young finally look at her instead of

the windshield and the passing scenery.

"What kind of things?"

Lila sighed, pressing her back into the seat while pushing against the steering wheel. "Are you ready for the job? Because if you're thinking you wanted a trial run today to see how things go, you're not going to like what I have to say."

"Pull over," Young said curtly.

Lila saw the seriousness in Young's features and flicked on the turn signal. She guided the car to the side of the road, threw it in park, then punched the hazards and the bar lights. They sat, listening to the lights click.

"I had to do a lot of soul searching," Young said after a bit. "Discover myself again." Her dark eyes flicked to Lila and held. "I'm more than the sum of my sins. What those women did is no reflection on me and what happened when I tried to stop them."

"Are you telling me you're coming back full-time?"

"Yeah, I guess I am."

Lila turned off the hazards and the bar lights. "Good." She pulled back out onto the road. "Wait until you see what we've got brewing."

KATHY MILLER'S FARM was another mile uphill, past the boneyard. Young asked about the line of vehicles parked along the road. After Lila's brief explanation, Young volleyed a slew of questions, many of which Lila had no answers for. The Spanish Inquisition didn't back off until Lila pulled into the pothole-ridden drive.

The farmstead was small in comparison to some of the other places Lila had the pleasure—or displeasure depending on the circumstances—of visiting. A few of the outbuildings looked dated, but otherwise, it was well-kept and appeared functional. In a lean-to encircled by a fence made of boards, a white-faced red cow watched as she parked next to Kathy's truck.

"That must be the wandering heifer who led her owner to the boneyard." Lila turned off the engine.

"Do you know what a heifer is?" Young asked.

Lila wanted to be offended. "I've lived here long enough to figure it out."

"Well, that's reassuring." A smirk turned up the corners of the deputy's mouth.

Lila struggled to stay annoyed with the sarcastic remark but failed. She exited the vehicle as an excuse to keep Young from seeing her succumb to the wit. It was good to see Young had maintained some semblance of humor.

They met at the front of the unit. Lila surveyed the property, then checked the time. Just past eight a.m. No one appeared to be home.

"Does she work?" Young asked.

"According to Meyer's report, she does not. The farm is her sole income." Lila pointed at the truck. "That's her only vehicle."

"Other than, say, a tractor?"

Lila gave her a droll look. "That's a given."

Young pointed at a small replica of the house stationed next to the tiny front porch. "She's got a dog. It hasn't come out to greet us."

"Or she had a dog," Lila debunked. "Or it's in the house."

"We'd hear it barking. Ms. Miller crosses me as the type to always have a dog. It's probably with her, wherever she is."

Lila glowered at Young. "Is that your Sioux sense? Or you just blowing hot air?"

The Native woman grinned. "Guess you'll never know which."

"One day, I'll call your mother and tell her to teach me how to smell out your bullshit," Lila muttered.

"Good luck with that. She's worse than me." Young sniffed the cool morning air. "Speaking of smell." She made a beeline for the pen.

As she studied the structure, she gave the heifer a nice head scratching. "Ms. Miller might be out riding." She pointed at the other side of the lean-to. "I smell horse."

"Just great," Lila muttered.

"Did you give her a heads-up you were coming?" Young asked.

"Nope."

Hot breath steaming in the cold air, Young left the heifer with a final stout pat on the neck and meandered back. "Looks like we're waiting."

"Guess we are."

Her neatly laid out plans for the day disrupted, Lila decided to do what any good investigator did in situations like this—kill time by reading over reports. Or in her case, write it up. She'd gone over Meyer's interview report earlier while she readied for the day. She had yet to write up her notes from yesterday.

Laptop and written notes in hand, she lugged the arm-load to the front of the car. Not in the mood to figure out a way to maneuver her laptop around the steering wheel and still combating a severe case of cabin fever, Lila preferred the brisk air outside to being crammed in her car. Using the hood, she made herself a makeshift desk and got comfortable.

Young picked up the folder with Meyer's name and report number scrawled on the front flap. "Mind if I get caught up?"

"Might as well. We're going to need all the fresh eyes on this mess we can get."

While Young read, Lila tapped away. The necessity of writing reports was the tedious, boring part of the job she hadn't really enjoyed in her law enforcement career. One thing was certain, no lawyer could ever discredit anything she'd ever reported.

Last night's reprieve with Kyle at least alleviated some of the disquieting voices in her head in regard to their relationship. Only some. Despite his assurances he wasn't going to use their shared time together to work through his troubling past, Lila sensed a disconnect with him. Something she couldn't put her finger on to give a name.

Maybe it was her own misgivings and she was trying to pass them off as his? Things had not been easy between them—a far cry better than her last disastrous relationship—but they had been good.

Lila pulled out of her wandering thoughts and focused on her report.

Shit.

She quickly deleted everything in the last two paragraphs. Intrusive thoughts on her sex life were not to be reported.

"Dayne?"

Pausing mid-deleting, she frowned at Young. "What?"

Young folded over the file and held it up face out for Lila. "You found a tunnel under a shack?"

"Yep." Lila went back to clearing out her waywardness.

"What's in the tunnel?"

Squinting at the computer screen, Lila bent closer. "At the moment, a whole lotta nothin'."

"Where did it go?"

Sighing, she straightened. "I'm trying to get that part down in my report, and then you can read all about it."

A pensive look fell over Young's tanned features. She turned the file back to her and peered at the report.

"What?" Lila demanded.

Young glanced at her. "What?"

"You act like there's something wrong. I mean, there is something horribly wrong about the whole situation. But what's with the"—Lila circled her hand in front of her face—"look?"

"It's …"

"It's what?"

Young pointed past Lila's head. "Incoming."

Lila looked over her shoulder and spotted a figure riding hell-bent for leather with a dark shape streaking over the ground, keeping pace with the horse.

"It's Kathy." Lila closed her laptop. "This doesn't look good."

She and Young moved to the edge of the yard as Kathy's

horse pounded past the lean-to and came to a rough stop. The dark shape turned out to be a speckled-coat dog. The squat beast let out a torrent of menacing barks.

"Rio, shut up!"

The dog ceased barking and sat, dark, beady eyes latched onto the deputies.

Kathy reined her horse around. "Deputy Dayne, am I ever glad you're here."

Lila and Young glanced at each other.

"Why's that?" Lila asked.

Kathy dismounted and dragged the heaving horse to the livestock pen. "You just saved me a heap of trouble trying to call you out here," she said as she led the animal into the open space next to the cow.

Lila's signal flags were going crazy. A bright, neon sign flashed *warning*. "Ms. Miller, what's going on?"

The older woman made short work of removing the horse's bridle and saddle, slinging the equipment on top of the fence as she left the paddock and latching the gate behind her. "I found something out on the river."

The older woman headed straight for her truck. "Get in, you two, I'll take you there."

Lila picked up her pace and followed Kathy to her vehicle. "Why don't we go in my car?"

"Your vehicle won't make it forty yards out there before it'll get stuck." Kathy pried open the driver's side door, then climbed onto the running board. "Need four-wheel drive to get back there."

"There's not enough room for all three of us," Lila protested.

"Someone can ride in the back with the dog."

The canine in question had long figured out what his owner was going to do and was now perched on the top of a spare tire in the truck bed.

Lila scowled at the thought of bouncing around back there with the savage runt of a dog.

"I'll do it," Young piped up and hopped into the truck bed.

The dog's heterochromatic eyes followed Young as she stepped past it and settled near the truck cab.

Kathy slapped the truck roof. "Let's go, Deputy Dayne."

With a dissatisfied grunt, Lila circled the back of the truck and climbed into the passenger side.

Everyone seated, Kathy brought the engine to life. She gave the dashboard a loving pat, and then put the vehicle into gear, not bothering to back up, just roaring forward. She guided the aging truck past the animal pen and out into the expansive field of dormant grass.

"What was it you saw on the river?" Lila asked, gripping the oh-shit bar as the truck bumped over rough ground.

"Don't know for certain."

Kathy navigated a tough patch, the steering wheel whipping back and forth. How she managed to get her horse over this without breaking a leg was a miracle.

"I saw a boat bobbing near the shoreline, and something was in it that didn't look right," she said after the truck evened out.

"Didn't look right how?" Lila pressed.

"I was on my horse too far away to tell. After what I found yesterday, no way was I taking a chance and checking it out myself."

Young pounded on the rear window. Lila peeked back, catching the signal to open the sliding pane. While they bounced over another bumpy spot in the field, Lila managed to get the window to slide over. Once they weren't attempting to put their heads through the roof, Young poked her face into the opening.

"What did she say?"

Lila repeated what Kathy told her. Young seemed to think on what she heard, not moving back from the window. Next to her, on the tire, the dog surfed the waves, doing a way better job of it than the humans.

Lila faced forward in time to be jolted upward. Her head smacked the truck ceiling.

"Ow!"

"Sorry," Kathy uttered.

Lila rubbed the bump forming on the top of her noggin. "What the heck are we going over?"

"Ruts." Kathy steered the truck to their right. "After it flooded, I didn't bother to have the field rolled. Didn't have time."

The field began to descend. Lila could see the trees past the nose of the truck. Between the leafless limbs, the sparkle of sunlight on the water's reflective surface momentarily distracted her.

When the hill leveled out, Kathy eased the truck to a stop and parked. "This way," she said before exiting the vehicle, not bothering to turn off the engine.

Lila hopped out of the cab at the same time Young swung over the side. Together, they followed Kathy and her menacing beast to the edge of the field. Kathy stopped at the mouth of a dirt path snaking down to the riverbank.

"The boat is gone," she said.

Lila scanned the shoreline. "It probably drifted." She led the way down the path.

She hit the rock-littered, sandy, mud bank and carefully walked closer to the water. Birds chattered in the trees above, unconcerned with the three women and the dog. Lila, hands hooked on her duty belt, studied the river.

Far to her right, Young checked the shoreline. Just off her left shoulder, Kathy picked a path over the slippery mud.

"I see something," Young called out, and she jogged along the river's edge.

Both Lila and Kathy followed carefully.

In a mess of downed trees and debris, caught up in a nook on the river, rocked an aluminum johnboat. Something bulky lay beneath what looked like a black tarp between the middle and rear seats.

"Told ya," Kathy said.

"How are we going to get to it before it gets loose and drifts away?" Young asked.

"Ms. Miller, do you have anything in your truck we can hook to the hull and drag it in?" Lila asked the woman.

"Maybe. Lemme go see." Kathy hauled tail back up the path.

Young sniffed the air. "Smell that?"

Frowning, Lila did the same but got a hit of chilled river water and dank mud. "No. What do you smell?"

"Decomp."

Lila eyed the woman. "First the horse thing and now

this. Do you have some kind of super sniffer?"

Young shrugged. "Maybe."

Tree branches scraping against the hull worried Lila. The johnboat was pushing hard against the debris holding it in place, the current giving it the extra incentive to break free. Lila peered up the hill.

"Hope she hurries up."

"We're screwed if she doesn't have anything," Young said and moved farther along the shoreline. "I can jump in and push it over."

"It's too cold to get wet," Lila said.

Kathy's dog barked, drawing their attention up the path. Kathy emerged carrying something in one hand and gripping a length of rope.

"Hammer and rope should do it," she said as she hurried down the path.

"Who's got the better arm and aim?" Lila asked.

"Lemme try," Young said, taking the items from Kathy. "Better stand back in case this thing slips free."

She secured the hammer with the rope, and then inched closer to the water's edge.

Lila and Kathy stood off to Young's far left and watched as she shook out the end of the rope attached to the hammer. The bobbing boat let out a wincing screech as it shifted among the debris, angling toward the freedom of open water. Young swung the hammer end around a few times and then chucked it out at the boat. The hammer fell short, splashing into the river.

Young reeled it in, flinging away the tree parts and reeds the hammer dragged with it. Then she gave it another shot.

Again the boat made noise, edging closer to the end of the debris pile. Lila's jaw ached as she waited for Young to make contact.

This time, Young's throw hit the side of the boat and slipped into the water. She uttered something in her native language, probably a curse.

"We're going to lose it," Kathy whispered.

"Hold your horses," Young bit out.

Once more she swung the hammer around, giving herself more slack, and this time flung it out like she would have thrown a loop at a cow. The hammer sailed through the air, passed the boat's side, and landed with a thud against the tarp. Carefully, Young reeled it in until the hammer hooked against the hull.

"Here we go," she said after giving it a tug to make sure the hammer stayed.

She began pulling the boat back toward the shoreline. Slowly, the boat worked free of the debris and started toward the shore.

Lila moved to Young's side in case she needed help, watching the boat inch its way through the maze of tree branches and browned reeds. Her breath hitched when the hammer began to slip.

Young muttered something and then eased off.

The forward progress was lost as the boat, caught by a current, slipped away.

Lila's fear of losing the boat came true as the hammer flipped over and flew out.

Before she could stop her, Young threw the rope aside and ran into the river, sloshing against the water to reach the boat. She was waist high and feet from the boat when she went under.

"Young!"

The woman's dark braid preceded her head as she broke the surface. She was closer to the boat and grabbed onto the side. The johnboat rocked hard against Young but stayed level. Spitting water, she hooked her arm over the side and hung there a moment.

"Are you okay?" Lila asked.

"Fine," Young said. "It's deep out here. Throw me the rope."

Lila grabbed up the discarded rope and reeled it in. She removed the hammer and threw the rope end out to Young. It took a few tries until Young managed to grab the line. She tied it off on a metal loop and then swam back to shore. Once she was out of the water, Lila and Kathy hauled the boat in. The bottom grated against the rocks as Young dragged it out of the water.

Young stayed next to the craft, panting.

"So much for keeping you dry," Lila said.

Young flipped her off.

If their banter continued, Lila could see herself connecting with Young at the friend level. The thought scared the crap out of her. She did not have friends. Friends hurt and betrayed you. She had yet to fully commit to a lover as more than just a guy scratching an itch. Befriending another woman meant another phase of trust Lila kept in short demand.

"Something is definitely rotting under this tarp," Young said between breaths.

"Ms. Miller, you should probably stay back and not see this," Lila said.

"Deputy, I've seen my fair share of dead bodies."

"I'm sure you have, but there's a fundamental difference between seeing the decomposing body of an animal versus a human being," Lila pressed. "I'd rather you not have those images …"

"Deputy, I'll stop you before you muck this up any further. I was an army nurse back in the day."

Young appeared impressed by this revelation. Lila begrudgingly had to admit that she, too, was impressed.

"Okay then."

Lila took a deep breath, catching the stench Young had warned her about. She dug around in her coat pockets and found one nitrile glove leftover from yesterday. Glove snapped in place, Lila reached for the edge of the tarp and found it firmly tucked under whatever it was covering. She had to feel around along the bottom of the boat, noting as she did that there was a certain shape to the lump, an appendage type of shape. Her fingers brushed against the lip of the tarp, and she followed the skirt, untucking it as she went, until she found a corner.

As she pulled, something scrambled out from under the tarp and scurried up her arm. Lila shrieked at the unfamiliar insect. She whipped her arm around, dislodging the bug, only to watch it spread out wings and fly off.

"What the hell was that?" Young asked.

Lila gaped in horror as more of the bugs escaped under the opening and crawled everywhere.

Kathy had come closer to the boat. "Those look like beetles."

"What kind of freaking beetle can survive these temps at this time of the year?" Lila demanded.

Kathy pinched one off the side of the boat and held it up. "The kind that likes to feed on flesh." She nodded at the tarp. "Better get it off, Deputy, so we can see what's under there."

Bracing herself for the upcoming horror show, Lila grasped the edge of the tarp and flung it aside, scattering the beetles.

"Oh my God," Young uttered in revulsion.

Lila had endured a lot in her life. She'd been privy to the horrors of the I-80 killer's trail of bodies and the worst that Chicago could throw at her. But she discovered in this moment something she'd never be unable to see for the rest of her life.

A trio of human bodies left to rot and be consumed by insects in a boat was forever seared in her memory.

CHAPTER FIFTEEN

I T FELT GOOD to be back in uniform.

Elizabeth hadn't realized how much she'd come to like being sheriff until it was nearly taken away from her. Oddly enough, by her own stubbornness. If there was one thing she'd like to change about the job—one thing only—it was the constant parade of dead bodies moving through the county.

Her morning of swearing in Joel and debriefing with Rafe on Dominic's status was rudely interrupted by her deputy detective's call-in. Elizabeth stood command over the bevy of techs and deputies swarming the beached johnboat.

Dayne had called over the DCI techs from the boneyard. They had been an hour into their work before Elizabeth arrived with Rafe in tow. At Dayne's behest, the forensic anthropologist had joined the fray as well, hemming and hawing over the three bodies.

Elizabeth squinted uphill at the truck parked there. Co-rey Young, her one deputy she'd yet to have a conversation with, sat in the cab along with the truck's owner. Young's dunk in the river had left her chilled, and she had to get out of the cold.

Next to Elizabeth, Rafe shifted, following her gaze. "Somehow I knew she'd seek out Dayne before you," he rumbled.

Seeming to sense their scrutiny, Young's attention fell on them. After a momentary stare down, she went back to doing whatever it was keeping her preoccupied inside the truck cab.

Elizabeth grunted and resumed her vigil over the beehive activity on the riverbank.

Before Joel had come into the office, Elizabeth had spent the better part of the predawn hours poring over Olivia's day planner. Not only did it contain a goldmine of phone numbers and addresses, but a journal of sorts. Elizabeth learned rather quickly that Olivia had family in Chicago. The phone number to the Remington home was old, but it still worked, and the man who answered revealed a side of Olivia no one in Juniper would have expected.

Dayne left the anthropologist and headed for Elizabeth and Rafe.

"Damn it," Elizabeth muttered.

Her undersheriff gave her a sharp look. "What?"

"Now is not the time for someone to abscond with my medical examiner."

"I'm beginning to think Olivia's abduction correlates with the discovery of the boneyard," Rafe said.

Dayne joined them and crossed her arms. "I'd have to agree."

"Who would orchestrate something like this?" Elizabeth asked. "And why?"

"The million-dollar question," Dayne replied. "Dr. Pembrook has asked the state medical examiner to come down. These bodies are too fresh for him. But he's highly fascinated with the ..." She dug out her notebook and squinted at the notes. "The dermestid beetles? Said they're a breed that's not really native to Iowa but will survive anywhere if given the proper food source and conditions."

"Which in this case are bodies covered by a tarp." Elizabeth made a face. "How does he know that much about beetles? He's not the forensic entomologist."

"I dabble in entomology, and it fascinates me, Sheriff." The man in question had crept into their con-fab. He thrust out a glove-free hand. "Dr. Steven Pembrook. We didn't get a chance to meet yesterday."

Elizabeth gripped his hand, and they shook. "We meet today." She pointed at the johnboat. "Want to fill me in to save my deputy the agony of trying to pronounce words she's not familiar with?"

Dayne pulled a fierce scowl and then shoved her notebook back into her jacket.

Dr. Pembrook chuckled. "I'll do my best to give you laymen terms. I'd like to get back to the other site and resume my work there."

"Let's wrap this up and get you to it."

With a nod, he faced the riverbank. "What is left of the bodies that the beetles didn't consume bear remarkable wounds. The beetles have chewed up the clothing, but there's enough to distinguish what they were."

"I thought they were flesh-eating?" Elizabeth asked.

"They will consume natural fibers, which is what they've done here. I'm not exactly sure how long those bodies have been in the boat and left with the beetles. Given the right conditions and the sheer quantity, they could consume a fully intact body anywhere from three days to a week. With three bodies in there, it's taken them some time. They started on the top body and were making their way down. The body at the bottom of the boat, a young Hispanic female, is missing most of her vital organs as well as her eyes."

Elizabeth frowned. "The beetles?"

"No, I don't believe so. It appears the organs might have been removed before the body was placed in the boat. I can't confirm the eyes, the medical examiner will be able to tell better than I can. If I was a betting man, and I am, I'm betting those were taken, too."

"Won't the beetles eat soft tissue first?" Rafe asked.

"Yes, it's possible. But as I noted, the bodies have wounds that, to my eye, look like incisions."

Whoa! Back up the information train here. Elizabeth lifted her sunglasses and squinted at the anthropologist.

"Incisions?" Dayne cut in. "Like surgical? Like someone with surgical capabilities left behind incisions? And you didn't bother to say this to me before?"

The good Dr. Pembrook had the grace to grimace at the deputy's battery of questions. "I hadn't fully pieced it together to say something until now. Apologies. I'm not the expert in this particular field. Most of what I'm telling you is hypothetical."

"We understand that, Doctor." Elizabeth took control, giving her deputy a warning look to back off grilling the anthropologist.

"If I may add one more thought to this," Pembrook said, his gaze bouncing between Elizabeth and Dayne.

"What's that, Doctor?" Elizabeth asked.

"These poor humans were used for other means and their remains left." Pembrook's features brightened. "Which could mean the other site was the dumping ground. If the dermestid beetles were used to accelerate the decomposition, it could mean the bones have not been there for an extended period."

"What could they have possibly been used for and then just discarded like waste?" Elizabeth pressed.

"Black-market organs," Dayne stated.

Pembrook's eyebrows lifted. "That would be a good deduction, Deputy Detective."

Elizabeth studied her investigator. She was well aware of Dayne's penchant for slow processing and extensive research before coming to any conclusions. Coming to this idea this fast was bothersome.

Dayne's pinched features were not reassuring either.

"Let's wait for the medical examiner to get here and let them do the autopsies before we jump down that rabbit hole," Elizabeth said. "In the meantime, I'll release the bodies for transport to the morgue. If we can get in."

"We'll be able to get in. I found Olivia's key card at the house. It's in evidence right now," Rafe said.

"I'll resume my duties down the road," Pembrook said. He looked at Dayne. "Will you be joining me there?"

"Once I'm done here. I want to go through the shack and the tunnel." Dayne ran her hands up and down her thighs. "We need to process the burned-out vehicle, too."

Seemingly satisfied with her answer, the anthropologist left.

Elizabeth didn't bother to watch him go, taking note of

Dayne's odd behavior. She glanced at Rafe, who was staring uphill.

"What's churning around in your head, Deputy?"

Her question pulled Rafe's attention back to them.

"We all know it's not coincidental that Olivia goes missing and Dominic is attacked the same day we find the boneyard. It's all connected," Dayne said.

Elizabeth met Rafe's steady gaze. He tilted his head to Dayne as if to say *she's going somewhere with this you won't like.*

"I agree, but you're not saying something," Elizabeth pressed.

Dayne's stony gaze flicked between she and her undersheriff. Her hesitation was the pin heading for the fragile skin of the balloon.

"Our good doctors are mixed up in all of this." Dayne's statement was the blunt instrument she intended it to be.

"Bullshit," Elizabeth spat.

"Sheriff, you can't take a personal side in this," Dayne warned.

"She's right," Rafe said.

Elizabeth pointed at him. "Enough from you. As for you"—her finger swung to Dayne—"there will be nothing of that nature stated to anyone. Hear me?"

Dayne, despite her short stature, lifted her shoulders and grew a few feet taller. Her sunbaked features hardened. "If you play the bias card in this investigation, pulling a repeat of what happened last Halloween, I will quit."

Elizabeth could only gape. Dayne quit? Where the hell was this coming from? She had come here years before, traumatized but determined to continue being a law enforcement officer despite a tragedy. She didn't quit then, why would she quit now?

What was this crap about bias? Elizabeth did not play those games. Ever.

"I've done what I need to here," Dayne continued. "I'm taking Young home to change, and then we're headed to the other scene."

At the mention of Corey Young, Elizabeth was brought out of her momentary daze. "Wait, when was it decided she was ready to come back to work?"

Dayne didn't bother to stop as she brushed past them. She gave a cursory glance at Elizabeth. "I guess when she was comfortable enough to tell me."

"Deputy Dayne!"

Her outburst drew curious stares their way. Lookie-loos enjoying the pending disaster. Out-of-towners primed to find cracks in the department's structure. Grinding her molars, Elizabeth hiked up the path to meet Dayne head-on. Rafe moved in time with her.

"I don't appreciate the attitude," Elizabeth forced past her clenched teeth.

The cagey flicker in the deputy detective's eyes made Elizabeth take both a physical and mental step back.

"Sheriff, I say this out of respect for what you've accomplished in the past. Get a rein on your emotions or take a seat and stay out of the way."

Feeling like she'd been riddled with shrapnel, Elizabeth was left to stare at Dayne.

Once the deputy crested the hill, she spoke to Kathy Miller, then hopped into the back of the truck.

The second the truck slipped out of sight, Rafe grabbed Elizabeth's elbow and hauled her farther along the path away from still-prying eyes. "What were you thinking?"

She jerked free. "Excuse me?"

Blue flames lit up his eyes. "Dayne's right. If you pull the same stunt you did last time, things will explode. You're hovering on the verge of an election cycle, and people are still gossiping about your reckless behavior."

"I couldn't care less."

"You should care," he snapped, the gravel in his voice grounding out the words. "I don't know what was going through your head to allow Joel to be deputized. Now this. If Dayne quits, we are truly up shit creek without a paddle."

"You're selling the rest of the department short," she shot back.

"I'm doing no such thing. Dayne is the literal investigative brains behind this whole department. We lose her, we lose any advantage we have in resolving these cases." He jabbed a finger at her. "You lose the next election, and we lose the thread holding this whole operation together."

Behind her sunglasses, she blinked, feeling the heat rising in her face. She forced down the scorching remarks burning her tongue, daring to be let out. Her skin prickled from the undivided attention zeroed on them. A fury she hadn't experienced in ages took hold of her.

How dare he! How dare he question her actions. Second-guess her authority. Stomp on her like she was some irritating beetle.

Rafe lowered his hand, his gaze still aflame. "Go back to

your car. I will finish up here."

She opened her mouth, and he jerked his finger at her again.

"Not one word," he growled, then pointed up the hill. "Go."

As abruptly as he barked his commands, he turned on heel and stalked downhill. The techs surrounding the johnboat flew into a tizzy, their soap opera concluded on a cliffhanger, and returned to their duties.

Elizabeth seethed. Between Rafe's heavy-handed usurping and Dayne's threats, she didn't know which made her angrier.

Screw them. Screw them both!

About-facing, she marched the rest of the way uphill and to her Interceptor. She pulled her cell free of its pocket and found the contact number.

He answered on the second ring. "Yeah?"

"I'm coming back to the department to pick you up. You're coming with me."

"Where?"

"Iowa City. I have a doctor to see."

CHAPTER SIXTEEN

A RATTLING WOKE Olivia.

She had fallen asleep with an open file on her face. Removing it as she adjusted her position, she noticed she'd been lying on the bed. A good thing, all things considered. She wasn't certain how long she'd slept. The pulsing pain in her arm was a good indicator it was way past time for the next round of OTCs.

A hesitant creak of hinges followed the rattling.

Olivia peered through blurred eyes at the doorway. Horatio's broad frame darkened the entrance. He was alone.

She struggled into a seated position, letting the files lining her body slip and flop to the floor.

"You have been busy," he said as he closed and locked the door.

Nausea uncoiled and slithered into her esophagus. Olivia swallowed the cascading saliva, pummeling the ugly serpent trying to beat a hasty exit.

"Liv," Horatio inquired softly.

She held up her palm to stop him, then pressed her hand to her lips. If she didn't move now, she was going to ruin these reports.

She made one disastrous attempt to get up. The next she was manhandled to her feet and dragged to the bathroom, her stomach convulsing as she went. She skipped the normal receptacle of choice for the sink, which was closest when her body gave in to the need to vomit.

Horatio remained at her side as she heaved, holding her loosened hair aside with each retch. When she'd finished, he helped her ease to the floor, where she leaned her sweaty cheek against the cool door. She closed her eyes, taking lung-cleansing breaths, listening to Horatio rinse out the sink.

The squeak of the faucet and the cease of running water brought her eyes open. Drying his hands on a towel, Horatio turned to her and then squatted.

"Your body is telling you it can't take the pain," he sniped.

"I'm a doctor, you idiot," she bit back weakly.

"Then take the damn Percocet, Liv."

"You don't listen, do you?"

Again, she closed her eyes and wished for the hundredth time she could go back to two days ago and prevent all of this from happening. The feel of a damp, cool towel on her forehead made her open her eyes. Horatio was watching her as he carefully wiped away the snot and spittle.

His actions were not that of the man who'd been raised in a world where tenderness and caring was a sign of weakness, something to be exploited and would eventually kill him. These were the actions of man who had fallen in love with a young woman hell-bent on changing her life and her world. That woman was long gone.

Olivia grasped his wrist and thrust his hand away. "I'll take the Percocet on two conditions."

His dark gaze gleamed with curiosity. "Name your

price."

"First, I want a full, detailed report on Dominic's current status and what led him to making a deal with you."

"That's two conditions in one," he stated.

"It's one," she retorted. "Second, I want to know what day it is and the time."

He studied her a bit, then tossed the towel into the sink and offered his hand. "You'll continue to take the Percocet until you no longer have need of it?"

She considered his offered hand and her current predicament on the floor. Grudgingly, she took his hand and allowed him to help her to her feet. "At least until tomorrow, then we'll see." She wobbled as her head swam from the effort. "It depends on what you tell me."

"Tomorrow is not long enough for a mending bone."

"Who's the doctor?"

A charming smile lifted the corners of his full mouth. "Why you, dear Liv."

"If you don't stop using *Liv*, I'll bash your head in with this cast."

"Even when sick, you're still feisty."

She glowered at him.

"As my first peace offering, today is Monday. It's midday. You've only been here for twenty-four hours." He gestured at the door. "Now, will you go sit down and take some meds?"

"Where's Adrian?"

Horatio shook his head. "Not part of the deal."

She swatted off any assistance from him and staggered out of the bathroom and to the table. The second she was settled, he produced two pills and a bottle of water. Olivia looked from the white ovals to the stubborn black wall. Sighing, she downed the pills, chasing them with water.

"Satisfied?" She slapped down the bottle, smug that she'd splashed water on him.

Horatio took the second chair and swung it closer to her, sitting with his knees brushing hers. He'd use any excuse to touch her. "I take no pleasure in seeing you try to muscle through this. It's not necessary."

"It is when I can't handle the drugs." She swept her hand around the room at the scattered case files. "Especially when I need to stay focused on the task."

"There's no rush on this."

"There is when you're holding me hostage until I solve this. You do realize I'm only a medical examiner. I'm not a detective. I don't do the legwork, interview people, find the evidence, test it and what not. I just get the bodies and find out the manner and why. Not the who or what."

"All of those things were done for you."

"No. Only part of it was done for me. These cases aren't completed. They're cold cases, the whole lot of them. You're asking me to do something I'm not trained to do."

"What I ask of you stems back to what Dominic has involved himself in," Horatio countered.

Here was where they came to the crux of her predicament and why Horatio had reentered her life unbidden. Olivia took a moment to center herself, staring at the man across from her, studying his broad features, the sweep of his eyebrows over dark, shadowed eyes, and the rounded nose. He wore no skull cap today, instead revealing his shiny dome. A diamond, nestled in his right earlobe, winked in the early-afternoon sunlight. Today's suit was a pair of dark-blue jeans with a soft gray cashmere sweater and dark-brown boots. The dark spot on the left sleeve was courtesy of her episode in the bathroom and his assistance. Too bad she hadn't managed to splatter more of her vomit on him.

She had to stop letting Horatio distract her. Despite the rift between herself and Dominic, she was married to him. She loved Dominic. Why else would she have stuck around when it was evident her husband was putting distance between them? Even though he tried not to act like it, Dominic still loved her. Obviously, Horatio knew something damning about Dominic.

"Tell me," she said delicately.

Horatio bent forward, resting his hands between his legs. "You don't look convinced you want to hear what I have to say."

She tilted her chin down and leveled her angry gaze at him. "Do not presume to know how I feel. Explain yourself."

Twining his fingers, he worked his mouth. Finally, a sigh of resignation blew past his lips. "Eighteen months ago, Dominic reached out to me with a proposition: help him and he'd owe me any favor cashed in at any time, no questions asked. I refused at first, until he became persistent to the point he showed up in Chicago on my front doorstep."

Olivia scowled. "When was that?" She couldn't recall any time in the past year Dominic had gone to Chicago alone.

"June, last year."

The date triggered a memory in Olivia. In June, she'd

been at a mandated training course in Des Moines to renew her medical examiner's license. Dominic had been home, alone, for a week. It was the perfect time to slip across state lines and pay a visit to Horatio.

"Eight months ago, you finally caved after all the previous rejections? Why change your mind?" she asked.

Horatio held out his hands. "Why any man in my position would." He rubbed his fingers together, the universal sign of greed. "Money. He was loaded with it, too."

"How much?"

"What he bribed me with or what came after?"

Olivia trembled, her steely control over her anger slipping. "Let's start with what he bribed you with."

"A half a mil."

Her heart seized. "Where did that money come from?" she choked out.

Neither one of them was living in the lap of luxury. They made enough in their respective professions to maintain their home and a comfortable living, but there were mountainous debts remaining on student and medical school loans.

Horatio touched her knee. Didn't appear to look offended when she jerked away from his hand. "Dominic didn't elaborate. He just asked me to launder it and the money yet to come."

"Launder it? Why?"

"He wouldn't tell me. Just begged me to make it go away." He tried again, this time palming her whole knee and squeezing it.

What was it going to take to get him to stop? Slapping him? She swept his hand from her knee.

He straightened. "When a man comes to me asking to make money disappear, it means only one thing." His eyes glinted black. "Blood money."

Olivia looked away, staring at the photos and papers hanging on the wall. What had her husband gotten himself into? She replayed the last few years over in her head, rolling back the edges until she recalled the night Dominic, in an uncharacteristic moment, lost his temper with her over a stack of patient files. It fit with Horatio's timeline when Dominic first made contact with him. She squinted.

At the time, she'd assumed Dominic's fury was over violating their mutual agreement to stay out of the other's practice. Olivia thought it odd he'd be so mad about it. Now, looking back, she wondered if he'd been hiding something more in those files and she'd tread close to the actual truth. In the days, weeks, and months following, he'd grown more distant, more caustic, leaving Olivia to believe she'd done something terrible, turning her away when she tried to talk with him and never apologizing for his actions.

A hand on her elbow brought her back to the present. She met Horatio's expectant gaze.

"You remembered something?" he asked.

"A moment. It still doesn't answer what my husband was up to. You still haven't told me everything you know."

"This is what I know. Dominic wouldn't talk about the money. The total sum I took in for him before I stopped figured close to three million."

Olivia clutched her stomach and bent forward. "Wh-what?"

"The money is rolling around in offshore accounts until I

can figure out what to do with it. I had one of my men follow your husband until he had some information for me to use. A meeting between your husband and two other men." He withdrew a photo from his jean pocket as if he'd expected to have this conversation with her today and needed his proof. He held it out to her.

She glanced at Horatio's face and then the photo. "I can't," she whispered.

"You wanted to know. Now take it."

She wiggled her good arm from between her folded body and took the photo. The glossy four by six quivered. Centered with his back to the photographer was Dominic. To his right stood another man, half of his body obstructed by a large, evergreen shrub, who settled one hand on Dominic's shoulder, his other held up like he was gesturing as he spoke. Directly in front of them, standing on what was probably a set of steps leading to a brick building, was a Caucasian male in a black uniform.

"Son of a bitch," she spat and threw the photo.

"Recognize the men with him?"

"Only one. James Ross," she hissed. "He's a police officer in Juniper."

"Such vitriol," Horatio said. "Problems?"

"A bigot and a prick are among his better qualities. Why would he be associating with my husband?"

"Couldn't get it out of Dominic. When I presented him with the image, he flew into a rage and cut off contact with me."

"When?" Olivia demanded.

"Three weeks ago."

Her head was growing light; the Percocet was taking effect. She had to hold out a bit longer before the urge to sleep took over.

"How long have you been gathering all of these files?" she asked.

"Longer than three weeks." Horatio stood and moved to the refrigerator. "A little birdie whistled a song in my ear, and I went searching."

"What birdie?"

He looked back at her as he pulled a bottle of ruby-red juice from the fridge. "That is not a confidence I'm about to reveal to you." He broke the seal on the bottle and returned to his chair. Holding out the bottle to her as he sat. "Drink this."

She rankled at the abrupt order but took the juice. She read the label, the words blurring as her fatigued eyes tried to focus. Giving up, she tipped the bottle and guzzled. It was tart and refreshing. Cherry if she didn't miss her guess. Finishing off the juice, she smacked her lips.

"Where's Dominic now?" she pressed, setting the empty bottle on the table.

"Adrian informs me Dominic has been hospitalized."

Panic overthrew the fatigue in her body. "Where? With what?"

"Iowa City at the university hospital. The diagnosis is unknown. It would have to be bad enough to life flight him, no?"

Her panic was replaced by fear. She bolted to her feet. "You're getting me out of here. Now."

Horatio stood. "I won't. The threat on your life is far

from over."

"You can't keep me locked away like Rapunzel. He is my husband and I need to be with him."

"He has more than enough people looking out for him. You need to focus on these case files and figure it out."

"I don't need to do a damn thing for you." She tried to push around him, but she wobbled.

Horatio wrapped a supportive arm around her midsection and steadied her. "Hate me all you like, Liv, but your safety is my main concern. Your husband chose badly, and you will not suffer the consequences."

Olivia beat her fist against his arm, the blows useless against his rock-solid form. She sagged, letting him support her full weight. He pressed his face close to hers, her crimped hair the only barrier between them. For a second, a mere blip in her life, she allowed herself to remember what it was like to be loved and cared for by this man. Her ancient feelings for Horatio scared her. How could she still feel this way about him when she was married to another man?

"I can help you," Horatio said in her ear. "Just say the word, and I'll take you away from all of this, and you can let Dominic pay for his sins. No more combing through dusty files. No more worries over anything. Just you and me."

Her eyes squeezed shut, Olivia let herself entertain his offer. If not for the flashes of her friends' faces and their worry over where she'd gone, she could almost see herself succumbing to Horatio's bidding.

Furious she had succumbed to his charms and even considered his proposal, she gathered her weakened bones and jerked free of his grasp. Facing him, she placed a hand on his chest to keep him at arm's length. "I won't leave my friends to suffer the consequences."

Horatio clasped her hand under his. "You were always too good to do bad."

Olivia pulled free. "I always will." She yawned, the fight drained out of her.

"Rest." He guided her through the maze of files and reports. "You can resume your work after the pain wears off."

"I need you to do something for me."

"I'm not letting you out of here."

"Not that." She sat on the edge of the bed and looked up at him. "I thought hard about this, and it's the only way I can make this investigation easier for me—and for the Eckardt deputies."

"I'm not going to like this."

"You need to make contact with Lila Dayne. Don't just show up in her home uninvited or you'll be shot. Approach her, alone, when she's alone, in public."

"The ex-detective from Chicago?" That he knew this didn't surprise Olivia. As Horatio stated often, it was his business to know everyone's business. "Why?"

"She'll be spearheading the investigation. And she knows how to keep quiet."

"What do you expect me to tell her?"

"I expect you to pass along things I've learned, then you'll tell me what she's learned. If you won't let me leave, I expect you to be my gopher."

"Sounds like you're volleying for a chance to escape."

"These are my terms." She lay her fatigued body on the bed. "What is your answer?"

CHAPTER SEVENTEEN

"**Y**OU THREATENED TO quit?"

On her hands and knees in the tunnel, Lila looked up, the headlamp she wore spotlighting the towering Viking blocking the entrance. With an eye roll, she went back to work.

"I don't need to explain myself to you," she said, sweeping a handheld metal detector over the loose dirt.

In the last two hours, she'd found earrings and rings, a few coins, and one chain necklace that was distinctly masculine in style. She had started at the mouth of the cave along the waterway and worked back to the shack. Her discoveries didn't prove a whole lot, except maybe that this tunnel was a path from point A to point B. But for whom? And for what exactly?

"Wrong," he grumbled.

Apparently, she wasn't going to get any further with her evidence gathering while he stood there. She turned off the metal detector and sat back on her legs, letting her hands rest on her bent knees.

"Who told you?"

"Young." Kyle crossed his arms. "Funny how she's the first to know these things."

"She was there."

"For God's sake, Lila, don't do this. Don't act like this."

She bolted to her feet and crowded into his personal space. "Don't act like what? Like I'm about to get a repeat performance from our sheriff and I get left with the steaming pile of crap to clean up?" She jabbed a dirty, gloved finger into his chest. "I'm still knee-deep in that fiasco from last Halloween. And where the hell have you been in the aftermath?"

"Excuse me? Did you forget that I was one of the men strung up like a piece of meat, waiting to be the next one sliced and diced? Or was your suffering more important than mine or my sister's?"

She backed up, biting her lips. Hands twined in front of her face, she pressed her fingers to her mouth and stared at him, getting her temper under control.

He knew better than to compare her trauma to his own. He damn well knew better.

Lila lowered her hands. "I will not grace any of that with an explanation. If the sole reason you came here was to pick a fight with me, then leave."

Their stare down was interrupted by a shout from the trap door.

"Dayne! You need to get up here."

Giving Kyle a parting glare, she grabbed up her evidence kit and shoved past him. She stomped up the steps and met Young topside.

She shoved the plastic tote into the other deputy's arms. "Take this out to the head tech."

Young's features scrunched. "You okay?"

The heavy tread of male boots behind her made Lila's

scowl deepen.

"Not now," she said softly and went outside.

She breached the corner of the shack, and a voice called for her. Lila spotted Pembrook waving at her.

"He found something you need to see," Young said as she walked past Lila.

"Lila," Kyle tried from the shack doorway.

Ignoring him, she headed for the anthropologist. Guess last night's booty call was just that. Should have known better. Four months without sex made one do stupid, irrational things. She completely missed the think-it-over-first boat last night during his visit.

Of course, he'd take the sheriff's side. After all, Kyle was practically tied by the apron strings to Benoit. Once more, Lila got the distinct impression she was being shoved into the outsider box again. Because nearly four years of service to this community didn't mean a thing when she couldn't trace her roots clear back to the Stone Age.

She rearranged her face as she neared Dr. Pembrook to keep from broadcasting her soured, bitter thoughts.

"What did you find?" Even she could hear the irritation lancing her words.

The good ole bone doc didn't seem one bit fazed. He picked up a white plastic tub and thrust it toward her. "This was buried under about five inches of debris and dirt." He pointed to a tree a few feet from where they stood. "Left under there. No bones were near it."

Inside the tub was a mangled, dirty black Nylon back-pack. It lay flat, indicating it was empty, and was large, probably something an adult would use. Lila pinched the edge of the closest flap and lifted it, noting the zipper had been ripped away from the fabric.

"Did you look inside?" she asked.

"No. Will leave that to you."

"Anything else left with it?"

Pembrook shook his head. "The tech who discovered it is still checking, but this, aside from the clothing left on the remains, is probably the only nonbiological item left here."

"Thanks," she said and walked back to the shack with the tub.

Kyle waited for her, a dark scowl clouding his face.

"We're not talking about anything other than evidence," she snarled at him as she moved around him to the table she'd set up outside the shack.

"Fine," he growled and joined her.

Lila removed the backpack from the tub and placed it on the plastic sheet covering the table, then set the tub aside. Lundquist moved to the opposite side of the table, steering clear of the light stand.

"It's like those hiking backpacks," he said.

She showed him where the zipper on the front panel had been damaged. "Wonder if it was ripped open." She peeled back the next layer and found a second pocket, still zipped. "This wasn't damaged."

Lundquist said nothing as she pulled the zipper back. It stuck a few times on clumped dirt gumming up the teeth. The interior was dark, smelling of dank earth and mold. Lila put her hand inside and felt around, then checked the front pocket.

"Empty." When she lifted the bag and shook it, she got

the sensation there was some weight to it. "Hiking packs tended to have reinforcement, right?"

"Usually." Kyle held out his hand, freshly gloved. "Lemme see."

She passed it to him and watched as he groped the bag. The motions sent her brain to places she didn't want to visit at this moment.

He stopped. "What?"

Her face fell. "What?"

Kyle circled his face. "What's with the face?"

Lila wrinkled her nose. "Nothing. It's nothing."

He didn't look convinced. Well, too bad. She resumed watching him inspect the backpack.

At the bottom of the bag, he hesitated and then patted the flattened surface. "There's something inside here." He reached behind him and withdrew a folded knife.

"What are you doing?" she demanded as he flicked out the blade.

"Locating a hidden compartment." He stabbed the point into the reinforced bottom.

Lila reached for the bag. "You're damaging evidence."

He moved it out of her reach, which wasn't far for him considering the table between them and her shorter stature. "Only if I find nothing here."

"Kyle," Lila snarled, "I'm going to kick your ass for this."

"You're not tall enough," he deadpanned.

If she weren't so infuriated with him, she might have found his quip funny. She slapped the tabletop. "Arrangements can be made."

Finished with slicing into the bag's bottom, Lundquist

folded the blade inside the handle and shoved his knife into his pocket. "Moment of truth." He delved inside the ragged flap.

Lila gaped as he withdrew a flat notebook. A slender item came out with the notebook and hit the table. Lila picked it up.

"A weird-looking pencil."

"It's a sketching pencil," he said, setting the bag aside and cradling the notebook. "This is a sketch pad."

The pad looked in remarkably good condition. Lila picked up the bag and felt inside the exposed compartment. A slick surface lined the pocket like some kind of sealant.

"Does it have any moisture damage?" she asked.

Kyle lifted the cover, and it came away cleanly. "Doesn't appear so." He turned the pages. "These are good." He lowered the pad.

The page he showed her was a detailed sketch of a woman's face surrounded by fauna and vines.

Lila tilted the pad closer. "It's so detailed."

He flipped to the next page. This drawing a landscape of a body of water and surrounding land. The reeds lining the shore looked as if they could move in a breeze. The next was another woman, this time looking through a broken window.

"Each of these are initialed and dated." Lundquist pointed to the right bottom corner of the pages. "Whoever did these wouldn't have just left them behind."

He flipped through to the final drawing in the pad. It was an extreme close-up of the human eye with something reflecting in the eye. "This is the last one. Dated"—he squinted at the numbers—"October." He met Lila's gaze. "Last year."

The rustle of boots through grass drew Lila's attention. Young joined them at the table.

"Whaddya have here?" she asked.

"The belongings of a potential victim," Lila answered. She studied the pencil lying on the table. "What are the odds we could pull DNA or prints from this?" She pointed at the pad. "Or that?"

Kyle turned pensive. "Maybe. It was protected inside the bag, but it was buried and left to the elements. The pad is surprisingly in good condition. I don't know if the same could be said for biological traces."

"DCI has all the neat little toys and tricks to do it," Young pointed out.

"So do I," he shot back. He focused on Lila. "Do you want me to check?"

"It's worth a shot. We can't pass up any opportunities."

"There's still the matter of those bodies we found this morning," Young said.

"Anyone heard from the state ME?" Lila asked.

"It's why I'm out here," Kyle replied. "He wants to speak with you. Seems no one knows where the sheriff went. And she's not answering her phone."

Lila groaned. "Where's Fontaine?"

"Which one?" Lundquist asked.

"What do you mean, which one? There's only one Fontaine who works at the sheriff's department."

"Not anymore." Kyle looked like he wanted to exit this conversation, quick. "Apparently, the sheriff deputized Joel this morning. He's now on the payroll."

"Come again?"

"Seems I came back to work at the right time," Young quipped.

Lila shook her head. "I can't effing believe this." She waved her hand over the bag and sketch pad. "Bag and tag. We'll deal with this later. Guess I'm going to the morgue."

CHAPTER EIGHTEEN

T HE UNIVERSITY OF Iowa hospital main lobby's carpeted corridor gave way to the easily sterilized vinyl flooring. A comfortable hush permeated the halls and waiting rooms, as if speaking too loudly would disturb the dead. It always gave Elizabeth a sad case of the heebie-jeebies, even when she was a patient herself.

Joel stayed one step behind her, allowing her to remain in command. Their drive to Iowa City had been spent in silence.

A blessing and a curse. It gave Elizabeth a chance to mull over, pick apart, and overthink her interactions with Dayne and Rafe at the riverbed. The cursed part came when she concluded—or maybe it was conceded—she was not being rational. When Dayne mentioned they should all consider Olivia and Dominic's connection to the boneyard and the bodies as nefarious, Elizabeth had overreacted. Bias was putting it nicely.

Reality, she was being a bitch.

Rounding the curving hall, they entered the general patient wing of the hospital. The University of Iowa hospital was a huge maze; it took Elizabeth three attempts and a threat of a warrant before she was able to get to the right area where they had roomed Dominic. Maybe, in some cases, being a bitch did work. Through the ordeal, Joel kept his silence.

As they approached the circular nurses' station, Elizabeth glanced over at her ex. His features were hard, mission centered, and he walked ... no, he prowled. This struck Elizabeth oddly. She didn't dwell on it as they were greeted by a brunette wearing dark purple scrubs and bright green plastic-framed glasses.

"Afternoon, Sheriff. What can I help you with?"

"Are you the charge nurse?"

"No. Give me a minute, I'll get her." She skirted around her chair and vacated the cubicle.

Joel braced an elbow on the counter and casually leaned against it. "How much you wanna bet they've already called up here with a heads-up you were coming?"

"If that were the case, the charge nurse should have been here waiting for me."

"Ten to one, the doc's doc is hot on her heels."

Elizabeth gave him a sidelong look, then focused on the direction the nurse had disappeared. "What's bothering you?"

"Nothin' is bothering me."

"Don't give me that crap. We were married for twenty years, and I know all your little tics and expressions. Something is bothering you."

Joel adjusted his posture from leaning to standing military precise upright. "You think you know me that well?"

Looking him up and down, she smiled. What was it about the Fontaine men that, no matter what uniform it was, they always looked so good? Their father, Jonathan Fontaine, had been a farmer, raised by a farmer, raised by a farmer, but all previous generations of Fontaines had served their country in one capacity or another. Joel and Rafe's father managed to miss being drafted into Vietnam, but he did pay his due diligence and joined the National Guard. He'd been a volunteer firefighter for the county. It was only fitting for his sons to choose a path putting them in uniform.

Elizabeth crossed her arms and settled into a loose-hipped stance. "I know you well enough. Can your newbie woman claim that?"

A twinkle popped in his eyes, and he gave her one of his slow, sugar-coated smiles. "Jealous?"

"Intrigued." She lifted her hand from the crook of her left elbow and circled her finger. "Spit it out."

A crescendo of voices coming up the hall saved Joel from admitting anything to her. The purple-scrub nurse chased the heels of another purple-scrub woman and a man with dark hair turning silver at the sideburns in a white lab coat. The charge nurse and the doctor didn't look 100 percent pleased.

"You've gone and done it now," Joel said in a low voice.

"Hesh up," Elizabeth hissed.

The doctor rounded the nurses' station. "Sheriff Benoit, is it?"

"It is."

He introduced himself as the head surgeon. "What can I do for you?"

"You're the surgeon who handled Dr. Dominic Thorpe's case when he came in yesterday?"

The man let out an exasperated sound. "I'm not at liberty to speak to you about the patient's case or treatment. We can only speak to the next of kin."

Elizabeth put on her best politician's charm. "Doctor, I'm well aware of the hoops and HIPAA and all of that. What you're not aware of is that Dr. Thrope has no known next of kin other than his wife, who is currently missing. As in, there is strong evidence to support someone has abducted her. We need to speak with him to find out what happened."

The surgeon hemmed and hawed, looking at his charge nurse, who seemed just as perplexed on what to do. He grimaced. "This is out of the norm for me."

"You've never had a patient come in here with a police escort before?" Joel asked.

"Not like this." The surgeon dug through a pocket and produced a folded sheaf of papers. Once unfolded, he shifted through them and pulled out one. "I have instructions here to allow only Officer Ross and Deputy Fontaine in to see Dr. Thrope. No one else." He looked back at the charge nurse for confirmation and got a nod from the older woman.

"Who said only those two were allowed?" Elizabeth pressed. Could she play against Lady Luck with Joel—Deputy Fontaine—going into the room in place of his brother?

"Officer Ross," the charge nurse answered.

"Explains why you had a hard time getting through the iron curtain," Joel muttered.

"Doctor, what's it going to take for me to see my witness and my county's only surgeon?"

"I'm sorry, Sheriff, but hospital policy is strict in these matters. Unless you can produce a warrant or have Officer

Ross make an amendment—"

A persistent buzz cut off the surgeon. Both nurses looked to a special panel set up on the desk where a red light was lit up.

The charge nurse frowned. "It's room 344," she told the surgeon.

"Okay, uh, Sheriff, excuse me one minute." He beckoned for the charge nurse and the two took off down the hall.

Another buzz and light sent the other nurse into another room.

Alone, Elizabeth inched closer to Joel. "Ideas?"

"Someone doesn't want you anywhere near the good doc."

She peered down the hall where the other two had disappeared. "I get the same feeling."

"What's odd is, they allowed Rafe access, but not anyone else."

"Want to pretend to be your brother?"

"If you want me to. It'll be real awkward later if he comes up and these same people are here."

Elizabeth gnawed on her tongue. What did she do? Was she willing to break the rules to get what she wanted? This type of scenario was precisely the kind of thing Kelley Sheehan would have done during his tenure as sheriff. The very thing Elizabeth swore she'd never do.

Why the hell not? She had sworn to let loose the dogs of war. And what better way to do it than by letting Joel ply some of his former trade on these unsuspecting doctors and nurses. One Fontaine was the same as the other.

Joel stiffened and tipped his head toward the hall. "Incoming."

Moving with a purpose he hadn't had before, the surgeon returned. His flushed features and steely eyes gave Elizabeth pause. Did someone usurp his authority?

"Sheriff Benoit, I've been instructed—ordered—to allow you to see Dr. Thorpe. You only." He looked pointedly at Joel. "Your deputy will have to remain here until you're through."

Elizabeth met Joel's gaze. Her ex said nothing and did nothing, but she got the message he conveyed loud and clear. Go, he had her back. She gestured for the surgeon to lead the way.

Turned out room 344 was Dominic's. And one Officer James Ross was stationed outside the door.

"Officer Ross. How is it you drew the short straw to stay on protective custody detail?"

"Police chief said it was only right for me to continue. He's real worried about Dr. Thorpe."

"I don't recall giving you or Ed any authority on the matter. Let's not forget, Eckardt County Sheriff's Department trumps Juniper police in this."

Next to her, the surgeon cleared his throat. Elizabeth ignored him.

"Well, you did say you needed me to keep watch over the doc," Ross countered.

"While he was in Juniper. Not here."

"That's not what your undersheriff said."

Elizabeth and Rafe would have a come to Jesus moment when she got back to town. Yes, it was true, he had been given authority and rights while she recovered, but this was going too far.

The door to the room opened, and the charge nurse emerged. "Excuse me, Sheriff. Dr. Thorpe wants to talk to you."

She caught the surgeon's eye. "When I'm through, you and I will be having a discussion."

"I have rounds, Sheriff."

"I understand. But we've got some adjustments to make."

She went to enter the room and sensed Ross shifting to follow. She stopped and glared at him. "I don't think so."

"It's only right," he said.

"Not on my watch." She pointed at the chair he'd vacated when she arrived. "Plant it. Don't move." Her edict rendered, she pushed into the room.

A sharp, unpleasant, and all too familiar odor assaulted her the moment she entered. Iodine along with the other typical hospital smells left Elizabeth off-kilter. For a moment, she was thrust back, remembering it was she who had been lying in a hospital bed, recovering from yet another round of surgeries. She would forever hate those odor-bearing reminders of what she'd put herself through.

Dominic, despite the array of cords, tubes, and an oxygen cannula, looked surprisingly better, and awake. He lifted an IV-strapped hand and crooked a finger.

Before she reached the bedside, she caught his glance at the doorway behind her. She chanced a look over her shoulder and spotted Ross framed in the narrow window beside the door.

Irritation flashed through her. She caught the edge of the privacy curtain and flung it around. The metal tracks rattled, making Dominic cringe.

"We don't need any lookie-loos," she said.

"Have you found Olivia?" he rasped.

"How do you know she's missing?"

He stared at her; the whites of his eyes were filled with broken blood vessels. When no answer was forthcoming, Elizabeth pressed a hand to her mouth and considered biting her fingers to keep from screaming. The hit of temper under control, she dropped her hand to her hip.

"What is going on, Dominic?"

Swallowing, he looked away.

Elizabeth snatched his hand closest to her and tugged, earning a wince from him, and his attention returned to her. "I'm at a point today where I'm not above applying some uncomfortable pressure to get straight answers." She squeezed his tape-wrapped knuckles. "Don't make me do it."

"What are you doing? This isn't you."

"No, it's not. For the last thirty-some odd hours, I've had my surgeon nearly drop dead at my doorstep, my closest friend disappear, a huge-ass boneyard discovered in my backyard, and then three more bodies discovered floating in the river. If you want to play stupid games with me, I'll dole out stupid prizes."

Dominic managed to free his hand and clutched it to his chest. He glared at her, but the effect was weak at best, probably from all the painkillers.

"You haven't found Olivia." The resignation in his voice matched the despair in his features.

"When you arrived at the Fontaine cabin, you were stabbed and had stumbled up a hill from a wrecked Jeep. A Jeep, I might add, that has never belonged to you and is now missing, along with your own vehicle and Olivia's. You passed out from significant blood loss. We didn't learn until you were already in the hospital that Olivia was abducted. From your home. There are no signs you were ever there at the time of the abduction. So, again, how do you know she's missing?"

"It was the terms." He covered his battered face and made a sound like a wounded animal.

For the briefest of moments, Elizabeth's compassion for his predicament powered through her anger. For a split second she second-guessed her actions. Then reality caved in, and she stuffed her tender side in a cage and locked it.

"Whose terms?"

Dominic choked, slapping his hands into his lap. He sucked in a breath and grimaced. The motion must have stirred up a stab of pain from his wounds.

"Walk away from this, Elizabeth."

"Why would I ever do that? You begged me, *begged*, to find Olivia before you passed out. Now you want to change your mind."

He looked at her sharply. "Walk away. Stop asking questions. Close your department's investigation. End it now."

"I can't."

"If you don't, more people will die. And so will Olivia."

CHAPTER NINETEEN

T HE MORGUE IN the Juniper hospital was Olivia's domain. Being here without her commanding presence to explain the findings felt horribly wrong to Lila.

The state medical examiner—who had introduced himself as Dr. Victor Bradley—was decent, if not a bit on the stuffy side, and further confirmed what Dr. Pembrook suspected. The victims had their vital, healthy organs removed before death.

"Can you tell if they were alive when it happened?" Lila asked, standing at the end of one gurney bearing the remains of a young male.

"If the organs were harvested for black-market purposes, yes, they would have to keep them alive up until they removed the heart," the medical examiner answered.

Which meant an expert in the field of surgery. Along with a sterile place set up to remove the organs where they could go unnoticed. That ruled out the shack. Nothing about the building and the tunnel suggested that was the place for operations to remove organs. More like the dumping ground. And a place to move live humans undetected.

"They would need access to some sophisticated equipment to make the setup work," Kyle said in passing.

Lila inched closer to the deceased male's head, noting

that the medical examiner's telltale Y incision was not on the youth's torso. "His chest was left open?"

"Yes. As was the young woman the beetles had not disturbed. The body the insects had been consuming showed similar signs. This could have been a rushed job, or they have never bothered to close the chest cavity after surgery. It would give the beetles primary access to the internal tissue without having to chew through the skin and muscle first. Work their way inside out as it were."

Absorbing this tidbit, Lila studied the young victim. His skin, not mottled by beetle bites and lividity, was a light tan coloration, his hair dark, nearly black, and his fingernails were jagged, with dirt built up against the nail bed. Who was he? Where had he come from?

"Other than removing their hearts, how did they actually go about killing the victims?" Lila asked.

The ME moved to a tray and picked up a small evidence bag. He passed it to Kyle, who stood closer to him.

"I'm ruling my cause of death as suffocation. I found those fibers in two of the victims' airways. I was also able to make out some bruising that was not livor mortis around the mouth and nose, which lends strong corroboration to suffocation. It's also possible the victims were allowed to bleed out and those fibers are from something else, and the bruising was from a tightly fitted oxygen mask."

"Either way would make the most sense," Kyle said, passing the bag to Lila.

She saw the two fine, possibly white, fibers clinging to the sides of the plastic case. They could have come from anything and anywhere. Processing those through evidence at DCI would take days if not weeks or months.

"Would the suspects save the blood?" she asked.

"Possibly. Our country and the world at large has seen a drop in blood donations."

"What about the eyes?" Kyle asked. "Were they removed perimortem versus being consumed by the beetles?"

Dr. Bradley tilted his head in thought. "There are clear signs they were surgically removed. Replacement corneas and in some cases the whole eye are in high demand."

Lila sighed and moved away from the gurney. "How does something like this happen in the US? Much less in the middle of freaking rural America? Under our noses?"

Dr. Bradley draped a privacy sheet over the young female. "It's more common than you think." The ME accessed Olivia's computer, having already explained that the hospital administration had given him special login credentials. "When the anthropologist asked me to come in on this case, he told me about his situation with your boneyard. I recalled a case a few years ago with similar findings."

"Dr. Pembrook hasn't mentioned there were any similar cases," Lila interjected.

"It's because he's new to DCI. Just came on late last year."

Lila, having inched closer to the medical examiner and the computer desk, froze. "Something like this has happened before?"

Dr. Bradley tilted his head to look at her. "In Iowa, no. It was across the river in Illinois." He returned to his search on the computer. "Here we go." A PDF opened on the screen, and the medical examiner stepped back. "The discovery was made three years ago."

Lila began reading the report, stopped, and looked at the ME. "I'm going to need all of these sent to my email."

"Done. You might also check in with other bordering states databases for the same thing."

"Why?"

The medical examiner crossed his arms and stared at her point blank. "There is no way Iowa or Illinois were specifically chosen for this. I bet my career there are other cold cases exactly like this in Missouri, Kentucky, and possibly as far south as Arkansas and Mississippi."

"Along the Mississippi River?" Lundquist asked.

"Precisely."

LILA STOOD OUTSIDE the hospital, lifted her face to the midafternoon sun, and soaked in the remnants of the day while clearing her lungs of the rotten smell of death.

"If Dr. Bradley's right and this goes back years, even decades, in multiple states, we're going to have to contact the feds," Kyle said beside her.

She peeled an eye open and looked sideways at him. "We go there as a last resort." She resumed her sun-basking. "Besides, I doubt this is even on the feds' radar."

"You can't know that for certain without asking," he prodded.

Lila gave up soaking in any more rays and slid on her sunglasses. "Some days, you're a real pain in the ass, you know that."

"I'm the pain in the ass? Have you looked in the mirror lately?"

"I have my reasons for not wanting to bring in the FBI, and number one on that list is we don't have enough evidence to prove this is a federal case."

Kyle crossed his arms, drawing himself up to his full height. "Then I suggest we take a deep, dark dive into those files Bradley sent and research for other places."

"You do realize the sheriff has more to say about that than we do," Lila countered. "With the way she's been freewheeling lately, I doubt she'd want the FBI here scrutinizing her work."

He shook his head. "Sheriff wouldn't turn down extra help."

"Yeah, evidenced by her appointing her ex-husband as a deputy. Which, I'm still trying to understand how that works if he's still attached to the army."

Kyle huffed, dropping his arms to his sides. "You'll find any excuse to avoid asking for help."

"When it comes to the FBI, damn straight I will." She went to walk past him.

"You and I are still going to have a talk about your propensity to shoot off at the mouth," he said.

"How does never work for you?"

Her smart-ass remark was waylaid by the loud growl of her stomach. Kyle's brows furrowed, plunging behind his own aviator-style sunglasses.

"When was the last time you ate?" he demanded.

Lila sighed. "You're not my caretaker."

"Don't give me that. Just answer the question."

"Well, aren't you testy?"

He didn't grace her comment with a response, merely kept a straight face.

But she wasn't in the mood for another battle with him. "A muffin for breakfast and coffee this morning."

A low rumble lifted from the depths of his chest. "Stay here. I'll get something from the hospital cafeteria."

"Eww, not there."

"What's wrong with their food?" He held up his hand. "You know what, never mind. Just stay here. I'll be back."

Before she could protest further, he stalked off to his vehicle.

With her own rumbled groan, Lila turned her back on his retreating figure and ambled over to a concrete bench stationed along the gravel walking path. The simple path circling the entire hospital complex had been completed last summer after a bit of a brouhaha on public health and wellness. Not one for a public display of her own physical fitness, Lila had never used the loop, preferring her home equipment.

Seated, she slumped down, shoving her hands in her jacket pockets and watched a pair of middle-aged women in workout gear stroll past, their idle gossip drifting back to Lila. Oh, how nice it must be to just meander on through life with nothing bigger to worry about than so-in-so's latest escapades at the name your club/organization's last meeting. Some days Lila missed the solitude of living in Chicago where one was a mere drop in the existence of millions of residents within the city's limits.

Tiring of watching the two women attempt to break the

world record for the slowest walk time, Lila reclined her head against the backrest and closed her eyes. Whatever idea Kyle had for a meal, she hoped he would bring the largest cup of the blackest coffee he could get.

The February breeze carried a tinge of spring. Lila had been enjoying the warmer days as of late and hoped the typical "third" winter didn't make another round. She was ready for spring.

What she wasn't ready for was the inevitable fiery circus of hell sure to come if they brought in the FBI to consult. The moment the media got wind of what they'd discovered here in Eckardt, it would explode. Every national outlet would swarm to Juniper, and chaos would reign. Speculation and rumor would become fact. And everyone working in the sheriff's department would find their carefully constructed lives picked apart and plastered about for clicks and ratings.

Kyle could demand and snarl all he wanted. Then again, if she told him what she was truly trying to avoid by involving the FBI, maybe he'd back off his insistence. She didn't doubt for one minute he'd rethink it if he knew he and his sister's turbulent lives would make good click bait for the social media dragons. And a juicy episode for all those true crime podcasters.

The sigh of clothing against the concrete bench infiltrated her rambling thoughts. She stiffened as a warm, exotic scent with a hint of what she could only describe as pipe tobacco teased her senses. Lila came alert, peeling her eyes open enough to peer over to her left.

The man seated inches from her was not from around here. A worn, dark-brown leather coat suited his imposing figure perfectly. The dark gray skull cap topped off the ensemble.

Carefully, Lila sat up, her right hand slipping to her side.

"I'm of no threat to you," he said, his deep bass carried the pull of Southside. He kept his gaze forward. "No need to draw your weapon, Deputy."

"I'll be the judge of that." Lila shifted to keep him in her line of sight. "Who are you?"

"For now, let's just say I'm a friend."

"I have no friends from Southside."

His face twitched, a slight smile drawing up the corner of his mouth. "I'm sure your former Jackson Park neighbors would agree."

A cold sweat prickled along Lila's neck.

"I did not come here to put you on edge, Deputy." He looked at her, fully exposing his face to her. "I was asked to approach you."

"By whom?"

"In due time," he said, his head swiveling away from her. "We have a mutual interest."

"I doubt that." She allowed her muscles to relax a fraction so as to appear unbothered by him. She doubted he was buying her attempt. "But I'm listening."

He held up his hands, then pointed at his opened coat. "I think it best to show you versus telling you."

"No games," she warned and gave him a nod.

He reached inside the jacket and withdrew a tri-folded sheaf of paper. He offered the fat stack to her. "The graveyard of exposed bones," he said. "It's not the only one."

She was well aware of that, but she had no intentions of

revealing what she knew to him. She studied the man next to her, and seeing he meant her no harm, she took the papers. When she pried the thick wad apart, only then did she let her gaze leave him.

In her hands, she held black-and-white maps with red flags pinned to precise places along the Mississippi River. Beside each flag was a date. She shuffled through the sheets, noting the oldest date went back ten years, the most recent, yesterday. The last page was a land deed.

She looked up from the mess. "What is this?"

"Your guide to the other boneyards. Every single site has a cold case file. Every single place a disinterested police force." He lowered his chin and narrowed his dark umber gaze at her. "Until now."

Lila pulled the land deed from the stack. "This isn't a map to a boneyard. It's a deed." She looked closer at it. "To a place in Iowa."

When he didn't elaborate on what she held, Lila scowled. "Why does a man from the Chicago Southside give two shits about bones left to bleach in the sun in the middle of nowhere?"

He chuckled and rose from the bench. "That, good deputy, is for you to figure out." He straightened, tilting his head just so, to the left. "Appears your man has returned. I'll be seeing you."

Lila hopped to her feet and watched his imposing figure swagger away, a strut born of the streets and pride. When he rounded the far corner of the walking path leading behind the hospital, she shuddered, releasing the tension coiled in her muscles. He was a man she shouldn't cross.

"Who was that?" Kyle asked the moment he joined her.

Lila stared at the map of boneyards slithering up the Mississippi River Valley. "I have no idea." She thrust the papers at him. "Whoever he is, he claims to be a friend and wants to help."

Kyle exchanged the greasy food bag for the papers.

The heavenly scent of piping hot potatoes fried in oil drenched in salt made Lila's stomach cramp in anticipation. She dove into the bag and dragged out the fries container.

"Did you get me a coffee?" she asked around a mouthful of hot spuds.

"In the car," Kyle said, his attention not wavering as he read through the maps. "These all look like photocopies." He flipped over one of the sheets to expose a light-yellow sticky note with a name scrawled on it. "Who's Booker Williams?"

"Beats me. We'll run it through the system and see if anything pops." She rammed more food in her mouth.

Kyle continued to study the maps and then the deed before he finally looked at Lila. "What did the guy say?"

She gulped down another generous helping of fries. "He said those are a guide to all the other boneyards. Every one of them are cold cases. And the police departments involved don't care."

"Until now."

"Bingo."

CHAPTER TWENTY

B LACK FINGERS OF night raked through the waning
daylight as Elizabeth and Joel returned to Eckardt
County. In two weeks' time, they would return to daylight
savings—leaping forward as they said—and the sun would
set later. Elizabeth couldn't wait for the arrival of summer.

Her trip to Iowa City to glean more information from
Dominic had been a bust, but not completely. After a few
phone calls, pulling some strings, asking for favors, she got
Officer Ross out of the hospital and banned as Dominic's
watchdog. The university hospital administration had
granted her some measure of leniency and provided a
constant rotation of security guards—some of them former
Iowa City police officers—to keep an eye on his room. If
anything occurred out of the ordinary, they were to contact
her immediately and no one else. All of this was accomplished after a drawn-out battle with the head of the
hospital's administration. The threat of bringing lawyers into
the mix seemed to temper their zeal to gatekeep her authority
in the situation.

In the end, Dominic remained tightlipped about the
events leading to his injuries and why his wife was in peril.
Elizabeth felt a revelation about the discovery of the boneyard and the mysterious tunnel under an abandoned shack

would either make Dominic clam up tighter or lie. But his ongoing refusal to enlighten her brought her dangerously close to caving in and spilling the whole sordid truth.

Try as she might to prove to Dayne and anyone else who agreed with the deputy detective that Dominic and Olivia were somehow not involved with the three victims and the boneyard, Elizabeth was beginning to waver. Dominic's behavior certainly suggested he had involved himself with something nefarious.

Which led her to driving directly to the Remington-Thorpe house when she and Joel returned to Juniper.

Elizabeth parked her Interceptor in the slightly sloped drive and killed the engine. Once the lights faded off, she sat there listening to her ex-husband breathe and stared at the darkened house.

Since her return to Juniper and her subsequent friendship with Olivia, Elizabeth had been to the Remington-Thorpe residence maybe ten or fifteen times. In more recent years, she hadn't been inside until yesterday when she came to survey the damage and find Olivia gone. Time had not allowed her the luxury of visiting friends. A byproduct of being sheriff in a large county with a growing homicide problem.

So consumed by her passion to see ex-sheriff Kelley Sheehan rot in prison and solve the deaths of her old high schoolmates, Elizabeth had missed something going on in the Remington-Thorpe lives. Now that nagging, insatiable need for answers was taking hold, replacing the void left with the resolution to Brendette Lundquist's murder.

"What are you thinking?" Joel asked when she still

hadn't moved from the SUV.

Elizabeth dragged her attention away from the dark house and redirected it to him. "I'm thinking if Dominic were hiding things, especially about who took his wife, he might find it safer to leave the evidence here at home." She returned to the red brick and white paneled split two-level. "He's got hiding places in there. We're going to dig them up."

"Then what are you waiting on? Approval to walk through a crime scene?"

"In a sense."

Eliciting a grunt, Joel opened the door and exited the SUV.

Guess that was her cue. Elizabeth followed him out and up the walk.

"You have a key?" he asked as he reached the front door.

She did, and she also had the code for the alarm system from Olivia. This was not how either of them anticipated using it. Elizabeth passed over the key.

Once Joel released the dead bolt and the handle lock, she squeezed past him to the beeping box along the foyer. The code entered, the beeping ceased, and they were free to roam about without gathering unwanted attention from the security company and the neighbors. The house was the farthest back on the cul-de-sac, a thick grove of fir and spruce trees horseshoeing the property, blocking the prying eyes of busybodies. However, a shrilling alarm tended to penetrate the stillness, letting all around hear it.

"Where do you want to start first?" Joel asked, turning on the hall lights.

Elizabeth blinked against the sudden brightness. Yesterday, she and Rafe had focused on only the hallway and the kitchen, gave cursory looks to the rest of the house where it didn't appear anything was disturbed. The plan had been for Dayne and Lundquist or DCI to do a more thorough search today. With the discovery of the three bodies, it didn't happen.

"They both have offices here," she said. "We'll start there."

"What am I looking for?"

She scowled at him. "I don't know. Something out of the ordinary for a doctor. Geesh, what's with the million questions?"

"You're sending me on a mission with next to no intel. This is what gets a man killed."

"This isn't one of your super-duper, top-secret classified missions. It's detective work. You look for things that are out of the ordinary."

Joel snorted as he passed her. "I can see why Dayne is the detective in this department."

"Bite me."

He sniggered. "Don't tease me with a good time."

Elizabeth groaned. Why did she saddle herself with a newly retired army guy? Why?

She followed him down the hall, stepping over the remnants of the fight near the kitchen entrance. The spot reminded her that she needed to have Lundquist run the blood sample. At the first door just past the kitchen, Joel stopped.

"Where does this go?" he asked, opening it.

"Upstairs. Their bedroom and one other room are up there, and a bathroom," she said.

He moved across the hall and opened the door there. "And this?"

"Ground-level floor. If I remember right, there's a den of sorts and a spare room. Laundry room, too."

"Which way are the offices?"

Elizabeth frowned, looking from one door to the next. "I'm not sure. Let's start upstairs."

She flicked on the stairwell light as she mounted the carpeted steps. It was a short flight.

The upper-level landing had a wall of windows overlooking the backyard and the grove of trees. Lining the floor in front of the windows was a veritable greenhouse of all varieties of plant life, some blooming, others with big, lush leaves. Bookending the row of potted plants were leafy, tree-like plants, their wide, glossy green leaves bowing to the visitors. Tall bookshelves loaded with medical journals and a beautiful audio system that included a record player with rows of vinyl records covered the adjoining wall to the windows.

"Someone's green thumb got carried away," Joel remarked as he headed for the first room.

"Olivia," Elizabeth answered.

He switched on the light in the room. "Who uses this?"

She peeked in, noticing the flourish of indigo, purple, and orange in the furniture, throws, art, and rugs. Olivia's favorite colors.

"This is Olivia's office. Might as well check it over."

Elizabeth continued to the next room on the same side of

the hall. It was the couple's bedroom. Across the hall was the bathroom. She turned on the bedroom light and began her search.

As she progressed, she noticed nothing of Dominic's was in the room. None of his clothing or scrubs. No shoes. No watches or tie pins or other masculine finery. Everything in the room was Olivia's and Olivia's alone. Giving up on the bedroom, she went across the hall to the bathroom. It was the same there. too. She turned off the lights and met Joel in the main area.

"Nothing," he said. "Just her stuff. Did find a locked safe."

"Won't be anything in there to help us." She looked back at the bedroom. "None of Dominic's things are up here. It's like he moved out."

"Ground floor maybe?"

With a humph, she headed down the stairs, across the first-floor hall, and down the steps. The lower level of the house was more enclosed, and the few lights in the den area struggled to illuminate the area.

"Check the entertainment center, too," she told Joel as she slipped along a dimly lit hall to the second additional room.

As she passed the laundry room that doubled as a spare bathroom, she paused and backtracked. The lighting in this room was brighter, and what it revealed gave Elizabeth a twinge. Towels with Dominic's initials hung on the shower door. Shaving cream cans and razors stacked neatly along the sink counter with an electric toothbrush and a half-used tube of paste.

Elizabeth abandoned the room and went next door. The room meant to be Dominic's office looked to be his bedroom as well. She took a step inside and was brought up short by a loud thump. The noise had come from the den.

"Elizabeth," Joel called, a bite to his voice she rarely heard.

She reeled out of the room and hurried back down the hall. She found him, weapon drawn, staring at the sliding glass doors opening out to the side yard. She rounded the corner and let out a gasp.

"Stand down," she barked at her ex and rushed to the door.

A young male, his upper body pressed to the glass, lay sprawled across the doorway. A streak of red smeared the window. He was wearing only a red-stained T-shirt and jeans.

Elizabeth struggled to disengage the lock and latch. Once she got it right, she slid the door open until she could stick her head out.

"Damn it, Ellie," Joel snapped and jerked her back. "Use some common sense."

With his Glock lifted, he squeezed through the gap, assessed the downed man, and then swept the yard. While he did his perimeter check, Elizabeth wormed her way between the door and the frame.

Squatting next to the injured man, she got the sensation of déjà vu, except she didn't know this bleeding human, whereas yesterday, it had been Dominic. Elizabeth dug out her pocket-sized LED flashlight and assessed the young man's injuries. He stared at her, the whites of his eyes bloodshot, and the pupils dilated.

"Where are you injured?" she asked, unable to make out where all the blood was coming from.

He lifted at red-slicked hand and clutched her coat sleeve. The strength in his grasp shocked her.

"Where ... is ..." he slurred, his voice trailing off.

"Young man, where are you hurt?" Elizabeth tried again.

His eyes began to droop. His grip on her coat slackened and his hand slid. Elizabeth caught it in hers and shook it.

"We're clear," Joel said when he returned.

"Call the EMS," Elizabeth ordered as the young man's eyes closed.

While Joel radioed for an ambulance, she set about searching the unconscious man's body for the source of the bleeding. As she peeled his blood-saturated shirt away from his stomach, it made a sucking sound. She gingerly rolled it upward and let out a groan.

The young man sported a gaping hole in his lower abdomen that looked like someone had tried to unsuccessfully use staples to mend the severed flesh. He was bleeding out, and she didn't know how much longer he would live.

"Joel, tell them to get their asses here. Now!"

CHAPTER TWENTY-ONE

L ILA HAD EVERY light on in the deputy's bullpen. She stood, a red Sharpie in hand, before a large paper map of the Mississippi River from Minnesota to the Gulf of Mexico.

With Kyle at his lab running tests, Lila had kept Young out on patrol and put Meyer to work going over the emails the state medical examiner had sent over. Together, she and Meyer combed through national databases, searching for similar indicators. Between that avenue and the sheaf of papers with marked spots given to her by the mysterious man, they'd found eleven sites along the Mississippi River.

Somebody or somebodies were using the massive waterway to move humans upriver. Taking them to places where their organs were harvested, the victims killed, and then disposing of their remains where no one was supposed to find them. By the reports coming from the anthropologist, and now the medical examiner, the victims were both male and female and mostly young, possibly as old as in their twenties. Prime age group to harvest the healthiest organs.

Lila sensed that there were locations farther south. Either they hadn't been discovered due to the significant predatory animal activity in the more southern regions of the Mississippi River or the population density scared away the would-be traffickers. Coming farther north would prove harder still with the lock and dam systems. It made more sense to shuttle the victims via the road and not the river.

Which explained the burned SUV. It could have been a vehicle used to transport. How it got to the river embankment was a mystery. DCI techs had not found any impressions in the dirt to indicate a heavy SUV had been driven through there, which was possible if it was done while the ground was frozen solid.

She turned her back on the wall and moved to her desk. She'd given the maps to Meyer. The oddball land deed she had kept for herself. Lila picked up the copy. Norwood. The family property where they had found their boneyard.

How did Mystery Man get a copy of this? And what did it mean in relation to the other information?

Lila let the sheet fall back to her desk and then checked on the other two.

At her post, the night dispatcher, Alexis Zachary, stared intently at her computer screen. Having relieved the decidedly sick Georgia over three hours ago, Alexis had been helping Lila and Meyer search the internet and social media for any news or information on other boneyards. Alexis was of the generation that had grown up with a device in her hand. Her savviness with the social media sites had proven to be a gold mine.

"Anything new?" Lila asked them.

Both looked at her with glassy eyes and shook their heads, then went back to work.

"You two look like you need a break," she said.

"No time," Meyer remarked. He paused in his search and his gaze returned to Lila. "We need to run down leads on the beetles. Someone must be spending a lot of money to keep that venture going."

"Lundquist said he'd talk with the forensic entomologist and chase that one. I want to talk with Dr. Pembrook more on it. He seemed to know a lot about those beetles." Lila jotted a note to herself to call the anthropologist.

"Isn't he supposed to be the bones expert?" Meyer asked.

Lila tossed her pen on the desk. "Guess he's a jack-of-all-trades."

A contemplative expression edged into Meyer's haggard features, then he slid a notepad under his hand and scribbled on it. "What about the burned SUV?" he asked as he continued to write.

"DCI techs are supposed to have it moved to a garage," Lila explained. "I'm hoping they can find a VIN or something tangible from the wreckage we can work with. Alexis, have there been any hits on the sheriff's BOLO for the Remington-Thorpe vehicles?"

"Not a thing."

Had those cars gone by the wayside like the mysterious Jeep the sheriff said had been made to do a disappearing act? How did someone make three separate vehicles vanish?

"Meyer, where are you at on that sticky note name?"

Meyer stretched his arms above his head and then rocked his chair back. "Striking out. Do you realize how many people in this country alone have that same exact name?"

"Thousands." Lila sighed. "Narrow down the search to the Chicago area."

"Are you planning to reach out to the locals LEOs at all of these locations?" he asked.

"Someone has to." Lila looked pointedly at the sheriff's vacant office.

"Did she really deputize her ex-husband?" Alexis asked.

Stomping boots proceeded a growled "She damn well did."

Lila watched Undersheriff Fontaine stalk by her desk, heading to his own. "Where've you been?"

Fontaine threw his coat at his chair and then stripped his Kevlar from his body, tossing the heavy vest on the chair. He resorted to jerking open desk drawers and slamming them shut. His oh-so subtle way of telling her to piss off.

Alexis and Meyer seemed to shrink behind their computer monitors. Lila was certain they had nothing to worry about from him. He was mad at the sheriff.

She gave a light sniff. Who wasn't these days?

He must have found what he was searching for. He dragged out a hard-shell case from a lower drawer and slapped it down on the top of his desk.

Lila stiffened at the sight of the lockbox. Oh, this was not good. Not one bit.

She glanced at Meyer. His eyes widened. He, too, was aware of what that particular case meant.

Fontaine removed his sidearm, setting it on top of the box, and began undoing the buttons on his uniform top.

Panic set in. Lila ventured forward. "Fontaine?"

The undersheriff halted midway in amputating his dark beige shirt from his torso. Leaving the tails to hang free and exposing his white undershirt, he smacked his hands down on each side of the black case. "What?" His bark echoed through the bullpen.

Alexis flinched and ducked.

With Fontaine's seething glare pinned on Lila, she pointed to the dispatcher and Meyer and motioned for them to leave. She didn't have to gesture twice. Alexis snatched the headset from her desk and hooked it over her ear as she scooted out.

Lila grabbed Meyer's elbow as he passed. "Call Lundquist and see where he's at," she said in a lowered voice.

He nodded and then followed Alexis down the hall.

"I don't need you running interference, Dayne," he snarled as she sidled up to his desk.

"Appears I do." She eyed the black leather holster encasing the matte-finished Glock. "What's going on?"

Fontaine straightened, took a step back, and stared down at her.

Normally when he did this, she got the impression he was trying to assert his towering authority over her. This time his gaze held a different look, a different feel. Like he was assessing how his next statement would come across to her.

"Would you actually quit?" he asked. "If she went too far, are you going to pull the trigger on that threat?"

Lila took her own step back from his desk and found a very interesting spot on the floor to study. When she'd hurled those words at Sheriff Benoit, she'd been in the heat of the moment. Her temper had risen as she listened to Elizabeth make excuses for people she was too close to, and the idea launched into Lila's head and flew from her lips. Later, when Kyle had cornered her on the ultimatum, she had been doing her best to not dwell on it. She had acted on a consideration that she'd been avoiding since the day she left Chicago—leaving law enforcement for good.

"Dayne?" Fontaine's gravelly voice deepened, pulling her back.

She lifted her head and met his troubled gaze.

"I haven't exactly been easy on you," he said. "We've had our differences."

An amused snort escaped. "You make it sound like they've been childish skirmishes."

He made a noise as if conceding her point.

She sighed. "To answer your question, I don't know."

Fontaine resumed his bent-over position and focused on his weapon.

"If you're thinking of doing what I suspect you are, don't," she said.

He tilted his head to look at her. "Why shouldn't I?"

"Because you're the glue holding this whole screwed-up place together."

He barked a somewhat amused laugh and pushed off the desk. "That's what I told Elizabeth this morning. Except it's her. Not me."

"Okay, look, I don't give you enough credit." Lila made a face at his scowl. "Fine, I never give you credit. Face the facts. If it weren't for you, we would've had to deal with some state-mandated interim sheriff who doesn't know crap about Eckardt. We hummed along fine with you at the helm. Don't sell yourself short." She glanced around and then leaned in. "And you're the only one who can handle the sheriff when she gets in one of her snits."

Fontaine rolled his eyes. "Are you high?"

She had to restrain the flinch. More than four years sober, and everyone in Eckardt tended to forget she'd been an addict before she moved here. A slight benefit of being the token outsider, no one knew her history in order to exploit her weaknesses.

"Some days I wish," she quipped.

"Aww, shit, I forgot. Dayne, I didn't—"

"Don't," she cut him off. "I can joke about it now, because it doesn't rule my life." She pointed at the sheriff's office. "You can't let her mood swings rule yours. Never did before, don't let it start now."

He frowned at her. "What do you suggest I do?"

The thought flitted through her head. She considered saying it, then looked hard at him and reconsidered. It would not go over well with him. Fontaine was not Kyle. But then again.

"I'm not liking the look on your face, Dayne," he said, crossing his arm and folding the tails of his uniform top.

The dispatch phone rang, giving her a much-needed breather. Wherever Alexis was hiding out, she answered on the second ring. The interruption over, Fontaine looked at Lila with lifted eyebrows, waiting.

She held up her hands. "Hear me out. And remember, I'm the last person you should ever take advice from in this situation."

His eyebrows lowered and a confused scowl settled in.

Lila winced. "Have you ever considered actually … Oh, God, I can't believe I'm saying this." She scrubbed her face and then snapped her arms to her sides. "Just do it already."

"Do what?"

"Do. It. You know?"

Fontaine's confusion deepened.

"Seriously? You're going to make me say it." Lila swallowed, nearly choking on her tongue. "For God's sake, Rafe, would you just screw her already and get all that"—she waved her hands in front of him—"pent-up tension out between the two of you?"

Abject horror replaced his confusion. "Are you out of your mind?"

"Obviously, if I just told *you* to go have sex." She groaned. "Now I can say it."

For the first time, she saw Fontaine go pale, then redden. Lila bit her tongue before she slipped up and pointed out the man's embarrassment. Never had she thought it possible.

He cleared his throat and then began rebuttoning his top. "Uh ... yeah. You ..."

"Deputies," Alexis broke in. "There's been an emergency call-in."

"Where?" Lila asked.

"The Remington-Thorpe house."

Fontaine's head snapped up. "What?"

"Sheriff found a severely wounded man there. EMS is enroute to hospital."

Fontaine hurriedly finished buttoning his top. "Dayne, you're with me. Leave your unit here; we'll take mine. Have Meyer hang back and continue with what you have going on here."

"Lundquist is already at the hospital," she said.

"Alexis, get in touch with him and tell him to meet up with the sheriff." With his shirt tucked in, he grabbed up his vest. "What was she doing there?"

"The better question is, where has she been all afternoon?" Lila pointed out.

He paused in strapping the Velcro and looked at her. "With my brother, I know that much."

"Is he the reason why you were about to pull the quit card?"

Fontaine's face fell.

"Wow. Nail meet hammer."

"Get ready to roll," he ordered.

"You really need to consider what I said."

He grabbed his coat from the chair. "Dayne, I'm not discussing this any further with you. Let's go."

CHAPTER TWENTY-TWO

OLIVIA WOKE TO a single light in a sea of black. After a moment to get her bearings, she realized the light was coming from the bathroom in her apartment prison. She remained on the bed, listening. No sounds came from inside or outside.

She was alone.

Her arm didn't hurt nearly as bad, but the throbbing lingered. She was certain Horatio had left the bottle of Percocet when he'd last been here, if she chose to take more. Yet the thought of getting out of the comfortable bed to even locate the bottle, or any painkiller for that matter, seemed an insurmountable hill she wasn't ready to climb.

In the end, the gnawing ache in her stomach and her parched throat won out. Olivia carefully sat up and vacated the bed. She paid a visit to the bathroom, where the shower beckoned once more. She vowed she would clean up this time. After she nourished her body and mind.

She left the bathroom, turning on lights as she went, and shuffled to the fridge, where she pulled out a water bottle and one of those packaged snacks of salami, cheese, and crackers. On the counter next to the white paper bag of over-the-counter meds sat the orange prescription bottle. Of course, it would have a childproof lid and she with only one good hand to open it.

After a bit of a struggle to peel away the plastic seal on the packaged snack, she slumped on a chair at the table. As she eased the ache in her stomach, she studied her array of case files with weary eyes. Hopefully, Horatio had done as she asked and approached Lila.

She mulled over Horatio's revelations. The stacks of money Dominic had him launder. The correlation with Dominic approaching Horatio about the money and the timing of his bizarre behavior.

Gulping down water, her tired and drug-addled brain suddenly clicked. She slapped the bottle down on the table, her spasming hand squishing the plastic container until water spewed from the top.

"Shit."

She shook her wet hand, sending water drops flying, then stood.

Dominic. The money. The boneyards scattered along the Mississippi River Valley. It had one significant connection. It was the only thing that made sense.

Black-market organ trafficking.

Olivia got up from the chair and inched closer to the case file timeline she had pinned along the walls. Dominic's skills as a surgeon would be sought after. He couldn't be connected to all of these cases. It wasn't possible. He could, however, be connected with what was discovered in Eckardt County.

So how did he get caught up in something this heinous? Dominic was a man incapable of harm. At least, she assumed the man she'd married was incapable. Except from what Horatio had told her, she was beginning to think she married a farce. Dominic always seemed above reproach, a man tied to his morals and scruples, someone the opposite of Horatio in every sense of the word. A man Olivia had loved deeply and believed in.

What could have possibly driven him to abandon his code of honor and take lives? Who could have convinced Dominic?

No. Not convinced.

Olivia turned her back to the wall of cases and scrutinized the room around her. No, her husband would never allow himself to be convinced of anything immoral. He had been blackmailed. Threatened with something so heinous it would force him to do the unthinkable.

What could Dominic have done to give someone that much power over him? Was it something from his past before her? Or something he'd done during his years through med school and residency? And who had the control to wield power over him?

Horatio said her life was in danger. Made it clear to justify kidnapping and sequestering her away in this apartment.

If that was true, she could see Dominic caving to a blackmailing scheme with Olivia as the incentive. In his own misguided intention, he would find a way to protect her further by creating a chasm in their marriage. A means to push her out of his life to keep her safe. Hurting her and himself in the process.

Olivia face burned, her eyes watering. "Why would you do it?" she asked the ceiling.

There was a soft knock on the door before the locks rattled. She wheeled around as the door opened and Horatio entered.

"Liv?"

"Don't call me that!" Her voice reached a fevered pitch.

He shut the door with a snap. She watched as he slid the keys inside his pocket. A plan formulated in her mind.

"What is wrong with you?" he asked.

With her good arm, she jabbed the air at him. "You know."

"What do I know?"

"You know why he did it. You know who is pulling his strings. You know who would threaten him by using me to get to him."

Horatio stared at her, his features like granite, his eyes coals, dull and black. She flew at him, slapping his cheek. He absorbed the blow, his gaze wavering a moment, then returned to the unfeeling killer she was well-acquainted with.

"Answer me," she spit.

"I don't know who it is," he ground out. His nostrils flared. "I do know what they blackmailed him with."

When he didn't elaborate, she stepped into his personal space.

"Tell me," she snarled.

Red infused his dark skin. A dangerous glint passed through his eyes. None of it deterred Olivia. Deep inside her, the part of her Horatio had loved, knew he'd never hurt her.

"When I said you didn't know your husband as well as you thought, I wasn't lying. Your man hides a past. He's been lying to you the whole of your relationship."

"You're wrong."

Horatio closed the gap between them. "Am I?" His gaze

roamed over her face. "What did he tell you, if ever, about his life? His family?"

"He has no family. He was fostered."

Horatio's derisive laugh scratched along taut nerves.

"So gullible," he mocked. "He had family, but it ain't the kind of family you wanted it to be."

"I didn't care where he came from," Olivia shot back.

"Oh, but you did. After you ran from me, you cared." Horatio's voice slithered into his menacing calm. "You wanted to believe him. To scrub your dirty past clean. His claims of a whitewashed childhood was what you wanted. Made your quickie marriage before a judge easier to explain than why he couldn't invite anyone from his side."

Olivia's breathing increased. The urge to scream in his face bubbled inside.

"He ain't Northside any more than I am." Horatio leaned closer, his lips a hairbreadth from hers. "He's as crooked as they come. Better yet, his dumbass brother is the crooked one. Ask me how I know."

She didn't take his bait, only sneered at him.

"I sent you a wedding gift. Remember? What was it?"

If she didn't answer him, Horatio would shake it out of her. "A bottle of ten-year-old brandy and snifters with our names … Bastard. You knew him. How?"

"Know of him. I'm in the business of knowing other people's business. That boy had some business."

"No." Olivia stepped back, but he moved right with her.

"Dominic's brother was a real piece of work. You know how your man got through med school and didn't have to work a job?" When she didn't answer, he gave her a malicious grin. "His big brother was the king of the con. Worked some money scheme, literally robbed people of their dough and paid Dominic's way through school. Kept his finder's fee, of course."

"That's harmless compared to what you've done. You've murdered men to gain power."

"I've only killed those who've needed killing. Dominic's brother left a more destructive path. Some of those con victims were people with families. Some of those men were so destroyed by what they'd lost, they killed themselves. And Dominic knew about it and did nothing."

She slapped his chest. "Stop lying."

Horatio grabbed her chin one-handed and squeezed. "I don't lie." His dark eyes glinted. "Never to you. Your man was the liar. Comes from a long line of liars and cheats. Had plenty of opportunities to come clean with you but never did."

His words rang true, yet Olivia couldn't accept them. Because if she did, she would have to face the reality that her marriage was nothing more than a sham. She had left Horatio to get away from the mistakes of her past and jumped right into the same blasted hot pan.

"I hate you," she ground out between his clenched fingers.

He released her with a jerk. "They all do, baby."

Olivia shoved him away and pedaled back. "Get out!"

"Get yourself under control, woman. I'll be back in the morning." He left, locking up.

Olivia remained rooted, listening to his fading footsteps. Hot tears rolled down her cheeks. She hadn't wanted to know the truth. Hadn't wanted to hear it from Horatio.

She lifted her good hand and stared at the keys she'd clutched in her fist. She had not grown up in his environment; hadn't learned the tools of the trade as a child like he had. But their years together at a vulnerable and malleable time of her life had taught her tricks Horatio was not privy to. Olivia was quite an accomplished pickpocket.

Ripping her heart further from her chest had been worth it.

CHAPTER TWENTY-THREE

"A RE YOU OUT of your ever-lovin' mind?"

Elizabeth, unflinching, gave her undersheriff a glance—noting Dayne's presence at his side—and resumed her search of Dominic's possessions. How ironic Rafe would channel his elder brother's insolent approach. "If you're here to bellow at me, do it outside. I'm busy."

"Doing what, exactly?" Dayne asked.

Elizabeth pulled a *Fischer's Mastery of Surgery* hardcover from the modest bookshelf next to the bed. "In not so many words, Dominic gave me the impression he's done something that has put Olivia's, and now our lives, in danger. I'm here looking for it."

"Where's Joel?" Rafe demanded.

"Scouring the perimeter for signs of where our latest victim stumbled in from." She pried open the well-read volume and let the pages fall open. "Why don't you help him out."

Rafe glowered at her. "If this is your way of getting—"

Dayne pressed a hand into his back and rerouted him. "Good idea, Sheriff." She gave Rafe a pointed look. "Tracking is more your forte."

He went to speak, but Dayne shoved him through the doorway.

Elizabeth was stymied by Rafe's willingness to be pushed

around by Dayne. A little extra perplexed that Dayne bothered to intervene in what would have turned into a verbal brawl. She and Rafe weren't usually buddy-buddy. More likely to bite each other's heads off than gang up on her.

Whatever the two were up to, Elizabeth didn't have the time to dwell on it. She flipped through the pages of the book and found nothing out of the ordinary.

Dayne came back. "Where have you already searched?"

Elizabeth returned the medical book and waved her hand at the shelf. "I've only gone through this."

She ceased flopping her hand and studied it, recalling how coated and sticky it had been earlier. The blood looked a brilliant shade of red, almost too red. It brought forward the recent memories of her own blood-saturated shirt. Her fingers smeared in it. Her palm pressed to her side, a feeble attempt to stop the weeping.

Elizabeth made a fist. "Took me a while to get cleaned up."

"Do you have anything specific in mind what you're looking for?" Dayne asked.

Reaching for the next book, Elizabeth shook her head. "I have no idea what I'm searching for. I just ..." She released the book's spine and shifted to look at Dayne over her shoulder. "I want to find Olivia."

Dayne must have heard the strain in her voice. The normally hard-ass woman's sharp edges seemed to soften. "We all do."

Elizabeth returned to the bookshelf and pulled out a ten-year-old copy of the *Physicians' Desk Reference*. "Your decision to quit on me was a flippant excuse to put me in my place?"

Her question hung between them, creating a silence that intrigued and disturbed Elizabeth at intervals. When Dayne released a soul-weary sigh it stirred the atmosphere, charging it with a sense of dread, keeping Elizabeth from opening the heavy book. She didn't look at her deputy detective. Couldn't bring herself to face the fact she might have irreparably created a fissure in their comradeship, or worse widened an already existing one.

"I spoke out of turn."

The blunt statement brought Elizabeth to her feet. She faced Dayne, who was standing in front of the open closet, holding a battered brown leather messenger bag.

"So, in a heated moment of disagreement with me, you blurt out you'll quit? It just came to you? On the spot?"

Dayne's edges hardened. She lifted her chin and kept her shrewd gaze lasered on Elizabeth.

"In my many years of dealing with a wide variety of humans, learning their subtle and not so subtle tics and moods, I know when I'm being placated. You don't threaten something like quitting without having first dwelled on it."

Dayne's silence stretched. Her features morphed into a pinched frown.

"I had a long drive to and from Iowa City this afternoon," Elizabeth continued. "He doesn't act like it, but Joel makes for a rotten conversationalist. Gave me too much quiet time to revisit our riverside spat."

She sat the book, spine down, on the bed, and inched to the footboard, putting herself closer to Dayne.

"When I brought you into the fold, I meant to provide you a place to last for years, if not the rest of your life. I don't want to be the reason you leave."

Dayne sighed, her shoulders drooping. She started to say something but stopped when her gaze darted behind Elizabeth. "What's that?" She pointed at the bed.

Elizabeth glanced back, saw the book had fallen open, and then focused on Dayne again. "One of Dominic's physician books."

Dayne made a face. "Sheriff, really?"

Her exasperated tone gave Elizabeth a swift reality kick. She turned around, and this time paid attention. The book had fallen open a quarter of the way to the end. A small, folded sheet of paper was nestled between the pages. Elizabeth was of half a mind to believe it was a note that Dominic had absentmindedly written down and then wedged in the book forgetting all about it. Or was it a clue to whomever or whatever was behind the fear controlling Dominic? Would they be so lucky?

She took it out, noting it was a sheet from a prescription pad.

Dayne set the messenger bag on the bed and joined Elizabeth as she unfolded the page.

Except for the header announcing Dominic's name, his two and three letter credentials, along with a distinct watermark to note it was an authentic script sheet, it was blank.

"Nothing more than a convenient bookmark," Elizabeth said.

"Well, that was a major letdown." Dayne turned away, grabbing up the messenger bag.

"I'm beginning to think I'm on a wild goose chase. If Dominic can keep his mouth shut about whatever is going on, what says he's likely to leave any clues lying around in his home?" Elizabeth shoved the folded sheet back in its place and flipped the reference book shut.

Dayne rummaged inside the bag, pulling out scraps of paper, old gum wrappers, and forgotten pens and pencils, and laid the mess on the bedspread. "It's not a bad idea. If you hadn't decided to come here, you wouldn't have encountered the half-dead guy."

Elizabeth watched her continue to scrounge through the bag a moment. Oh, the deputy was a cool one, deflecting from the grilling and redirecting. There was no way Elizabeth was going to let her off the hook.

Before she could press the matter, Dayne held up a medium-sized pad of note sheets.

She squinted at it. "There's no address or name, just a symbol and a phone number. Wonder if this is from his former practice before he moved here?"

"Let me see it." Elizabeth took the proffered pad and looked it over. "Maybe. Or it was a place he did an internship with?"

Dayne took the pad back. "It's a Chicago number. Do you know if he worked in Chicago? Or lived there?"

"Olivia was from there, I think. Might be how they met."

A guarded look fell into place on Dayne's face. Sensing this conversation turning down the wrong road, Elizabeth straightened the wheel and kept going forward.

"Wanna call it?"

Dayne checked her phone. "It's kinda late to be calling anyone, but I'm game if you are. Let's see what the message says." She dialed the number and then held out her phone with the speaker on.

The line rang three times before the answering service picked up. "You've reached First Health Chicago, the medical offices of Dr. Asa Pryce and Dr. Samuel Alderman. If this is a medical emergency, please hang up and call 911. If this is a nonemergency call and you are a patient of Dr. Pryce or Dr. Alderman, please call back during normal office hours of nine a.m. to five p.m. Monday through Friday. Thank you."

Dayne ended the call. "Well, guess we know who to try again tomorrow during normal office hours."

The thud of men's boots and the low rumble of their voices breached the quiet of the house.

Rafe entered the room first, making sure to keep his older brother behind him. "Found something you both should see."

"Who found it?" Joel grumped from the hall.

Rafe kept his attention zeroed on Elizabeth, his features tight. If she didn't know better—and oh how she knew better when it came to those two—she guessed they'd bickered and sniped at each other out there.

Why did she let Joel sweet-talk her into this setup? The brothers never got along when they were together and were barely cordial with each other when Joel lived hundreds of thousands of miles away.

Dayne dumped the messenger bag on the bed. "Lead the way."

A CHILL LANCED the night. Meteorologists were calling for a new cold front to shift through overnight and bring with it a chance of snow tomorrow.

Elizabeth was wishing she was home right now, curled up on the sofa with Bentley and a hot cup of cocoa.

She had to look away from the big dark stain in front of the patio doors when their group passed by. Too many reminders dredged up flashbacks.

Was she experiencing the beginnings of post-traumatic?

No. It was too late for that.

Wasn't it?

Rafe led them to the tree line and paused. His and Joel's bright Maglites fell on the blood spot under the spiky branches of a fir tree.

"He must've laid here for a time," Rafe explained, then moved his light to another point fifty feet away. "Looks like he came from that direction."

"What's out there?" Dayne asked.

"Miles of pasture ground, timber, and a farmstead here and there," Rafe answered.

"Smack in the middle of it is the Fontaine hunting cabin," Joel added.

Elizabeth stepped between the brothers and walked toward the edge of the light's beam.

"I didn't realize this cul-de-sac was so close to your place," Dayne was saying.

Joel said something to Dayne, but Elizabeth had stopped listening. She became aware of Rafe's presence at her side as she kept walking, past the next blood spot and toward the edge of the unknown.

She was brought to a halt by a barbed-wire fence. It was old, sagged in places, and some of the trees had grown around the wire, making it a part of the tree itself. Here divided the residential from the rural. This pathetic, neglected wire keeping the civilized from encroaching on the untamed. Beyond the fence was a tangled mess of grasses, weeds, and wildlife. Farther still were more trees, a veritable hunter's paradise.

"He climbed through here," she said.

Rafe touched her shoulder and pointed to their right. She followed him to the place where the young man had passed through the wire, using an old hedge post to support his weakening body. A bloody handprint covered the top of the post.

"I'm calling Des Moines County tomorrow," Rafe said. "They have a tracking K-9."

"I'll call them. Sheriff's the one who needs to get the authorization," she reminded him.

They stood in silence, staring out past the light's edge. The wind blew through the trees, making a whooshing sound and shaking the boughs, its winter bite chilling Elizbeth's cheeks.

"You think this leads back to the cabin?" she asked after a moment.

"Right to where you saw the Jeep," Rafe said.

Elizabeth didn't need light to see it. She sensed it. Felt it. Her county was mainly farmland and choked areas of timber. Somewhere out there, her wounded victim had struggled through the catch of grasses and low-slung trees to get to this point.

"Whoever is behind this has had more than twenty-four hours to pack up and move on. If their little butcher shop is out there, we're not going to find them in it."

"They'll still have made a rushed job of it. We could get lucky."

Elizabeth huffed, her breath clouding in the cold. "I have my doubts."

She turned to head back to the house, but Rafe stopped her with his warm hand on her arm.

"We need to call it a night," he said, his voice lowering.

"I should check on the victim."

"Lundquist is there. He and Dayne can follow up." Rafe looked toward the two figures in the distance, then back to her. "I'm taking you home."

Elizabeth tilted her head just so and looked at him side-eyed. "Why?"

He gave a grunt, and then started back toward the other two, tugging her along with him.

"Rafe?"

When they met up with Joel and Dayne, Rafe laid out orders.

"Dayne, take my car and Joel back to the department. Do whatever you need to there, and check in with Lundquist. We're locking up here, and I'm taking the sheriff home. I'll get my car tomorrow."

Elizabeth protested at his hurried movements as he dragged her along. As she passed Dayne standing in the halo of Joel's flashlight, she noticed a smile cross the other woman's face.

Now what was that all about?

Back inside the Remington-Thorpe home, Elizabeth trailed Rafe around as he locked up and turned off lights.

"Mind telling me what the hell you're doing?" she demanded as they were exiting the garage. Her Interceptor was the lone vehicle sitting in the driveway. "Dayne left fast."

"Good," Rafe said and latched onto her arm, dragging her to him.

Shocked at his brazen move, she leaned heavily into him. "Raphael Fontaine, you better explain—"

His mouth was hot and possessive against hers. Elizabeth's frazzled brain took three seconds to finally catch up with what was going on before she returned the kiss. Rafe gave her a few seconds more, and then broke off.

"We're going home," he said.

She didn't know what brought it on. But it was about damn time.

CHAPTER TWENTY-FOUR

Day 3, Tuesday, February 27—48 Hours Missing

A FTER PALMING HORATIO'S keys, Olivia used them on the lock and found she'd struck gold. The latches gave way, and she was able to step outside into freedom. Her first inclination was to bolt, but caution kept her from acting on instinct. She didn't have a clue where she was, and she wasn't about to go running around looking like a crazed drug addict.

She locked up and searched for fresh clothing. The scrubs she had worn when Horatio took her were three days old and smelled ripe. In a small closet in the bathroom, she found a clean set of what looked like her own scrubs and huge, fluffy towels. She also found a pair of slip-on Crocs in her size. While she never wore the ugly shoes—preferring comfortable dress shoes or runners—she was grateful she didn't have to worry about how to tie laces with one hand.

After twenty awkward minutes, she managed to relieve herself of the filthy clothing and cover the cast with a plastic trash bag.

The hot shower felt good and helped take her mind off the burning throbs coming from her broken arm. She took longer than she had planned in the shower, but the delay was partially from the fact she had to do everything one-handed.

The other excuse was to plot her route of escape and let her mind relax. She did everything in her power not to dwell on Horatio's revelations about Dominic. If she did, she would fall apart and be useless.

Forty-five minutes later, after another clumsy bout drying off and getting the clean scrubs on, she hurried to the kitchen to down more over-the-counter pain meds. Between the change of clothing and the shower, she'd overdone it. But she refused to take any more Percocet. She needed her wits about her if she was going to escape.

While she waited for the pain meds to kick in, she ate a few granola bars and drank a cup of tea. Next, she tackled the timeline walls, shoving her notes and some of the reports into a plastic grocery bag Horatio had left behind. In the insulated bag, she dumped in a few water and juice bottles, along with any packaged food items that didn't require refrigeration, and the OTCs. She placed the plastic-covered pages on top of the groceries and zipped close the insulated bag. Carefully, she slipped her casted arm through the handles and hiked it onto her shoulder, satisfied with the weight on her injured side. She would have to take it easy, but she couldn't afford to hinder her good arm by carrying the bag on it.

One last look around at the tiny apartment and Olivia was assured she had all she needed. It was time to bust loose.

Part of her plan was to leave a few lights on to give the perception she was working. Also to relock the door and leave the keys inside on the table. Her hope was the lights would fool Horatio if he came back before sunup, giving her more time to put distance between them. The keys were a reminder that he'd overestimated her, again.

How she wished she could see his face when he realized she'd slipped her prison and his grasp. Olivia smiled.

Once outside the relocked apartment, she paused and took in a deep breath of cold air.

Freedom.

It was cold, and she hadn't been lucky enough to find a coat. She'd have to grit her teeth and bear it. Maybe if she got cold enough, it would numb the pain in her arm. A good doctor always knew when ice was the best policy.

Using what little of the apartment light afforded her, she cautiously descended the steps. The wooden stairs groaned under her weight. She paused each time it creaked and listened for sounds of approach.

Horatio could have a guard posted somewhere or cameras. Olivia had to outthink him, and she wasn't reckless enough to believe he thought her fully safe. He would have some means to track someone's approach if anyone discovered her whereabouts. Yet she still held out hope her pressure to get him emotional and reveal Dominic's shadowed past would make Horatio careless.

Reaching the bottom of the steps, she paused to take a breath and assess. The dark was eerily quiet. Olivia had lost track of time. It had to be close to dawn. It was the middle of the week. If she was near any kind of roadway, she should be able to hear morning traffic.

Adjusting the bag straps on her shoulder, she then felt her way along the wall with her right hand until her fingers met air. She peered around the corner. Off in the distance, a faint glow rekindled her lagging optimistic nature. Could be a streetlamp. Or someone's home.

Olivia moved on, using the distant glow as her guide. She was following an older, narrow road, one that must have been gravel in the past and had been sealed. Her path was going downhill. She would have to avoid the occasional downed tree limb or other random debris blown and deposited along the road. The farther she went, the more she got a sense of where she was at. Her earlier suspicions of this being an older section of a town were holding true. It was also abandoned.

Olivia stopped and turned back the way she had come to squint uphill through the dark. So why had Horatio remodeled an upstairs apartment in an abandoned building? Had she not been the first person to be trapped there?

Or … or was it a bolt-hole of sorts for him? The idea of a sanctuary for Horatio made sense. He would need a place to disappear to if things got hot on his home turf. One could disappear in Chicago given half a chance. But Horatio was too high profile. He'd need places even outside of Illinois.

Places like out-of-the-way holes in the middle of nowhere where he could hide and not worry about needing to blend in. Like a rural area of Iowa that had parts of towns shuttered forever with abandoned homes and buildings no one cared about any longer.

She shuffled her way along her self-made path. Creating a refuge somewhere close to her would be another reason.

The glow intensified as she drew closer. Olivia made out what it was now. A small, single-story house that could only be described as a shack stood alone among the sea of black. A sole remaining streetlight towered over the insignificant home, illuminating an intersection. For some blessed reason, someone had decided to keep power flowing to this one light.

Her grassy path ended at the edge of a crumbling portion of the road. A cracked and pothole-ridden street lay to her left. To her right, the same seal-coated road continued downward.

While Olivia mulled her next steps, the breeze shifted and brought with it the scent of burning wood with an undercurrent of tang, like freezing cold river water. She glanced around, sniffing the air and catching the scent again. Could it be? Was she close to a major river? The Mississippi perhaps?

The wood smoke smell attracted her. A wisp of smoke appeared at the edge of the streetlight. Though there was no sign of anyone living in the house, someone obviously did and was using a woodstove.

If she went into the house, she ran the risk of meeting up with one of Horatio's thugs or the man himself. Or it could be any random person who was sticking it to the man by living out in a part of town that should be bulldozed in. Or worse, a squatter with no compunction whatsoever to attack someone disturbing them.

Olivia had to make up her mind what she was going to do, because standing here freezing her ass off wasn't going to get her any further along in her escape.

"Screw it," she muttered.

Her freedom was not to be put at risk. She'd freeze to death before she allowed herself to be attacked or imprisoned again.

She looked beyond the lamp to the darkened road. Out there was a better option. A chance to get closer to her husband.

And to the answers for the questions swirling inside her head.

CHAPTER TWENTY-FIVE

Day 3, Tuesday, February 27—51 Hours Missing

THE BED SHIFTING roused Elizabeth. A warm arm wrapped around her midsection and tucked her against the wall of muscle at her back. She smiled as Rafe nuzzled her neck.

"'Bout time you woke up," he said.

She squeezed her eyes shut. She didn't want to wake up nor did she want to leave this bed. She wanted to remain here with him, wrapped up in him. Or better yet, relive every blessed second of their night together.

A dog huff in her face made Elizabeth peel her eyes open. Bentley, with her snout propped on the bed, stared, her wet nose centimeters from Elizabeth's. The dark-brown gaze flicked back and forth between her owner and the man she adored, who settled his prickly chin on Elizabeth's bare shoulder.

"I think we're being paged," Rafe said.

Elizabeth petted her dog's head, then pointed at the door. Bentley obeyed the command and sashayed out.

Elizabeth rolled over to better look at Rafe. The rising sun backlit him as he stared down at her, his hand running up and down her thigh. She grasped his roaming hand and stopped his exploration. She took a moment to study his face.

"Why now?" she asked softly.

She didn't have to elaborate. He knew precisely what she was asking.

Rafe freed his hand and rolled onto his back, bringing her with him. She was propped on his chest, staring down at him.

"I don't know why I waited," he said.

"That's not answering my question."

He played with her mused hair, then ran a finger along her jawline. Elizabeth shivered at the light touch. Rafe smiled and cupped the back of her head to pull her down to him.

His kiss was equal parts gentle and passionate. She sagged against him.

She broke their kiss and rested her forehead against his. "More words, less actions."

"Does there have to be a reason? We've both wanted this for a long time."

"With you, I always need a reason." She let out a gasp as his hands began to play with her body. "Rafe," she groaned.

He nipped her lips. "Yes?" He kissed her again.

She was losing this battle. His strategy of seducing her was a brilliant move. When he dragged her on top, Elizabeth succumbed to his spell.

Later as she strolled out to her kitchen fresh from a shower and wearing her uniform, she found him finalizing breakfast, while Bentley was going to town on her kibble.

Elizabeth took the coffee mug handed to her. "Are you ever going to answer me?" She lifted the mug to her lips and peered at him over the rim. She sipped the coffee. He always knew how to make it just right.

Rafe gave her a crooked smile. "You're not going to give it up, are you?"

"Not any time soon."

He leaned forward. "Don't get caught up in the whys and what-for. For once, just go with it." He ended his statement with a peck on her lips.

Elizabeth lifted an eyebrow. "You know me better than that. No pat answer and a kiss on the lips is going to make me stop."

When he didn't answer, just stared at her with his own upraised eyebrows, she sighed.

"I'm going to ruin it, ain't I?"

He grunted.

"Okay." She held up a hand in surrender. "This is me backing off."

"Good." Rafe turned back to the counter. "Dayne checked in. The victim is still in surgery and considered critical."

"Is she still at the hospital?"

"Both she and Lundquist stayed." Rafe passed her a plate loaded with scrambled eggs and a buttered English muffin. "Little tidbit—you need more food in your house."

"I would have plenty if I'd been living here the last two weeks." She took the plate. "Where'd you find the eggs?"

"Marnie."

Leave it to her sister to look out for her. Living close by had its perks when she could raid her sister's cabinets.

Instead of sitting at her table, Elizabeth set her coffee mug down on the counter and stayed standing to eat. Rafe shook his head and went to let Bentley out into the yard.

Elizabeth had left Bentley at home yesterday, when normally the collie would ride along everywhere her owner went. Marnie had come over to the house and allowed Bentely to hang out with her in the bar. Today ... well, today Elizabeth would bring her companion.

"When I get into the office, I'll call the Des Moines sheriff," she told Rafe between bites of English muffin.

"Wish we could find room in our budget for a K-9 team," Rafe groused.

"I'm hard pressed to get anyone to squeeze out two pennies for office supplies half the time." Elizabeth finished the last of her food and set the plate in the dishwasher. "Did Dayne or Lundquist say anything about evidence from the boneyard site?"

He shook his head. "I'd imagine Lundquist would still be running tests while they waited."

"Any news from the office?"

Bentley pawed at the door and let out a sharp bark. Elizabeth went to open it for her dog.

"Meyer rolled out around midnight to get some sleep. Young is reporting this morning. Apparently, she's back full-time."

Elizabeth shrugged. "I'll take what I can get. If Young feels more comfortable with Dayne, we should probably assign them coinciding shifts."

She watched him as he cleaned up. During her shower, she'd contemplated telling him what she'd learned yesterday about Olivia, but she wasn't sure she wanted to sour the mood. Once she revealed how long she'd been sitting on this information, he would get mad. But she couldn't keep it hidden any longer.

"Rafe."

He turned off the faucet. "Yeah?"

She didn't say anything. He faced her, his brows furrowed.

She had to get this over with. "I found contact information for Olivia's parents."

He shifted to cross his arms and lean his hip into the counter. His cue for her to continue.

"Before I swore Joel in yesterday morning and we discovered the bodies, I called and spoke to her father. They haven't seen or spoken to Olivia in more than twenty-five years." Elizabeth eased back against the opposite counter. "They'd given her up for dead because she got caught up with some Chicago low life when she was eighteen and left. With the kind of lifestyle he led, they thought she'd been killed at some point."

"Did they give you a name of this guy?"

"They believe what they'd been told was an alias. When they tried to find her after she ran off, they got the usual runaround. *She's eighteen, she's an adult, the police department didn't have time for them.*"

Rafe considered what she said. "What did you tell them?"

"Who I was. Why I was calling and how I was connected to her. They didn't have much for me to go on. And they didn't seem to know how to react or what to say. I don't blame them. How would you react after more than twenty-five years if you found out the daughter you thought was dead is alive and she's made a whole new life for herself and can't seem to reconnect with you?"

"It puts a perspective on things," Rafe said. "Maybe this dude was the one who abducted her? She obviously got away from him and married Dominic. Maybe he finally found her and came back for her?"

"Who's to say Dominic wasn't the criminal?"

Rafe frowned. "Are you serious?"

"I don't want to be. But Dominic's behavior makes me think he had a hand in making Olivia vanish. And I know he's involved with that boneyard somehow. We just have to press him harder."

From its position on the counter, Rafe's phone chirped. He checked it and scowled.

"Joel?" she asked.

"On his way to the office now." He tucked his phone in his pocket. "Why did you let him talk you into this setup?"

"Really had no choice."

The expression he pulled made Elizabeth wince.

"You had a choice," he said. "Joel knows how to manipulate, and he's had your number for years."

"Now who's ruining a good thing?"

Rafe sighed, gripping her arms, and looking down at her. Elizabeth was by no means a short woman, but both Fontaine men were taller than her. When Rafe did this, at least he wasn't condescending about it like Joel typically was.

"Ellie, for the sake of peace, I will be civil about Joel working in the department. I still can't figure out how he pulled so many strings so quickly, but it's neither here nor there." He bent forward. "You have to remember you outrank him." He gave her a kiss. "And you're off-limits."

She chuckled. "You do realize your brother has been pushing us together the entire time he's been here."

Rafe gave her a skeptical look.

"I'm serious. He claims he's got a new lady in his life."

"I'll believe it when I see her." Rafe released her and headed for the living room. "Don't forget, he is a master manipulator."

"And you tend to act like a sore loser," she said after him.

"A jealous one, too," he remarked, stopping at the door. "You coming?"

Elizabeth called her dog and followed him out the door.

CHAPTER TWENTY-SIX

L ILA YAWNED.
Next to her, Lundquist downed his cup of coffee as if his life depended on that black substance for survival. They had remained at the hospital waiting for word on the victim's status.

There had been no time to life flight him to Iowa City— he was too unstable. A surgeon from the Burlington hospital rushed over and was doing her best to keep the poor man alive. It didn't look favorable. The entirety of the Juniper hospital wasn't equipped for this kind of life-and-death situation, especially with their emergency care surgeon himself severely injured.

Lila yawned again, reaching for her own cup of joe.

"You should get some sleep," Kyle admonished.

"You first," she hit back and threw down some coffee.

They'd hung out in his little out-of-the-way lab Olivia had specially designed for Kyle to do his own testing. Of the two of them, he was the more scientifically minded investigator. He could run preliminary or simple tests here, while shipping off the more intricate and specific tests to be done at DCI in Des Moines.

In the corner, one of the machines was purring along, running a DNA test from the victim. He had a hunch, and

Lila was letting him have full rein with it.

She, in the meantime—while attempting to keep her eyes from falling shut on her—was flipping through the sketchbook they'd discovered the day before. She hoped to decipher where the sketches were done, maybe to get an idea of where the artist had been from. Her soul ached at the thought of this life being snuffed out for something as evil as stealing their organs.

His warm hand on her back, rubbing the aching muscles, Kyle leaned closer. "I know that look."

Lila propped her cheek on her hand and looked at him. "What look is that?"

"Your pensive I'm-going-to-solve-this-damn-thing-even-if-it-kills-me look."

"So, I have a look?" She sighed, her gaze dropping to the image of the woman peering through a broken window. Lila tapped the page. "What do you wanna bet this is a rendering of our artist?"

"What if it's a woman close to the artist and not the artist themself?" Kyle countered.

"I don't get that impression. There's something about this one." She flipped the sketchbook closed and sat back, her chair squeaking. "How much of a DNA trace did you get off this?"

"Not much. The bag protected it from the worst of the moisture damage, but it's questionable."

Lila exchanged the sketchbook for the plastic tub storing the bagged items of evidence. Yesterday—God, was it yesterday already?—Kyle had swabbed and photographed each piece of evidence she'd collected from the tunnel. Most of the jewelry was a bust for trace, but he had managed to find two strands of hair snagged between the necklace's links.

She picked out the bag containing the coins she'd found. Lila hadn't paid any particular attention to what type of coins they were when she'd uncovered them. Some were pesos from different Central and South American countries, and there was one Canadian. A few American coins were in the mix. But what caught her attention now was a silver one with Cyrillic print.

"Is this Russian?"

Kyle reached for the bag, and she handed it over. He examined the one she noted. "It looks like it." He returned the evidence bag. "I didn't look at them too closely when I cataloged them."

"I wonder if Dr. Pembrook can tell if the bones came from a particular ethnic group?" she hemmed.

His laptop chimed with an incoming message. Kyle rolled his chair over to the computer. "You'll have to ask him." He leaned toward the monitor.

Lila grinned as she returned the coin evidence to the box. "You keep that up and you're going to need reading glasses, old man."

He tilted his head around the edge of the laptop and glowered. "We're the same age. And I don't need glasses." He resumed his reading. "Got a report back on the hiking bag." He sat back. "Looks like it's an American-based company that stopped making this particular style eight years ago."

"Which could mean our sketch artist is American? Or not and somehow got this bag." Lila drove her fingers through her greasy hair. She needed a shower. "In other words, it's a dead end."

"There's still the DNA option. And the beetles." Kyle pushed away from his computer desk and rolled closer to her. "The entomologist is looking up known buyers for those particular beetles in our area. He hoped to have a list for us today."

Lila sighed. "I need to check in with the DCI tech working on the burned SUV." She wrinkled her nose. "Didn't Fontaine give you a blood sample to run from the Remington-Thorpe house?"

"He did, and I've got the prelims back on the blood type and DNA. And"—he sorted through some of his printouts and found what he was looking for—"it belongs to an Adrian Landry, New Orleans criminal extraordinaire."

"New Orleans? What's he doing clear up here in Iowa?"

He handed her the rap sheet. "Maybe he's Mystery Man?"

Lila looked at the mugshot. "Nope, not even close." She scrunched her nose in thought. "Could be an associate of Mystery Man. It fits. We might as well add him to our list of rabbit trails to follow."

Kyle scribbled a note for himself. With his head dipped down, she studied his profile. She had been teasing him about the old man needing glasses, but on a closer look, she spotted some gray in his beard. She reached out and smoothed her thumb along his cheek.

He turned into her touch, his brows bowing. "What?"

"Nothing." She drew her hand away.

It had been months since they'd spent this much time

together. Alone. They still hadn't hashed out the brief spat over her rash comment to Benoit.

Now or never, Lila.

"I'm not going to quit," she blurted.

He set his pen down. "Then why'd you say it?"

"Because all I could see was the recent past rearing its ugly head and Benoit losing her mind again. I got mad and I let my tongue run away with me. I like Olivia and Dominic. Hell, I trust Olivia. But I also know from firsthand experience that even good people do bad things when they're pushed into a corner."

"Sheriff know this?" he asked.

"While we were going through Dominic's room last night, I told her as much."

A slow smile curved his lips. "Good. I didn't want to have to make a rash decision myself."

"What rash decision?"

His eyebrows shot up, and he scooted back to his laptop. "I wonder if the ME was able to finish the autopsies on those three?"

"Nothing like changing the subject," Lila groused. "What are the odds we're going to figure out who the victims are before we know who the perpetrators are?"

"Slim to none."

"At least you're honest." She rose from the chair and wandered to the single window in the lab.

The lab was on the ground level of the hospital. Her view outside the window was of the walking path. Lila focused on the bench where she'd sat beside Mystery Man the day before.

Where had he gone? Would he come back?

The thought had crossed her mind yesterday to pull a few strings back in Chicago and see what she could dig up on the guy. With the I-80 killers deceased, she had no worries about keeping her distance from Chicago. But her trusted contact with the police department was gone, and Lila wasn't too sure anyone would bother to give her the time of day. In the long run, her decision to seek answers about her unexpected guest was waylaid by the search for the other boneyards along the Mississippi. The maps he'd given her were proving to be more fruitful than any fact-finding mission on a Black guy from Chicago's Southside.

"Maybe we're looking at this from the wrong angle," Kyle said.

Lila turned from the window and frowned. "How so?"

"You said the sheriff was going through the Remington-Thorpe house last night, searching for a clue to what Dominic was up to. There has to be something there to give us an idea about this whole business. Black market always means money."

"True. But we need to hold off for the time being. The sheriff and Fontaine wanted to get a K-9 unit to backtrack the victim's path to the Remington-Thorpe house. There might be more clues out there we don't know about." She suddenly remembered the phone number. What time was it?

She yanked out her cell and checked the time. Shit. It was only seven thirtyish. Too soon to call the doctor's office and ask about Dominic. So much for that idea. Lila shoved her phone back in its pocket.

"Be nice to have actual people to interrogate," Kyle said

as he swiveled his chair around when one of his machines beeped.

"Gotta figure out who the people are to interrogate."

"Think Meyer will have any luck getting in touch with all those police agencies?"

"Hope so. Remind me to have Meyer dig into that land deed, too." Lila turned back to the window.

She startled when she spotted a figure sitting on the bench. Had Mystery Man returned? She backed from the window and headed for her coat hanging on the back of a chair.

Kyle turned from his work and followed her progress to the door. "Where you going?"

"Outside. Be right back," she said as she rammed her arms into the coat sleeves. "If the staff gives an update, holler at me."

"You do realize it's going to snow," Lundquist said after her.

"I'll make do." With that, she pushed out of the lab and into the hall.

It was a short walk to the nearest exit. Outside, the wind caught her hair and whipped it about her face. Lila drew the hood of her coat over her head and stopped the whiplash.

The figure remained seated as she approached. When she rounded the edge of the bench, he looked up.

"Sheehan? Isn't it too early for snakes to come out of hibernation?"

The craggy features crinkled in wry amusement. "Always quick with the witticisms."

"Didn't you know—it was a prerequisite on my job application. Number one reason the sheriff hired me, my witty repertoire."

Lila spotted the first flakes of snow coming down. She drew her coat closer to her body. Sheehan sat in his typical getup, snakeskin boots and snug jeans. The edge of a dark-green flannel peeked over the collar of his heavy wool and leather coat. It was the knitted stocking cap that had thrown her; Sheehan was the kind of man who didn't cross Lila as stocking cap wearer.

He looked out at the pond, shoving his gloved hands into his coat pockets. "Your smartassness isn't going to do your sheriff and this damnable department any good this time around."

"What's that supposed to mean?"

The snowfall thickened. Big, wet flakes splatted against their forms and the ground. Sheehan glanced up at her and then at the seat next to him before resuming his watch of the pond, where a pair of Canadian geese were floating.

Scowling at his implied orders, Lila sat, staying near the edge of the bench. "What do you know?"

"Whatever it was your lot discovered two days ago has kicked up a hornet's nest."

"You don't know what it was we discovered?" Lila asked incredulously.

"Do you know what you discovered?" he countered.

She swatted away his remark and a few flakes tickling her face. "You didn't come here to play twenty-one questions. You know something, and you need to get it off your chest." She frowned. "Don't you usually harass the sheriff when you do that?"

"Elizabeth and I aren't on speaking terms. She still blames me for her sister's downfall."

"She's got a point."

Sheehan's gaze narrowed. "You're the more reasonable one of the two." He turned his head and directed those reptilian eyes on her. "So be it."

Lila dipped her chin. "It's cold out here. You tracked me down. So spit it out."

He withdrew his left hand and held it across his body. From between his fingers dangled a key.

"What am I supposed to do with that?"

He removed his other hand, grabbed hers, and slapped the key into her palm. "You open a lock with it."

"A lock to what?" Lila studied the key. Nothing special about it. A silver-plated key on a single ring attached to a red plastic fob.

Sheehan pointing to the building behind them had Lila turning.

"The hospital?" She turned back to him. "Where in the hospital? And who gave this to you?"

Sheehan hoisted his tall, scrawny frame upright. He looked down at Lila from over his pointed nose. "A terrified individual gave that to me upon my release from the hospital. Told me to only reveal it to one person."

Lila frowned.

"You," he said and walked away.

Lila hopped to her feet. "Hey!"

Her shout startled the geese into flight, and they honked their displeasure.

"You didn't tell me what exact lock this key goes to," she

yelled after Sheehan.

"Not my circus, not my monkeys," he called back.

Lila gaped at his fading backside. "Son of a bitch."

She gripped the key and peered through the heavy snow at the hospital. "Guess I'm going on a scavenger hunt."

CHAPTER TWENTY-SEVEN

"SOMEONE'S TAILING US," Rafe said as he turned down the street to the Remington-Thorpe's cul-de-sac.

They were meeting up with the K-9 unit at the house.

Elizabeth peered at the Interceptor's sideview mirror. "Can you make out who it is?"

"No. Before you ask, the vehicle is a dark-gray sedan, Missouri plates, and tinted windows." He slowed the SUV to take the rounded street and pulled into the Remington-Thorpe driveway. "I caught sight of them when we left your place. They followed us to the department."

They had been at the office for an hour before coming this way. It would be another twenty minutes or more before the K-9 team arrived.

"Apparently, they waited for us to leave." Elizabeth was glad she left Bentley in Georgia's loving care instead of bringing her out here.

Rafe parked in front of the garage and killed the engine.

"Where are they?" she asked.

"Pulled into another house. They're behind a privacy fence and bushes; I can't see them. Either they'll camp out there to wait us out or leave as soon as we're out of sight inside. When you get out, go straight to the house."

"Then what?"

"Then we watch to see what they do. We'll have backup soon."

Backup being Joel and Young, whom Elizabeth had assigned to this detail. They should be coming any time now.

"Go," Rafe told her.

She exited the SUV and did exactly as he requested. She let herself inside with the key, and as soon as she began entering the security code, Rafe joined her, closing and locking the door behind him.

He had his phone out and was texting. "Alerting Joel," he said by way of explanation.

Elizabeth left the foyer and came to a halt at the entrance to the living room. "Rafe."

Bookshelves were toppled to the floor, their contents spilled among the wreckage of broken and desecrated furniture. The sofa and armchairs were included in the massacre, their fabric covers sliced and stuffing ripped out. Anything breakable had been shattered. The TV dangled by two cords, the weight of it pulling on the sheetrock.

"What the hell?" Rafe snarled.

Elizabeth glanced down the hall, spotting more debris added to the signs of Olivia's abduction. She abandoned Rafe in the hall and hurried to the kitchen. A peek past the swinging doors revealed more of the same carnage.

"Whoever did this came through the kitchen," she said, entering the room.

Porcelain shards and shattered pieces of glass crunched and popped under her boots. The glass pane in the patio door was nothing more than jagged edges splintering outward.

"Ellie," Rafe called.

She stepped out of the kitchen and wandered to the upstairs steps. Rafe stood at the top.

"Everything is destroyed," he said, his voice gruff.

"Dominic's room," she gasped and bolted down the steps to the lower level.

She stepped on the cracked remnants of a wooden side table. Stepping over the debris, she headed for the room Dominic had been staying in. Everywhere she looked there was destruction. She could imagine all of the priceless mementos in Olivia's office had been ruined, too.

Dominic's room looked as if it took the brunt of the searcher's wrath. Even the mattress had not come away unscathed. Elizabeth stood there, feeling like there was something she should remember.

She looked down at the remnants of a book lying at the tips of her boots. She squatted and pulled the tattered pieces into her hands, flipping the hardcover over. *Fischer's Mastery of Surgery.* The thing she was trying to recall hit her head-on. The notepad with the Chicago-based physician's office.

Elizabeth chucked the ruined book aside and searched the debris for the pad of paper. Last night, Dayne had left it on the bed. Elizabeth focused her search there. After a few minutes, she came up emptyhanded. It was either destroyed, or whoever tossed the house took it. At least Dayne had called the number last night; she should still have it on her phone.

Elizabeth backed down the hall and stopped by the ground floor exit. Oddly, the sliding door remained intact, the bloody smear from the victim dried to the pane.

The creak of weakened wood under considerable weight jolted her. She looked over as Rafe traversed over the wreckage.

"Dayne just texted me," he said and joined her to stare out the window at the backyard. "They didn't break this?"

"Strange, I know. What did Dayne say?"

"She and Lundquist went to Dominic's office in the hospital. It's been ransacked too."

"What about Olivia's office?"

"Untouched. The target apparently was Dominic."

"Why destroy her things here, but not her office?" Elizabeth asked.

"Whoever did this had an ax to grind." Rafe took a step closer to the unharmed sliding door. "I think they threw the patio furniture onto the lawn."

Elizabeth looked about the room. "They were searching for something."

Rafe's phone dinged. He made a face at the message, then turned the phone to her.

"Dayne was given a key," he said.

"To what?"

He drew the phone back. "Unknown. But I bet it belongs to whatever our vandals were looking for."

"Or they have the locked item and they were looking for the key." Elizabeth pinched the bridge of her nose and drew in a shuddering breath. "The malice with which this was done." She dropped her hand and met Rafe's gaze. "Dominic told me to walk away. To leave it alone and close the investigation."

His phone dinged again.

The look of defeat on his face made Elizabeth's gut twist. "What is it?"

"Dayne just got word our young man died during surgery."

All that effort for nothing. She had hoped the team at the hospital could keep him alive long enough for someone to get information out of him. But it wasn't meant to be.

Elizabeth stared at the mess surrounding them, her gaze eventually drifting to the blood smeared on the sliding glass door. The poor young man managed to keep himself alive long enough to make it to the Remington-Thorpe house. Maybe his determination would produce a better result once they tracked his path backward. Maybe his death would not be in vain.

Remembering the phone number, Elizabeth pulled out her phone and texted Dayne to send her the number. Two minutes later, Elizabeth tapped the underlined digits and called it.

"First Health Chicago, how may I direct your call?"

"This is Sheriff Elizabeth Benoit of Eckardt County, Iowa." Elizabeth paused, noticing she'd garnered Rafe's full attention. "I need to speak to one of your doctors."

"I'm sorry, Sheriff, did you say you were in Iowa?" the receptionist asked.

"I did."

"Okay, um, this is highly irregular." The receptionist sounded flustered. "What's your call regarding?"

"An active case. I'd rather discuss with whichever doctor has been there the longest."

"Oh, well, that would have been Dr. Alderman, but he's

no longer with us."

"But your after-hours message states he's still there."

"Yeah, we're sorry about that, it hasn't been updated. Dr. Alderman retired more than a year ago."

How lazy to not update their messages for that long. "Would Dr. Pryce be available to talk?"

"Let me check his schedule." Through the connection, Elizabeth could hear the receptionist typing. "I'm sorry, Sheriff, but he's in surgery all day today. He won't be available until tomorrow."

"He's a surgeon?"

"Yes."

"Was Dr. Alderman a surgeon?"

"Yes?" The receptionist sounded wary.

"May I ask how long you've worked there?" Elizabeth pressed.

Her side of the conversation had fully piqued Rafe's interest, and he was standing before her, waiting.

"I've only been here for three years, Sheriff."

Well, that was a dead end. Elizabeth sighed. Guess this wasn't going to get her any answers. "All right. Guess that's all I need, then. Thank you."

"You're welcome," the woman stuttered. "Are you sure?"

"Unless you can get me a phone number for Dr. Alderman, yeah, that's it."

"Sheriff, you said you're in Iowa?"

"I did."

"I don't have access to a way to contact Dr. Alderman, but I do know after he retired, he moved to Iowa."

A little flicker of hope came to life in Elizabeth. "Did he

now?"

"I hope it helps."

"Oh, it does." Elizabeth ended her call with the clinic receptionist and tucked away her cell.

"What was that all about?" Rafe asked, but his phone dinging kept Elizabeth from explaining. "Joel and Young are here." His brow furrowed. "Per Joel, whoever was following us is gone. Or they've moved to another position out of sight."

In her shock at seeing the ransacked house, Elizabeth had let it slip her mind about the tail. "What do you bet our stalkers are responsible for this?"

"If I were a betting man," Rafe said, "Las Vegas would run out of money."

CHAPTER TWENTY-EIGHT

O LIVIA'S DOWNWARD WALK turned uphill. She made her way in what she assumed was a general northerly direction until she ended up at a well-maintained cemetery. By then, the sun was up, hidden behind a thick bank of gray clouds. She was chilled and calling herself all kinds of brainless for doing this without proper clothing. Moreso when she'd been walking through a spit of snow earlier.

She slid the bag off her shoulder and over the cast, then placed it on the ledge of the brick entry post. Olivia dug to the bottom of the bag to grab up a bottle of water and the pain meds. While she downed more OTCs and drank the water, she studied her surroundings.

The general area was rural, but she was seeing more homes with a farm-like look to them. Homes where she spotted indications people lived there. The road she'd been following had gone from being sealed to actual gravel. If she was near a town, she was getting farther away from it.

Olivia squinted at the cemetery's entry. The metal working arched over the single-lane drive didn't give her a whole lot to go on about where she was. The cemetery's name was probably from some founder of the area. By the looks of the stone monuments nearest to her, it was old, mid-nineteenth century old.

She returned the empty bottle to the bag.

"Now what?"

Which direction? As she'd continued to walk this morning, the scent of water had faded, giving her the impression she'd gotten farther away from the source. She was all kinds of backward and mad at herself for not thinking this through better.

God help her, she didn't even know how to get back to Horatio's prison.

Olivia was a city girl. Born and raised in the beautiful village of Flossmoor, she'd had no outdoors experience outside of suburbia until she moved to Iowa, and that experience was limited before she moved to Juniper. She was at her wit's end.

A rumbling sound made her stiffen. She grabbed the bag, holding it flush to her body as she listened. The rumbling noise was joined by the rattle and squeak of metal. A vehicle, an older one by the sounds of it, was coming this way. Olivia glanced around.

Hide? Or flag down the driver? What did she do?

The boxy front end of a truck nosed around a curve in the road, bringing the full body into view. Olivia couldn't clearly make out the driver, but they didn't appear to be overly tall.

Snowflakes began falling again as the truck rolled closer. Shivering, Olivia made a decision. God help her if it was the wrong one.

She moved away from the cemetery entrance and bolted toward the gravel road. She stopped within inches of the edge just as the truck lumbered up a slight rise in the ground.

Olivia met the driver's gaze at the same moment the driver spotted her. The startled look on the driver's face was comical. The elderly lady hit the brakes, locking them up. Thankfully, the truck hadn't been going fast, but it still fishtailed and weaved to a stop yards past Olivia.

Olivia waited a few seconds while the truck idled on the road, then hurried over to the driver's side. The driver rolled the window down and gaped out the opening at Olivia.

"Missy, you're real lucky I didn't run you over."

"I'm sorry about that, ma'am, but I didn't know of any other way to flag you down."

The woman's hazy eyes narrowed as she studied Olivia. "What are you doing out here on a day like this with no coat on?"

"It's a very long story. Could I get a ride from you?"

The driver shook her head. "Get in." Then she reached her hand out the window with a tsk. "Give me that bag."

Olivia hesitated. She couldn't afford to lose any of the items within.

"I ain't gonna mess with your things. You won't be able to open the door with only one good hand if you're holding that." She nodded at Olivia's cast.

"True." Olivia carefully handed over the bag.

She hurried around the front of the truck and climbed into the cab. Once she was settled, the lady returned her bag.

"Thank you so much."

The driver held out her hand. "Name's Marjorie."

Olivia awkwardly reached over her body and shook the woman's hand. "Olivia."

"Well, Olivia, I was heading into town for my doctor's

appointment. Where would you like me to take you?" Marjorie looked pointedly at the cast.

"Actually, what town is it you're going to?"

"Fort Madison."

Olivia stared at the older woman in stunned silence. All this time, she had been one county away from home. "Wait. Where are we right now?"

Marjorie frowned at Olivia, looking at her as if she were daft. "Missy, you're across the river in Illinois."

Then not that close to Juniper.

"You wanna explain to me how you ended up out here in the middle of nowhere without a coat?" Marjorie frowned. "You running from a man?"

Olivia choked. In essence, she was running from a man. So whatever story she cooked up to tell Marjorie would ring with some truth. But did she dare beg Marjorie to take her to the physician's office with her? Or avoid it all together?

If Horatio was right that the dangerous people Dominic had aligned himself with were after her, exposing herself in public like that would alert them to her whereabouts. Not to mention the risk it posed for Horatio or Adrian finding her.

Marjorie cleared her throat, looking at Olivia expectant-ly.

Olivia broke eye contact and pressed into the seat. "Yeah." She sighed. "I'm running from a man."

CHAPTER TWENTY-NINE

O NCE THEY'D BEEN assured Dr. Bradley would perform the autopsy on the young man, Lila and Kyle headed for the University of Iowa hospital. Sheriff Benoit had received a phone call from Dominic's medical team and was warned he was well enough to be released. She wanted Lila and Kyle there to bring him home.

Before he was released, Benoit wanted Lila to grill him. The sheriff hoped if Lila pressed, Dominic would finally cave and tell them what was going on.

They were ushered to the floor where he was roomed. He'd been moved to a wing where the less serious cases were kept. Good, but surprising considering how bad he'd been when he'd arrived forty-eight hours before.

As they were walking along the corridor, a thought hit Lila. She came to a halt, grasping Kyle's coat sleeve and dragging him to a stop. The administrator leading them kept going, unaware they weren't following.

He turned to her. "What is it?"

"I just realized something. We should have gotten a picture of the victim to show Dominic."

He blinked at her a moment, then comprehension dawned on him. "You think it's someone connected to him somehow?"

She dug out her phone. "Exactly." She keyed in the phone number to the morgue. "What are the odds the ME is already working on him?"

"Pretty good," Lundquist said coming around to her side.

The administrator, a none-too-happy look on her face, returned. "Deputies?"

Lila lifted a finger and flashed a tolerable smile just as the line was picked up.

"Morgue, Dr. Bradley speaking."

The administrator crossed her arms and shot a perturbed look at Lila.

"Dr. Bradley, this is Deputy Dayne. I forgot to snap a photo of our young victim. You haven't begun the autopsy yet, have you?"

"I was just reviewing the surgeon's report and looking over the surgical site," Bradley said. "I can send you a photo now if you wouldn't mind giving me your cell number."

"That would be fantastic." Lila rattled off her number and ended the call. "Sorry about that, ma'am."

The woman's irritated features morphed into one of disconcertment, her arms sliding down to her sides. "What was that all about?"

Lila's face flamed hot. She was such a thoughtless fool. She'd have to blame it on the lack of sleep and the copious amounts of caffeine coursing through her. This poor woman was nothing more than an office manager who did not face criminal violence on a daily basis. She'd been kind enough to assist Lila and Lundquist from point A to point B, not be privy to a gruesome conversation.

Kyle touched the woman's shoulder and gave her his most flattering smile, the one he used when reassuring a victim's family members or the public. "It's an official police matter. We're not at liberty to speak about it."

Lila's phone vibrated. A photo message came through from Dr. Bradley. She nodded to Kyle.

"Ma'am, if you would," he said in a cajoling voice.

Lila's phone rang, and they started forward once again. This time, the administrator slammed to a halt and turned glaring eyes on Lila.

"Sorry," she said and took the call. "Make it fast, Meyer."

"I got a hit on Booker Williams that might pan out. Fifteen years ago, there was an arrest made on a Booker Williams in Humboldt Park, Chicago, for suspected check fraud. He wasn't convicted because the evidence disappeared. But that's not what caught my attention. It was the name of the person footing his bail: Dr. Samuel Alderman."

"That name sounds familiar." She met Kyle's expectant gaze. "Alderman? Does that ring a bell?"

He shook his head and shrugged.

"I looked him up," Meyer said. "He's a surgeon out of Chicago."

Lila's bell dinged. "Wait, I remember. I called his office last night. Sheriff was going to try again today."

"Want me to do it?" Meyer asked.

"No, let the sheriff. You dig deeper on those connections." She hung up after Meyer accepted his call to duty.

The administrator eyed each of them. "Are we done?"

"Again, ma'am, we're sorry," Kyle appeased her. "We're in the middle of two investigations."

The woman huffed and shook her head before waving them onward. With her back to them, Kyle made the *yikes* face at Lila.

The assigned security guard held out a clipboard. "Sign in, please."

Lila noted the long list of names who had already entered and exited the room in the last twenty-four hours.

"These have all been medical staff?" she asked the guard.

"Yes, per your sheriff's orders."

"I assure you, Deputy," the administrator added, "everyone who's entered here has been on the hospital staff for years and highly vetted."

"Can't be too careful," Lila said and turned to Kyle. "Here's my warning to you, I'm probably going to be the bad cop in there. You think I'm crossing a line, say something and I'll end it."

"You sure you want to do that?" he asked.

"Have a heart. He was stabbed," she said and pushed inside Dominic's room.

The man himself was propped up in the bed, staring out the bank of windows. The room overlooked the backside of the University of Iowa's football stadium.

"You shouldn't be here," Dominic said by way of greeting.

"Neither should you," Lila answered. "But we're your escort to go home."

A home Dominic had nary a clue was destroyed and now a full-on crime scene.

Kyle stationed himself next to the door while Lila went to stand at the end of the bed.

Dominic dragged his gaze from the window and gave her a scowl. "Every time one of you comes to see me, you put Olivia's life in further danger."

"The longer you keep your secrets locked up inside, the more danger you put everyone in," Lila countered.

"I'll tell you what I told the sheriff. Drop it. All of it. Move on as if you never knew a blessed thing."

She shook her head. "Sorry. Can't do it." She withdrew the key and held it up. "Especially when you decided to involve me in this whole fiasco."

His eyes widened. He held out an IV-strapped hand. "Give that to me."

Lila clutched the key and tucked it inside a vest pocket. "No can do. You passed it onto Sheehan for a reason with instructions to give it to me. I'm here to find out what I'm supposed to do with it."

"Nothing. You do nothing with it." He gestured as if begging. "Give me the key, Lila."

Hands evenly spaced on the bed's footboard, she leaned into them and white-knuckled the plastic bar. "Forget it, Doc. Whomever you were trying to hide it from is searching for it. They ransacked your office at the hospital. And according to the sheriff, they destroyed your home."

His features blanched. He let his hand fall to the bed and looked away.

"How do you expect us to find Olivia if you can't give us the information we need to locate her?"

"Stop it now, Lila."

She pushed off the footboard. "It's too late for regrets, Doc." She glanced at Kyle, who lifted his chin in approval.

"What's your connection to the boneyard out in the middle of nowhere?"

Had she not been watching for it she would have missed the slight twitch in Dominic's body. She pressed forward.

"Found the tunnel under the shack near the boneyard. Then someone decided to dump three bodies in a boat and float it down river. Bodies covered with dermestid beetles. Beetles, I'm told, that consume flesh and material pretty rapidly, especially when there are thousands of them."

Dominic seemed to curl inward, as if trying to protect himself from her barrage.

"So, I ask again, Doc, what's your connection to all of this?"

He continued to avoid her, pursing his lips into a thin line.

"Who is Adrian Landry?"

"How am I supposed to know?" Dominic said.

Slightly bolstered she got a reaction from him, Lila released her death grip on the footboard. "He's gotta mean something to you. Evidence places him in your home at the time Olivia went missing."

He appeared to relax at the mention of this Landry guy's connection to Olivia. Lila pounced on the shift in Dominic's posture.

"You know who it is. You know why Olivia was taken. And I bet my last dollar it all stems back to that boneyard. What is going on, Doc?"

Dominic remained mute. Anger surged through Lila. She left the foot of the bed and stepped into his line of sight.

"Answer me," she snapped. "Or so help me ..."

His gaze flicked up and connected. "Or you'll what, Deputy?"

Lila heard it. It was subtle, his carefully constructed voice slipping with his anger, but she caught it. The hint of an accent she'd grown up hearing. A drawl she'd encountered many times on Chicago's streets. An infliction she'd been reintroduced to the day before.

Southside.

Dominic held her gaze, his tightly controlled features giving nothing away, even as his carefully constructed life was crumbling around him. Yet he held fast to his stubbornness. How much of his soul had he given up?

Lila pulled out her phone and brought up the photo the state medical examiner had sent her. Her ace in the hole.

"If Olivia's plight won't change your mind, maybe this poor soul's will." She turned the phone to him.

He lost the determination to keep up the facade. He lowered his head and buried his face in his hands.

Some of Lila's anger dissipated, but she didn't lower the phone. "This half-dead kid hiked through God knows how many miles of timber and pasture to get to your house last night. He nearly bled to death before the sheriff found him. The hospital tried to keep him alive, except … he died on the table."

Dominic's shoulders sagged.

Lila went on, doing her best to stay indifferent about the whole situation and drive a response out of the man. "The preliminary report from the surgeon states he was missing both kidneys, most of his liver, and his pancreas. And it looked like someone was about to start in on his bowels."

He flinched at her description.

"Who is he, Dominic?" Lila inched closer to the bedside. "Where did he come from?" She reached out and grasped his wrist. "How did he know to get to your home?" She jerked his hand down. "Tell me."

He dropped his hand and ripped free of her hold. Fire mingled with tears in his eyes. "He's nobody."

"He's somebody. To you. And to someone out there who loves him."

"You need to leave," Dominic ground out.

She was about to give him his out when she remembered her call with Meyer. "Who's Booker Williams?"

He jerked hard enough to make the bed rattle.

Lila pounced. "You know who that is."

"Leave me alone," he said in a low, menacing voice.

"It's a long drive back to Juniper, *Doc*."

"Lila," Kyle warned from his corner. He'd certainly waited long enough.

She straightened her spine and took a step back from the bed. Dominic continued to glower at her, the control back in his face.

"I hope whatever it is you're hiding from everyone is worth the price of your soul." She turned for the exit. "I hope it doesn't cost Olivia her life."

Lundquist opened the door, holding it for her.

"You have no idea what you're getting into," Dominic said.

Lila looked back at him.

"If you continue to pursue this, you'll face something that will make the I-80 serial killer seem like a cakewalk. Neither you nor the sheriff are prepared for what will come."

"We relish the challenge."

CHAPTER THIRTY

MARJORIE HAD INSISTED Olivia come inside the physician's clinic with her—more like demanded she get her arm checked out. Olivia balked. There was no way of knowing who in the clinic would know of her or Dominic. Nor whether anyone there would have connections to the shady characters Horatio alluded to.

But the elderly woman would not be dissuaded from her determination. Olivia caved and went inside, but not without her bag.

Sitting here among the infirmed, young and old, Olivia felt conspicuous. Those who waited to be seen by their physicians seemed absorbed in their own worlds. But every so often Olivia got the sensation she was being studied. When Marjorie's name was called, she urged Olivia back to the exam room with her. The nurse kindly asked after Olivia, and Marjorie's quick answer that she was a recent acquaintance who moved in next door to her and didn't have a car rang true enough. The nurse dropped the subject.

After a quick rundown of Marjorie's reasons for seeing her doctor, Marjorie cajoled the nurse into asking the doctor to give Olivia the once-over. The nurse said she'd ask and escaped the room. Olivia was never given a chance to rebut. Marjorie was a force of nature no one seemed able to reroute.

They sat in the silence of the exam room, staring at each other.

"I'm perfectly fine," Olivia said softly.

"And you know this how, Dr. Olivia?" Marjorie quipped.

Olivia gnawed on her lips to squash the smile. She cleared her throat. "Actually, I am a doctor."

Marjorie gaped, her jaw dropping. Then she coughed out a laugh. "Well, you sure do a fine job of hiding it."

"You make it difficult to insist otherwise."

Olivia eyed the office phone stationed on the wall next to the single desktop computer. It was getting rare to see desktop computers in exam rooms, as most offices and hospitals used a laptop or tablet system the doctors and nurses carried with them. Olivia and her staff were no exception to this rule. What wasn't rare were the phones.

While the nurse had logged in to admit Marjorie, Olivia was struck by an idea. Since Horatio had informed her that Dominic was at the University of Iowa hospitals, she had a way to narrow down her search. But it was going to require a phone call.

If only it were legal and ethical to use her own credentials to access his information via the hospital programs. It would have certainly been faster and quieter.

She eyed Marjorie. Would her kind rescuer aid and abet her?

"Are you up to something?" Marjorie asked.

Olivia blinked. "If I was?"

The lady crossed her arms and settled back in her chair. "Would it be illegal?"

"No. The oddball variable is you."

"What are you plotting?"

Tongue tucked between her teeth, Olivia vacated her chair and sat in the rolling chair at the desk. "Finding my husband," she said softly.

Marjorie scowled. "He wouldn't be the villain you're running from?"

"He would be the man I'm running to." Olivia glanced at the exam room door and picked up the handset. "He's been injured and hospitalized." She pressed the receiver to her ear and listened to the dial tone. It wasn't the typical steady buzz waiting for a phone number to be entered. It had the intermittent tone waiting for an in-office code or the single digit to dial out.

Marjorie leaned forward. "How are you planning on finding him?"

Olivia had no idea what number this office used for the dial out. A second problem—she didn't want the reception desk seeing this exam room phone in use. It would bring someone in here sooner than she liked.

She set the handset down and returned to her seat next to Marjorie. "Do you have a cell phone?"

The elderly woman picked up her ginormous bag and plopped it in her lap. "I do." She reached inside the monster's mouth.

Olivia wondered if Marjorie's hand would emerge or if the bag would devour it.

Out came the woman's hand, and clutched in her grip was a dinosaur of a cell phone.

Ring, ring, the twenty-oughts are calling. They want their flip phone back.

Marjorie thrust it at Olivia. "Do you need me to keep watch for the doc so you're not overheard?"

Olivia took the flip phone. "If you don't mind? I'd appreciate it."

Giving her a conspiratorial grin, Marjorie got up from her seat, placed her large bag on the chair, and shuffled over to the door.

Old habits died hard. Even one-handed, Olivia was able to flip open the phone and thumb in the number she'd memorized to the University of Iowa's main call center. Being a doctor who had to consult with others from Iowa's premier hospital paid dividends.

Any time a call was made about a specific patient, it tended to be recorded in their online medical chart. Olivia was banking on Dominic having her on his HIPAA release and cashing in her privilege as his wife to gain access to his information and not have her search recorded. She might be damning herself and allowing someone to track her movements. But she didn't know how else to find Dominic quickly.

The call center was able to connect her with his surgeon's office. One of his nurses answered. Olivia related who she was and answered all the required questions before the nurse would continue. There was a brief pause as the nurse seemed to trip over her words.

"Mrs. Thorpe"—Olivia didn't bother to correct the woman—"there's a note here on your husband's chart stating that you're unavailable and that Sheriff Elizabeth Benoit is his contact."

Olivia glanced at Marjorie, who continued to keep her ear pressed to the door. "That would be correct. She's our backup."

Another long pause. A bead of sweat tracked between her breasts. Hopefully, this nurse wouldn't get too serious about this and bring in the surgeon. Olivia would have to hang up, because by then Marjorie's doctor would be here. Too many people being in on this meant a higher risk of discovery.

"No, no, that's fine. I just thought you would want to be aware," the nurse continued. "It would seem that Dr. Thorpe is to be released today."

"Really? I was told his injuries were more serious than that."

The nurse gave her a quick rundown on his surgery. His surgeon was satisfied with her husband's recovery and felt he would heal faster at home.

"Are we releasing him into your care?" the nurse asked.

Olivia stared at her cast. How would she care for her injured husband when she was recovering herself? She couldn't even drive. Except for this nurse, no one was aware of where Olivia was at or that she was free and not missing.

"Oh, sorry, I see there's a note here from the sheriff that she has someone coming to pick up Dr. Thorpe," the nurse added.

"That will work. Thank you." Olivia didn't give the nurse a chance to reply and snapped the flip phone shut.

The most logical person or persons to release Dominic to would be Elizabeth or Rafe. If they took him home, that was where Olivia needed to go.

But home meant danger. And Horatio.

"Shit."

Marjorie pulled herself from the door. "Problems?"

"A multitude. My husband is to be released today."

"Wouldn't that be a good thing?"

Olivia dropped Marjorie's phone back into the monster's mouth. "Normally, yes. I need to get back home."

"And home is where?"

"Juniper."

Marjorie flinched. "Incoming," she whispered and scurried back to her seat just as a knock at the door proceeding its opening.

"Good morning, Ms. Marjorie. I hear you have a friend with you today?"

The young male doctor took one look at Olivia, and she felt elation. She had never seen this man in her life and doubt he knew her.

He eyed her cast. "Did you break your arm?"

Olivia cleared her throat and tempered her response from the sarcastic remark on the tip of her tongue. "Yes, you could say that happened."

"Well, then let's see to Ms. Marjorie first, and if you don't mind, I'll have a look at it."

Olivia cradled the bag close to her body. He could consider taking a look all he liked, but there was no way she was going to let him.

She had to get through Marjorie's exam and get out of here. Hopefully, Marjorie and her truck were up to a longer drive.

CHAPTER THIRTY-ONE

T HE K-9 LED their little troop right to the Fontaine hunting cabin and down the hill to the place where the mysteriously missing Jeep had crashed.

Elizabeth wanted to scream.

The dog was able to pick up a scent leading into the trees yards from where the Jeep had been, but that was where it stopped.

Elizabeth and Rafe stood among the trees and dormant foliage and stared back the way they had come.

"He was with Dominic when he crashed out there."

"It would certainly explain the amount of blood Joel said he saw in the vehicle," Rafe said.

Elizabeth shook her head. "According to him, it was only the driver's seat. I don't know if he looked in the back seat." She huffed. "Every time I think we have something to grasp on to, it turns to smoke and *poof*. Gone."

"This isn't a bad thing. We can place the victim with Dominic at this point." Rafe began moving out of the woods. "He probably crawled out of the wrecked Jeep and staggered over here to hide. Maybe Dominic told him to do it?"

"And maybe the victim wasn't with him but back wherever those other three were. Maybe the jerkoffs behind this whole ordeal weren't able to kill him off in time, and instead of leaving him with the other bodies, they dragged him back out here intending to leave him to die."

"It's a possibility. Whoever is pulling the strings behind this is smart. They've been doing it long enough to get away with it."

"To hell with it!" Elizabeth stomped out of the timber and stalked back up the hill toward the cabin where the K-9 deputy and dog were waiting.

They had left Joel standing guard over the Remington-Thorpe house, watching to see if the car tailing Rafe and Elizabeth returned. Young, having been given a GPS locator to track them, was dispatched to retrieve them from their current location.

Rafe rushed to catch up to her. "I know you're worried about Olivia."

"I keep expecting us to stumble onto her body at some point." She slowed her pace. "The way Dominic behaves, I don't think she had anything to do with this. She's collateral to keep Dominic in line. For all we know, she's already dead."

Rafe caught her arm and pulled her to a stop. "This doesn't sound like you. You've never been a defeatist."

"I've also never had to face something like this before. Dominic's right. We're in over our heads."

"We're not," Rafe said harshly. "Let's regroup, get something hot to eat, and see where Meyer is at and check in with Dayne and Lundquist."

"What good is that going to do?"

"The good it'll do is get your head back in the right

space. It needs to be there before we go pay a visit to some-one."

"Someone who?"

"Sheehan."

THEY FOUND HIM. In his usual spot. The king presiding over his tiny little kingdom in The Watering Hole.

It was 1:30, and Marnie was getting the bar ready to open at five. She glanced up when Elizabeth and Rafe blew in with a gust of chilly wind. Leaning into the bar top, Marnie scowled.

"I'm not here to stir up trouble," Elizabeth said by way of greeting.

From his favored spot, Kelley Sheehan rose from his chair. "Elizabeth. Why don't you join me."

Marnie shook her head, threw a bar towel in the sink, and stalked into the back storage room.

Elizabeth mounted the steps to the raised seating area. Rafe stationed himself on the stairs, leaning against the wrought iron railing installed when Marnie had renovated the bar after she first purchased it.

The table Sheehan vacated was littered with receipts and bank statements, along with a handwritten and detailed ledger. When Marnie said he was a partner in the operation of The Watering Hole, it apparently meant the financial partner.

"If you're here about the key I gave to Dayne this morn-ing," Sheehan said, "I know nothing more than what I told her."

Elizabeth glanced at Rafe, then focused on Sheehan. "That's not why we're here."

Those whiskey-amber eyes regarded Elizabeth. He'd always been a man who could see more in a person than they wanted to reveal.

"I'm most certainly aware you have knowledge of what's been going on the last three days," Elizabeth said.

"I've heard rumblings."

"Did those rumblings come from anyone in particular who would give you pause?" Elizabeth asked.

"Give me pause in what way?" Sheehan countered.

"Oh, I don't know, maybe someone who spoke to you about it? Someone you would have never suspected?"

He chuckled, a low sound that tended to make Elizabeth's blood pressure rise. With a flick of his wrist, he gestured at the main floor of the bar. "Take your pick of any such person who walks through that door as someone *unexpected*." Sheehan moved to another table behind him with the chairs placed on the floor. He picked up a thick ceramic cream-colored mug and a stainless-steel carafe, then poured steaming coffee into the mug. "Elizabeth, people come here to drink. When they drink, they start talking." He set down the carafe and faced her. "When they start talking, I listen."

"It's why you hide out here so much," Rafe said.

Sheehan flicked an irritated look toward her undersheriff. "I don't hide. I own a share of this bar. I have every right to be here."

"Along with your part ownership in the Dew Drop?"

Elizabeth remarked.

He gave a sly smile behind his cup, then took a sip of the hot brew.

"I'm not here to play word games with you, Kelley. We have a crisis on our hands, and you're the one person who always seems to have some tidbit to help me resolve whatever catastrophe has befallen our sheriff's department," Elizabeth said.

Sheehan's gaze narrowed as he studied her. Slowly, he set the mug on the table next to the carafe. His attention flicked behind Elizabeth to the bar, then with a jerk of his head, he indicated for her and Rafe to follow him as he headed to a back door under the staircase leading up to Marnie's apartment.

Their trio stepped out into another bout of falling snow. Sheehan closed the door and waved them on.

"Where are we going?" Elizabeth asked as they trailed him down the alley between The Watering Hole and the neighboring building.

"Away from Marnie's eavesdropping," Sheehan said.

He rounded the backside of the brick two-story building next door and passed through a tall metal arbor to enter a dormant garden. During the spring and summer, this was a lush bee and butterfly garden; the pollen-loving insects flew here in droves to sip from the delicate petals. The owner also ran a novelty shop in the brick building at their backs.

Sheehan continued through the garden and ducked under a shorter arbor at the end of the garden's path.

"Haven't we gone far enough?" Rafe asked, bending at the waist to navigate his tall frame through the arbor.

Sheehan withdrew a set of keys and stepped up to another brick building's rear door. "In here."

Rafe met Elizabeth's eye before they followed him inside to a back entry. Sheehan closed and locked the door behind them. A refurbished staircase led down to a well-lit basement. A pair of steps went up to an old heavy wooden door with an antique handle and lock, probably the original hardware. From below, the furnace ran, heated air filling the building.

"This way." Sheehan went downward.

Rafe leaned close to Elizabeth's ear. "Isn't this the old general store some gal is turning into a boutique?"

"I think so."

Halfway down the steps, Sheehan paused and turned. "Today, you two." And on he continued.

Elizabeth huffed and followed.

The building's foundation was fashioned out of river stone and mortar, key components of nineteenth-century building construction. Despite the heat coming from the furnace, a damp odor lingered in the basement—residue from heavy rains and past floodings the building had endured, along with the passage of time.

Two bare bulbs hung on each end of the main area of the flooring. A wall constructed of wood panels divided the width of the room. Two-tiered skinny tables topped by antique lanterns bookended a door in the wall. To Elizabeth's right stood an old wood-burning furnace, a neat row of split wood stacked in a metal rack next to the furnace.

"Why are we down here?" she asked, watching Sheehan open the door in the wall.

He held the heavy door open and indicated for them to enter.

Elizabeth went first. The other side was done up as a sleeping area with a camping cot, thick blackout curtains over the windows, and a small metal table and lawn chair near the center.

A tiny figure wrapped in a dark green wool blanket huddled on the cot. A pair of wide, dark-brown eyes peeked around the edge of the blanket.

Elizabeth gaped at the hooded form. "Kelley, what is this?"

Sheehan must have gestured at the figure, because they slowly lowered the part of the blanket covering their head to reveal a teen girl.

"This, Elizabeth, is a terrified young woman who has a story to tell."

Elizabeth wanted to coldcock Sheehan.

"How long have you been hiding her here?"

The girl cowered then threw the blanket over her tangled dark-brown hair and hunkered up against the stone wall.

Sheehan shifted closer to the cot and sat beside the girl. "Since last night." His whiskey stare bore holes in Elizabeth. "Found her stumbling about at my place."

"You couldn't be bothered with alerting any of us she was here?" Elizabeth snapped.

"She doesn't speak English."

"As if that justifies you not reporting her?"

"Ellie," Rafe said softly.

Elizabeth composed herself, shoving away her anger when she noticed the blanket-covered girl trembling. Where had her compassion gone? Where had her need to comfort and assure victims and the distressed go? Had it been depleted from her as she hemorrhaged and bled out on Halloween night?

This was not how she behaved. What had she, Elizabeth Benoit, become?

Sheehan pointed at her. "This reaction is the exact reason I said nothing to any of you." He looked at the girl. "And the accusations that I somehow have a hand in the current fiasco blowing up in this county because she was on my property."

Elizabeth blew out a shaky breath. "Sorry. It's been a trying few days and nothing seems to make sense."

The startled expression on Sheehan's face was comical, except she was far beyond being amused.

She pressed forward before either man decided to question her sanity. "If she doesn't speak English, what does she speak?"

"It sounds like Spanish. Can either of you speak it?"

Rafe shook his head. "Not my forte."

"I can." Elizabeth waved Sheehan off the cot and took his place.

The girl kept her head down and the blanket tucked tight to her body.

"Hello, my name is Elizabeth. What's yours?" The girl poked her face between the dark-green folds and gaped at Elizabeth's Spanish fluency.

That old nurturing sensation, the one she'd get when dealing with the younger generation, fell over her. Having never been a mother herself—having children was something she and Joel never got around to doing and eventually decided it was best they not—Elizabeth still had the instincts. This girl was bringing it all forward. Maybe Elizabeth hadn't lost her compassionate nature after all.

When the girl didn't speak, Elizabeth took a new tact. "My friend, the man who saved you and brought you here, he's worried about you. He asked me to come check on you."

The girl looked to Sheehan and then back to Elizabeth, pulling the blanket farther away from her head. Up close, Elizabeth could see the girl's tangled hair was more matted than twisted. A certain sharp, tangy odor clung to her.

Blood.

"You speak Spanish?" the girl asked.

Elizabeth smiled. "I can. I have friends who taught me a long time ago." Once again, she could surreptitiously thank Joel and his years in the army for giving her opportunities she would never have had by remaining in Juniper and Eckardt County.

"Where is my brother? Do you know where he is?"

Elizabeth sensed Rafe shifting near them. She gestured for him to stay back, then leaned closer to the girl.

"What's your brother's name?"

"Javier." The girl pressed her hand to her chest. "I'm Elena."

"Elena, I'm not certain where your brother is, but we'll find him." Elizabeth touched the girl's thin arm. "Can you tell me how you got to my friend's house?"

Elena looked up, probably at Sheehan, and then leaned forward, the blanket falling past her shoulders and revealing the blood-streaked shirt. "I was running from the demon men."

"Demon men?"

"Yes. They were going to rip my insides out. Like they hurt Javier." Elena grasped Elizabeth's arm. "Don't let them get me."

The girl's terror was palpable, dragging Elizabeth into the pit with her.

"I won't let them," she assured Elena. "We will do everything in our power to make sure the demon men can't hurt you." She took the girl's hand in her own. "Do you remember where you were when you ran from them?"

Elena shook her head forcefully. "It was dark. I was scared." She stiffened, then pawed at Elizabeth's hand. "Trees. There were lots of trees."

"Good. Anything else?"

Elena's breathing increased, her gaze bouncing around. Elizabeth waited, certain the girl was trying to remember, trying to pull things from her head.

"Javier was bleeding so badly. He told me to run this way and he would go another. Keep the demon men from following me."

"Where was this at?" Elizabeth asked.

Elena trembled, her tiny body shaking. "There were so many trees," she cried.

Elizabeth pulled the girl into her arms and hugged her tightly. "It's okay. You don't have to remember."

The girl jerked suddenly out of Elizabeth's hold. "No! I need to remember." The voice bounced off the stone walls.

"Elena, let's talk about something else and maybe it will

come back to you," Elizabeth tried.

After a moment of contemplating, the girl nodded. "Yes, yes."

"How old are you?"

"Thirteen."

Revulsion beat against the walls of her stomach. She was almost too afraid to hear the answer to her next question. But it had to be asked.

"How old is Javier?"

"Seventeen."

A picture was forming in Elizabeth's head. The scent and streaks of blood on the girl. Her fear of how she would be next. The age. The location of where she was found in juxtaposition to where the K-9 had stopped earlier. It was more than coincidental.

As Elizabeth continued to study Elena, she was beginning to see it. How close-set the eyes were to the bridge of the nose. The prominent cheekbones. The dark-brown eyes and hair.

God help them. She knew who Javier was and where he was residing at this very moment. If she was wrong—please let her be wrong—there was no sense in upsetting Elena any more than she was now. Time for a redirect.

"Elena, I know it's scary to think about this, but can you tell me what the demon men looked like? Did you see them?"

Terror filled the girl's eyes. "I did not." She waved her hand in front of her face. "They wore masks."

"What kind of masks?"

Elena looked around the room as if searching for what

she meant. Elizabeth looked with her, not certain what the girl hoped to find in the room's spartan furnishings.

"Masks," Elena muttered, then made a two-handed gesture across her mouth, nose, and chin. "Mask." Then repeated her action.

A lightbulb snapped on inside Elizabeth's head. "A surgical mask. Like doctors use?"

Elena nodded vigorously. She pointed to her hair and smoothed it back. "They had on hair rags."

"An actual rag? Or was it more like a cap?"

"Rag. Like one you tie." Elena made the motions at the back of her head as if tying something.

"What's she saying?" Rafe asked.

Elizabeth held up a single finger to him.

"Elena, these are really good descriptions. It's okay if you didn't see them. Your description of what they wore helps me out a lot."

Her encouragement seemed to bolster the girl. She grasped at her filthy clothing and pointed at Elizabeth's.

"Did they wear something a doctor would? We call them scrubs."

"Only two," Elena said. "The others wore clothes like ours."

That brought Elizabeth to her next line of thought. "How many demon men were there?"

"Four." She shook her head and thought some more. "No. Six. There were six."

"Does that include the two men in scrubs?"

"No, just one man in scrubs. The other one was mad at the others. He was yelling at them. I don't think he liked them very much."

Elizabeth bent forward, getting closer to Elena. "Did you understand what he was saying to the other men?"

The girl's dark hair swung back and forth. "While they were fighting, Javier took me outside and hid me in a truck."

"A truck?"

"Yes, something one of the demon men drove. Javier was with me. He was bleeding. I don't know what they did to him." Elena's voice broke and tears escaped from the corners of her eyes.

Elizabeth's hurting heart raced. "Elena, honey, stay with me. Did you see anything around where the truck was when Javier hid you?"

"A little. We were taken to a building."

"We? You and Javier?"

"And the others." Elena dropped her gaze to her lap. "The others the demon men killed."

She had to mean the three bodies they discovered in the floating boat. Elizabeth glanced up at Rafe, whose grizzled features were screwed into a scowl. He had to be getting extremely impatient with getting no feedback for this conversation.

"Elena," Elizabeth continued, "can you describe the building for me?"

"Brick. It was small. Smelled bad." Elena wrinkled her nose. "Like death."

Decay, maybe? If Dayne's thoughts on the black-market organ transplants were right, then this building where they had taken Elena and Javier was the likely place where the unwilling donors were taken, and their organs harvested.

Which meant Javier and Elena were trafficked there.

"Was there anything special about this place, besides the smell, that you can remember?"

"It was old. The grass was long. Some of the cement was broken and cracked."

"Ellie, what is she saying?" Rafe pressed.

She swung her head around and looked up at him. "Do you know of any old run-down places that are made of brick?" She glanced over at Sheehan. "Do you?"

"In Eckardt?" Sheehan asked.

"Or in a neighboring county? She says she and her brother with several other people were taken to some place like that."

Rafe frowned, looking at Sheehan. "Could it be that old medical clinic where the original hospital was?"

Sheehan pinched his lips, his features tight. "Maybe," he said behind his hand.

"The old hospital," Elizabeth said. "I thought they bull-dozed the entire complex."

Sheehan dropped his hand. "Not all of it. Some outfit out of Des Moines tried to make a go of it with the old clinic as a drug rehab facility. County, then the state came in and deemed the building hazardous. Should have been torn down and leveled, but no one wants to spend the money to do it."

Elizabeth stood. "We need to check it out."

Rafe nodded at Elena. "What about her?"

"Keep her here. It's the safest place for her." Elizabeth shifted to put her back to Elena. "I'll explain more as we drive to the old clinic."

Rafe grunted his response and moved to the other room.

"Thank you for rescuing her. And bringing her here," she said to Sheehan.

"Is she gonna be okay?" he asked.

His concern sounded genuine. It was unnerving. Sheehan had always been a man to grate on Elizabeth. He was a man of the past, one who scorned and mocked women. Or so she thought. In the last year or more, Sheehan had shown her a different side. One she was beginning to think was his true nature. A side Marnie obviously was privy to, and it made sense to why she would align herself with him.

"For now." Elizabeth sighed. "I can't believe I'm going to say this, but here we go. Tell Marnie about her and get her down here. Marnie is fluent in Spanish, too, and you're going to need a translator. The girl's name is Elena." She peeked back at the girl, who had pulled the blanket up over her head once more. "Don't press her any more for answers. She's dealt with enough already. Get her some food. Something to drink. And keep her safe."

"What are you going to do, Elizabeth?"

"What every sheriff should do. Round up the bad guys."

CHAPTER THIRTY-TWO

OLIVIA HAD MARJORIE circle the cul-de-sac, drive past her home, then park along the street leading out of the residential area. There had been no signs anyone was at her house, no cars parked in the drive, no crime scene tape festooned to doors, not even a hint Dominic had been brought home yet. Yet, Olivia wasn't certain what lurked in the shadows of her home.

Horatio abducting her had made her wary.

"What are you looking for?" Marjorie asked.

"Something out of the ordinary." Olivia twisted in the seat to look out the truck's back window. Her home was too far out of view.

Marjorie did the same. "Do you see it?"

The cul-de-sac, normally a bright, cheery place, was gray and glum. A sad place. A scared place. The on again and off again snow only worsened the depressive state. Olivia loved her little community. Everyone knew each other here but abided by the strictures of everyone's need for privacy. This swirling sense of doom made her more anxious.

Something was not right here. She checked the time. 3:18. Most of the residents were at work, school, or generally not at home.

"I don't know what I'm seeing," Olivia admitted.

Marjorie turned around and as best she could, faced Olivia. "Missy, you got yourself a problem then. You need to …"

"I need to?" Olivia asked when she didn't go on.

A wry grin played with the woman's mouth. "In the immortal words of my late husband, God rest his soul. Shit or get off the pot."

Olivia bit her lips, but she couldn't contain her amusement. A soft laugh escaped. "How exactly do you expect me to execute this?"

Marjorie flipped herself around and started the truck. "I suggest we go to your home and check it out."

"Marjorie, this isn't your problem. You should go home."

"And leave you all by your lonesome when you've got troubles? What kind of Christian woman would I be to allow such nonsense." She pulled away from the curb and guided the truck down the street.

"I really appreciate your help. But I can't in good conscience let you become even more embroiled in this."

"How dangerous is this man?"

Olivia was watching the sideview mirror when she spotted movement. Without alerting Marjorie, she shifted, acting as if she were in pain, and situated herself where she could see into the rearview mirror.

"He's very dangerous."

Horatio was a threat to anyone but her. She couldn't shake the dread he'd given her when he spoke of the people Dominic had aligned with. People Horatio knew nothing about. The fact he couldn't gain the information was disconcerting.

Or was he playing her? He did know and he wasn't telling her because he had an ulterior motive?

"Maybe you and me should go to your sheriff's office," Marjorie stated, keeping her truck at the residential street's speed limit.

Olivia flicked her gaze between the sideview and the rearview mirrors. Then it emerged.

A dark-gray sedan swung around a car parked streetside. For the last two blocks it had been weaving in and out from behind the vehicles stationed along the curb. Olivia couldn't make out the plates.

"Which way to your sheriff's office?" Marjorie's question broke through Olivia's concentration.

"When you rounded the street at my cul-de-sac, did you see any dark-gray sedans parked at the houses?"

The older woman glanced at Olivia. "No. Why?"

What had she been thinking coming here? By now Horatio would know she'd escaped. His first inclination would be to stake out her home and wait for her to come back. If by some miracle he wasn't aware she was missing and he wasn't searching for her, could the driver of this car be the shadowy dangerous people who were after Dominic?

"Marjorie, I want you to stay on this street."

Marjorie frowned, the deep grooves making her flesh sag. She must have heard the slight quiver in Olivia's voice.

Olivia could only hope that if they stuck to the residential streets, they could reach the sheriff's department unscathed.

"When this street tees, we're taking a left."

"Olivia, you gonna tell me what's wrong with your voice and why you keep looking in my mirrors?"

The gray sedan was pulling closer. Olivia's heart thumped against her breastbone.

"Put your seat belt on." How had she not noticed the straps not crossing Marjorie's body?

"Olivia, you're worrying me." She reached across her body to grab the belt.

Olivia chanced a look back. The sedan's front fender was hidden by the truck bed. She swung around.

One minute she was hearing the loud click of the metal clasp of the buckle locking in place, the next there was ear-piercing screech of metal on metal. The truck wrenched sideways. Glass exploded around them.

Olivia was thrown into her seat belt, her head smacking the side of the headrest. Her ears rang. Blackness closed in on her, then there was nothing.

CHAPTER THIRTY-THREE

"THIS IS NOT the way to my house," Dominic snapped from the back seat of the borrowed SUV.

Kyle had borrowed Georgia's car to bring Dominic home. Neither his nor Lila's vehicle would be able to accommodate the surgeon's request that Dominic be able to lie back in a seat to relieve pressure on his sutures. Georgia had agreed only if Kyle drove. Apparently, Lila's short legs and need to have the seat closer to the steering wheel were a bit of a problem for the taller Georgia.

"No, it's not," Lila said, looking out the passenger side window at the passing small acreage with a quaint, yellow-painted house. "Your place was ransacked and destroyed, remember. I told you this at the hospital. There ain't nothing to go home to."

"I still need to see it and find some clothes."

Lila twisted in her seat to look at him. "Maybe we'll consider it. *If* you tell us what the key is to. Or better yet, you explain to us what the hell is going on."

"I will not be blackmailed into going to my own home."

"And I don't negotiate with dead men." Lila caught the amused expression on Kyle's features as she faced forward.

Dominic muttered, but Lila couldn't make out what it was. Probably best she hadn't.

"You know," she said to Kyle. "It's been a hot minute since the sheriff has checked in with us."

He frowned. "I don't think Fontaine has either." He looked at the rearview mirror for like the hundredth time. "No one from the department has."

Lila pulled out her cell phone. "I'll let Georgia know we're in town and ask her if she's got any updates."

"Forget the updates," Lundquist said, touching her arm. "Tell her to send backup our way."

Her flesh pebbled at the chill in his voice.

"What's wrong?" Dominic asked.

"Ditto," Lila added.

"The same black SUV has been tailing us since I passed county lines."

Lila's eyebrows rose. "Is that why you've been taking all the back ways?" She thought he was dragging out the trip by driving on the rural edges of town in order to get Dominic to talk.

"I had to make sure we were being followed. I'm dead certain now. Get backup out here."

She abandoned her cell and radioed the department directly. "Dispatch, this is Dayne. Anyone available?"

The radio cycled, but no one responded. Lila hailed the office again.

"Lila."

She peeked at Kyle. His knuckles were turning white. "Oh God, what?"

"There's another one."

This time she wrenched herself around to see out the rear windows. There was the initial black SUV. Just to the right of it drifted another large SUV, this one a dark blue.

Dominic had copied Lila's position, then he faced her. "They're after me."

"Who's after you?"

His fear pulsated through the vehicle.

"Damn it, Dominic, who is it?" Kyle snapped.

Suddenly, their SUV pitched forward. The belt yanked Lila's skewed body against the car seat, wrenching her neck and shooting pain down through her shoulder.

"Go faster," Dominic yelled.

Kyle sped up. "Hang on."

Lila watched the black SUV gain on their bumper. "He's closing in." She hailed dispatch once more.

"Brace yourselves," Kyle said as they were rammed again.

Their vehicle fishtailed slightly, but Kyle was able to maintain control. The years of training to chase and stop fleeing suspects came in real handy in this situation.

"He's moving to the outside," Lila warned.

"Where's the other one?"

Once the black car moved into the left lane, Lila spotted the dark blue one. "Right behind us. They're going to try to box us in."

"How do you know that?" Dominic demanded.

Lila reached to unbuckle her belt. "It's what I would do."

"Don't take that off," Kyle warned.

She watched the black SUV pull alongside them. The tinted windows protected the identity of the driver and any passengers. She peered back at the dark blue one—it maintained a comfortable distance back but stayed in their lane.

"What are they doing?" she asked.

"PIT maneuver," Kyle shouted.

Lila's gaze darted back to the black SUV as it lined up with their front bumper.

"Slam on the brakes!"

Lundquist did, jerking the steering wheel to the right. The tires squealed and barked as they locked up. Behind them, the dark blue SUV darted into the other lane but wasn't in time to avoid clipping their rear bumper. The impact forced their car off the pavement and into the shallow ditch.

The SUV plowed into a barbed-wire fence, ripping the strands from the posts and wrapping the front end in sharp barbs. Kyle managed to navigate the vehicle over the bumpy cow pasture until the tires went flat. He angled the SUV so that the driver's side faced the road and brought the vehicle to a lurching halt.

"Shit, shit, shit!" Lila spewed, releasing the buckle on her seat belt.

The black SUV backed up, coming in line with them. It was at least five hundred yards out. Enough space for them to escape the interior of their car but not enough to race across the pasture.

On the opposite side of the road, the blue SUV was end up in the air, stuck in the ditch. The black SUV parked, the doors opened, and the occupants spilled out.

"Out!" Kyle yelled as the black-dressed figures raised weapons.

Lila shoved her door open and fell onto the ground. Beside her, Dominic dropped from his seat, his legs crumpling when his feet hit turf.

"Out of the way!" Kyle bellowed.

Gunfire erupted as he hit the field beside her. Bullets riddled the SUV's body, splintering glass and piercing the metal frame.

Lila ducked her head and scrambled toward a flattened tire. Wire snagged her pant leg and bit into her flesh. She tried to shake it free, but the wire only tightened its hold.

Hunkered down behind the rear tire, Kyle shielded Dominic's body. The gunfire continued, coming closer.

"Kyle!"

Abject fear filled his eyes. As a seafaring man, he had never been in the midst of a firefight before. His fear was justified.

Lila, on the other hand, had been in a few in her time as a beat cop in Chicago, but she hadn't faced off against the shooters without backup and a lot of it. Her hand went to her sidearm and unsnapped the leather strap securing her weapon in the holster.

Kyle's gaze dropped to her hand and then up. "Do it." He reached for his radio and began hailing for help.

She managed to free her leg from the wire and drew her weapon. Lila got herself situated facing the SUV's hood and readied to pop up over it.

There was a lull in the gunfire, and she reacted.

The shooters had moved within ten yards of their cover. She fired, hitting one of them, and adjusted her shot for another. Her second shot struck the second target's leg before the others turned their weapons in her direction. Lila ducked down as a hail of bullets rained against the SUV.

"They're circling to the back," she told Kyle.

He drew his pistol and positioned himself between the oncoming shooters and Dominic.

Another round of gunfire erupted, interrupting those shooting at them. The shouts of surprise were cut short.

Lila met Kyle's bewildered gape with her own. She turned back to the hood and popped up, her pistol at the ready. Four bodies were sprawled on the ground, the weapons being kicked away from their reach by a pair of men.

The front man, a familiar man, strode toward them. His partner, a familiar-looking Black man with bright white tape stretched over his nose remained where he could monitor the downed shooters.

Lila glanced at the road. The black SUV was gone. She lowered her weapon and straightened.

"What the hell?"

"Deputy Dayne," the familiar man said, "if you would so kindly relay to Deputy Lundquist that we're not the enemy."

She glanced down at Kyle. "It's that mystery man I told you about."

She noticed the hard expression on Dominic's face. Before she or Kyle could aid him, he scrambled awkwardly to his feet.

He stumbled out from behind the crippled SUV. "Horatio!"

Kyle bolted after the injured surgeon, catching up with and stopping him before he could go any farther. Lila joined the two, pulling up short when the second man lifted his rifle.

"Stand down. They're not a threat," said the one Dominic called Horatio as he holstered his sidearm.

His partner complied.

"Where's my wife?" Dominic demanded.

An ugly look crossed Horatio's broad face. "They took her, you stupid fuck."

Adrian Landry, the man behind Horatio, smirked.

Lila's gut pitched. "Who took Olivia and how?"

"I don't know *who* they are," Horatio snarled, his darkened gaze never leaving Dominic. "Olivia slipped my protection and managed to get back here. By the time I located her, *they* had wrecked the truck she was riding in and took her."

"You damn motherfucker. You swore to me she ain't gettin' harmed. You told me you'd protect her," Dominic screamed, his cultured voice slipping.

Horatio closed the gap between him and Dominic and glowered down at the weakened surgeon. "I did what we agreed. We both underestimated our woman."

"She ain't your woman," Dominic spit.

"She was always my woman."

Lila intervened, slipping between the two men and pushing Dominic toward Kyle. "I don't know what you two are talking about, but standing here in the middle of a cow pasture isn't going to get Olivia back."

Horatio adjusted his immaculate coat and lifted his chin. "Our little deputy has a point."

"Call me little again and I'll make sure you sing soprano for the rest of your life."

He chuckled, then turned to his man. "Adrian, get the car." He looked down at Lila. "We're leaving."

"Wait!" Kyle barked. "We can't leave these bodies here."

"What do you expect us to do?" Horatio asked. "We don't have time to deal with them."

"We should at least see if we know any of them," he insisted.

"Be my guest. You have as long as it takes for Adrian to get the car out of the ditch and back on the road." Horatio turned on his heel and walked back to the road.

Lila holstered her weapon. "We need to get out of here. Whoever was driving the black SUV will come back."

"Get out your phone and we'll get pictures," Kyle said.

"Why?"

"In case their bodies do a disappearing act when we leave, we'll at least have photo evidence."

Together, they removed the tactical-style masks and photographed each of the dead men. As they were finishing up, Lila noticed that Adrian almost had the car out of the ditch.

"Notice a trend here?" Lila asked as she jerked off the last man's face covering.

"They all look like they're of Hispanic background," Kyle offered.

"And they all have a tattoo." She tilted the dead man's head to the side and lifted his ear lobe to reveal the tattoo of a cross on his neck. "Think it has a certain meaning?"

Kyle snapped the photo. "Guess we'll find out."

"They have the car on the road," Dominic said.

Horatio watched them while he stood by the dark-blue SUV as she and Kyle assisted their injured surgeon over the ravaged terrain and into the back seat.

Lila met Horatio's dark gaze as Kyle climbed in, too. "Thank you."

"I wouldn't thank me. I had selfish reasons."

"Selfish or not, we wouldn't have survived that ambush. They had every intention of killing us."

"They did." Horatio moved as if to slide inside the car. "They're cartel. They never leave anyone alive."

CHAPTER THIRTY-FOUR

THE HUM OF a generator drew Elizabeth across the cracked and weed-infested pavement. The scattered bouts of wet snow had melted. What little remained clung to patches of tall grasses or bent stalks. No snow meant no prints, from either she and Rafe or the people they were seeking.

Rafe had parked the Interceptor along the edge of the old hospital lot. Walking up the slight hill, they'd passed a weather-beaten stone sign, the last feature of the once-proud hospital.

"Hear it?" she quietly asked Rafe. "Generator."

He drew his pistol and held it pressed to his chest, in a move much like something his brother would do when he wanted his gun ready but not to fire. "Be cautious. We're probably not the only ones here."

No more than two hundred yards before them was a squat, red brick building where the medical clinic had resided. The double-breasted entry doors were boarded up with slats. All windows facing them were covered in plywood. Young trees and overgrown bushes choked the walkway. If the demon men Elena mentioned were using this building for their nefarious means, they weren't coming through this direction.

Elizabeth armed herself. "If they are here, where are they hiding their transportation?"

Rafe pointed to their left. "Once upon a time, there was an ambulance barn behind the hospital, remember?"

How was she expected to remember that far back? The original Eckardt County hospital had been forced to shut down when she was a kid.

"I don't remember much of anything about this place," she admitted. "If they are using it, they're probably entering the facility through the backside."

"Makes sense." Rafe's head moved as if on a swivel. "From this side, their activities would be spotted."

"We're going to have to go around." She paused to survey the area. "Where is our backup? Someone should be here by now."

Rafe glanced at his watch. "Try them again."

A tremendous crash of metal came from inside the old clinic, startling them. They raced for the nearest tangle of wooded shrubbery closest to the building and hunkered down.

"Guess we're not alone," Elizabeth whispered.

After a quick perusal of their surroundings, Rafe leaned closer to her. "I bet they're moving whatever equipment and such they have in there. Next step would be to burn this place to the ground and destroy any remaining evidence."

"Not on my watch they ain't." Elizabeth pressed her radio mic. "Dispatch, this is Sheriff Benoit." She released the button and waited for the reply. Nothing came. Frowning, she tried again. "Dispatch, this is Sheriff Benoit, report." Again, eerie silence. "Georgia?"

More clattering of metal followed by an irritated shout drifted out of the old clinic.

"What do you suggest we do?" she asked her undersheriff.

Sounds, louder because they were closer, reached them. There was a definite distinction between heavy things being moved and people speaking to each other.

"It's your call," Rafe said. "We have no backup and no idea why we can't reach anyone."

"Think we could sneak in there and spy on them?"

A chuckle, low and very male, came from their right.

"I would advise against that, Sheriff."

Elizabeth gaped at the trio of men facing them, two of which held wicked-looking rifles pointed right at them.

"Things have already gotten messy enough. Don't make me add your bodies to the equation."

CHAPTER THIRTY-FIVE

L ILA INSISTED HORATIO'S man drive them to the sheriff's department. Horatio resisted at first, but a snide comment from Dominic made the man relent.

After the adrenaline from the shootout had faded from Lila's system, the realization that no one had acknowledged her radio summons began to gnaw at her. She couldn't say anything about it for fear of creating a stir when there was none.

As Adrian guided the SUV down the street toward the center of Juniper, Lila's sense of dread exploded into horror. Firetrucks, police cars, and ambulances were parked in haphazard fashion all over the streets around the courthouse.

Fires burned in the courthouse parking lot, the fire crews doing their best to contain the carnage. The remains of all their vehicles turned blackened by flames.

Lila and Kyle were out and running the moment the SUV stopped.

"What happened?" she demanded, startling a fireman rounding his truck.

Out of nowhere, the Juniper chief of police stepped into their path.

"Deputy Dayne, Lundquist. Wait!" He caught her arm before she could rush past him. "Hold on."

"Ed, so help me," Lundquist snarled coming back to free Lila.

"You two need to stay out of there."

Lila whirled on the chief. "Why?" Spittal flew from her mouth, hitting the man in the face.

"Lundquist! Dayne!" It was Joel marching across the lawn, heading right for them.

It hit Lila as he drew closer the dark blotches splattered over the man's uniform and face were the dried remnants of blood.

"Oh my God," she gasped.

"Joel," Lundquist rasped.

The elder Fontaine held up his hands—those, too, were coated in blood. "It's not mine, and it doesn't belong to any of our people."

"Then whose blood is it?" Lila choked out.

"The men who tried to murder us and my dog." The cold way Joel said it made Lila's head swim.

"What did you use to stop them?" Kyle asked. "A knife?"

An odd, feral expression crossed Joel's face. He was all special operations man, trained by some of the best of the best the United States Army had ever had the pleasure of calling their own. The man had also trained those who followed in the art form of protection with both gun and blade.

"Who was all in there with you?" Kyle continued.

"Now, Joel, you shouldn't be answering that," Ed intervened.

"I'll answer however I like, Chief. They're my people, and my ex-wife and brother are still missing."

Lila shook free of her shock. "Wait, what?" She shouldered Kyle out of the way. "They're missing? How?"

"I don't know for a fact they're missing," Joel amended. "We weren't able to follow up on Elizabeth's orders because we were attacked."

"What was their last known location?" Lundquist asked.

"LKL, they were on their way to some place northeast of here," Joel said. He squinted at Kyle. "You know where the old hospital site is?"

"I do. Why would they go there?"

"Beats the hell out of me."

From behind Joel came Meyer and Young—they, too, looked blood-spattered and dirty. Bookended by the deputies was Georgia, draped in a blanket the fire crew kept on hand, and next to her legs trotted Bentley. Georgia moved robotically, the shock evident on her face.

Ed reached out and drew their dispatcher close to him. "Georgia, I think you should go to the hospital and make sure you're okay."

"Ed, I told you once, I'll tell you a thousand times, I'm fine," she chided.

"Georgia, he's right. You should go," Kyle said.

Her eyes narrowed; Georgia stared him down. "Where's my car?"

Lila let him handle the explanation. She met Young's dark gaze. The woman had barely been back on the job and she was thrust into the middle of a gunfight.

"Young?"

"Dayne," Young responded, her voice hard.

"She's good, Dayne," Joel interceded. There was a hint

of pride in the man's voice. "She and Meyer handled themselves as well as any soldier I've served with."

Bentley had extracted herself from Georgia's side and was sitting at her former owner's feet. Joel crouched and scratched the dog's ears.

His words left Lila feeling cold inside. They were not soldiers; they were law enforcement officers. Of their group, Kyle was the solitary person with a military background. When had this little piece of Iowa become a war zone?

The cold seeping through her turned icy. Dominic had warned them at the hospital, assured that what was coming was worse than anything she or the department had faced before.

Alarm slithered down Lila's spine, and she turned back to the street where she and Kyle had left Horatio's vehicle. It was no longer there. She scanned the entire area. Nothing. She broke from the pack forming around her and jogged back the way she'd come, disregarding Kyle's call-out.

"Did you see a dark-blue SUV back here?" she asked a passing fireman.

He shook his head and resumed his duties.

Lila ran to the end of the block and pulled up short of stepping onto the street. It was gone. For how long, who knew. She let out a guttural shout.

"Where did he go?" Kyle asked, joining her.

"I don't know," she lashed out. "They probably left the moment we were out of the car."

"Think they knew what happened here?"

"Dominic wouldn't have, but that Horatio, maybe." Lila grabbed his arm. "Find us some usable vehicles. We need to get to the sheriff and Fontaine."

Meyer, who had joined them, cleared his throat. "Lila," he said, his voice roughened by either emotion or abuse. "I need to tell you something."

"Can it wait? We need to find the sheriff."

"No," he snapped.

Taken back by the force he used, she squared up to him. "Okay, what is it?"

"Before we were ambushed, I found out two things." He swiped his hand across his forehead, leaving behind black streaks. "First, the land deed you asked me to follow up on. The long-distant relative to the Norwoods is James Ross."

"Like Juniper PD Officer James Ross?" Lila asked.

"Apparently one and the same," Meyer confirmed. "Second, I did some digging around on that Dr. Pembrook, the anthropologist."

"Why?" Lila inserted.

"Something wasn't right about him. I called every single police agency involved in the discoveries of all those other boneyards, and three of the five confirmed that a Dr. Steven Pembrook was the forensic anthropologist on record to document the sites. Two of the other sites had on record a Dr. Samuel Alderman as the anthropologist."

Lila knew better than to interrupt Meyer when he was laying out information, but the Alderman name snagged her interest. "Alderman—that was the name of a doctor from a Chicago-based medical office." She groaned. "The sheriff called there, and I have no idea what she found out."

"I do," Meyer said. "Dr. Alderman retired more than a year ago from his practice and moved to Iowa. I couldn't find records of an Alderman who was a surgeon moving here, but I did find Dr. Steven Pembrook, formerly of Chicago, Illinois, had moved here and took over the forensic anthropologist."

Lila glanced at Lundquist, seeing the same confused look on his face she was certain was on hers "What are you saying, Meyer?"

"I'm saying, the guy is fishy. I wasn't able to find any photos online or a history. Why is a general surgeon listed as a forensic anthropologist? One other thing, on one of the case reports, Dr. A. S. Pollard, a forensic entomologist, from the University of Tennessee was on site. I called the university, and they told me there isn't and never was a record of anyone by that name associated with their forensic entomology department."

"Wait," Kyle interrupted. "A. S. Pollard? Our entomologist discovered that was the name associated with multiple purchases of the dermestid beetle."

Lila held up her hands. "Hold it. You're bombarding me with too much scattered information."

"Sorry," Meyer said. "What I'm saying is, this guy might be behind all these boneyards. And he's being backed financially by those asshats who just tried to kill us."

Lila couldn't place the man she'd worked with briefly at the boneyard as a man capable of running a black-market organ trafficking ring. "Guys, I'm just not seeing it."

"See it or not, we don't have a lot of time," Kyle reminded her.

"Fine, we roll with what we were told. We know the asshats are a Mexican cartel," Lila said.

"Who told us that?" Kyle demanded.

"Horatio."

Meyer held up a blackened hand. "Who's Horatio?"

"Don't have time to explain," she said. "We need to confiscate vehicles and get to that old hospital. I don't have a good feeling about the sheriff and Fontaine."

CHAPTER THIRTY-SIX

OLIVIA WAS PULLED from unconsciousness by fiery pain roaring through her head and her right leg. When she managed to open her eyes, there was a red haze in her right eye. She tried to move her arm, but it wouldn't move.

A clanking sound joined the thunder pounding in her ears. She blinked, managing to clear the haze, and regretted even opening her eyes. The sight next to her was bloody carnage. As her throbbing brain began to function, she realized the carnage was her arm, and it was latched to a steel pipe by a pair of smeared handcuffs.

She was seated against something hard, cold, and damp. Olivia shifted and groaned as a new wave of pain rocked her body. Breathing through the agony was her only recourse until numbness washed over her. Finally able to focus, she peered at the lower half of her body. She stifled the urge to weep at the mangled mess that was her right leg.

What happened to her?

The sound of footsteps penetrated the whooshing in her ears. A pair of tan tactical boots came into view. She lifted her head, a miracle in and of itself because if the sight of her bloodied appendages was anything to go off of, she should have a severe neck injury. The radiating pain was too much to tilt her head up any farther; she could only view the legs.

The owner of the boots tsked as he lowered himself. "Ya should've stayed where that Black bastard hid ya."

That voice. She knew it.

He grabbed her chin and forced her head up. Her damaged muscles screamed in agony. James Ross's ugly face came into view.

"That's better."

"Let. Go."

He bent closer. "Give me what I want, then I'll consider it."

"If … I don't?"

His free hand moved to her leg. Olivia's breathing accelerated. His hand hovered over the exact spot she saw bone protruding through flesh.

"You think you hurt now, bitch? I can make you scream." Ross's mouth was a hairbreadth away. "Make you wish you'd died."

Summoning a strength Olivia thought had vanished when she married Dominic, she glared back at Ross. "I can't answer what I don't know."

"We'll see about that." He inched back, giving her some breathing room. "Where's the money?"

Olivia schooled her face, despite a new wave of pain roiling through her. "What money?"

Ross's fingers skimmed over her shattered leg. The sensation overwhelmed the agony and made her whimper.

"You know what money. Your husband took it to that Chicago thug. So, what did he do with it?"

"I don't know."

Ross pressed a finger into her flesh. Fire screamed from

the point, and Olivia cried out.

"Just a taste. It's gonna get a whole lot worse if you keep this up."

"I swear … I don't know."

The pressure increased. She screamed. Four agonizing seconds went by before Ross released.

Tears cleared what red remained in Olivia's eyes as she sobbed.

"Where's the money?"

"I don't know. He wouldn't tell me."

Ross moved to touch her leg.

"Please, God, don't. Please."

"James, that's enough."

Ross pulled his hand away from her leg, and his gleeful expression melted into a hateful one. He dropped Olivia's head and straightened.

"You don't get anywhere coddling them," he snapped.

"She has a compound fracture and countless lacerations, along with, I'm certain, one doozy of a concussion. Creating unnecessary pain and more suffering will only make her pass out. Then where does that leave you?"

Ross moved away from her and stopped in front of whomever he was trading words with. "For a sadist, you sure do have a soft spot for this one."

"*Au contraire*, I am a pragmatist."

There was a scuffle, and Ross was forced backward until he was slammed into the wall near Olivia. She flinched.

"I find you inflicting any more harm on her, I will gut you."

She heard the slap of flesh on flesh and looked up. Ross

was pinned against the cement wall by a tall, towheaded man. From her advantage point on the floor, she couldn't tell anything more about the other man.

"This whole operation has turned into a huge fiasco. Escobar wants his money," Ross spat.

"He'll get it. Along with Thorpe's head on a silver platter," Towhead said, his voice dripping with venom.

"We'd already have Thorpe if that thug hadn't showed up."

Towheaded guy grabbed Ross's face and pinched his cheeks in. "And who's fault is that? Not only did Thorpe get away, but those damn deputies are still alive."

Ross tried to speak. His tormentor released his mouth. "I warned you it was a bad idea picking this area. That bitch sheriff is like a fucking dog with a bone."

"Ahh, speaking of which." Towheaded guy stepped back from Ross, freeing the crooked cop. "I come bearing gifts." He turned, keeping his back to Olivia and walked away.

Ross glanced down at her, smirked, and then followed.

Olivia watched them until they merged with the shadows. Unable to keep her head up, she let it drop, her chin cradled against her chest. God, how she wished for the oblivion of unconsciousness. Or even the luxury of a Percocet stupor.

Their voices echoed through the darkened corridor, but she couldn't make out what they said. Moments later, they returned.

Olivia forced her head upward and let it rest against the cement wall behind her. She made out the two men and a third form between them. That form wasn't walking, they were dragging it.

When they emerged into the dim lighting Olivia recognized the uniform. Fear numbed her agony.

The men unceremoniously dropped Elizabeth's body on the floor next to Olivia. Blood crusted the left side of Elizabeth's head.

"Lookee what we have here," Ross said as he reached down to slap a second set of cuffs on Elizabeth's wrist. "You won't have to die alone." He hauled Elizabeth closer to the same steel pipe trapping Olivia, slung the cuff through the gap, then secured Elizabeth's other wrist. "We get your husband and we'll complete the set."

Her fear slithered away, and in its place came the fury. "There are people still out there who'll hunt you down."

Towhead bent at the waist and stared into her eyes. "Oh, I'm counting on it. I especially look forward to locking horns with Deputy Dayne." His smile was too large, too clownish. Psychotic in a way. "That woman's mind fascinates me."

"Ross is right. You're sadistic."

He winked. "It's only the tip of the iceberg, Dr. Remington-Thorpe."

CHAPTER THIRTY-SEVEN

Day 3, Tuesday, February 27—5:28 p.m., 2 Hours Missing

DESPITE ED'S PROTESTS, the five remaining deputies confiscated two Juniper police vehicles. Joel managed to talk one of the volunteer firefighter slash paramedic guys into letting him use his truck—a tricked-out rig equipped with bells and whistles one would find in an actual ambulance—as long as the owner came with. The guy agreed.

Lila didn't disagree. With the way this day had gone, they were all in need of a few extra medically trained hands.

Before she left the courthouse, she made Ed promise to call in the Iowa State Troopers and send them to the scene where they'd left Georgia's destroyed SUV. Once there, they were to relay their findings. Lila hoped there were four dead guys and a disabled car. But Lady Luck was being a real bitch lately.

Her radio chirped. She glanced at the top screen. Joel. She hit the mic. "You need something, Fontaine?" She cringed. So weird.

Next to her, Kyle grunted, never taking his eyes off the darkening road.

"We just got a radio call for a second accident scene."

Lila swallowed, refusing to look at the man driving. "Where was it?" she asked into the mic.

"Three blocks from the Thorpe's cul-de-sac. Report says it was an older model pickup. No signs of another vehicle."

"Horatio mentioned Olivia had been taken," Kyle said. "Think that's how they did it?"

"It's how they came after us," Lila said absentmindedly. She got the sense Joel wasn't telling her everything. She pressed the mic button. "Is that all?"

In the seconds it took for Joel to answer, Kyle killed the headlights and pulled into an old parking lot left for Mother Nature to overrun.

"The driver's deceased."

Lila closed her eyes and hung her head.

"It's not Dr. Remington-Thorpe," Joel followed up. "It was an elderly woman."

It didn't make it any better to hear an innocent bystander had been sucked into this hellish nightmare and lost their life. One more candle added to the countless hundreds already extinguished.

"Dayne, the accident wasn't what killed her," Joel said over the radio.

Lila brought her head up. Liquid heat surged through her. "Then what did?"

Lundquist parked in the middle of the lot. Meyer pulled up along their right side, and Joel swung the truck off to their left and parked perpendicular to the other vehicles.

"Gunshot. Execution style."

Lila let go of the mic and slammed her palms against the dashboard. "Fuck!"

She sat there, breathing hard, letting the fury fuel her. Kyle remained quiet, his hands still gripping the steering wheel.

"We do this smart," he said, reaching down to turn the key.

They exited the car together and headed to the rear hatch. A large black storage box sat in the cargo area. Paraphernalia every cop would potentially need on the job for every situation was laid out neatly inside the box's top drawers. The larger, bottom drawer held a shotgun and a rifle along with ammo for each. Kyle let Lila take the rifle, and he handled the shotgun.

Armed, they met up with the others in front of the vehicles. Their backup paramedic was ordered to stay with his vehicle. If he was needed, they'd call him.

In the red glow of their muted flashlights, Joel looked expectantly at Lila. "Here's your battlefield promotion."

"I don't do in charge," she stated.

He scowled. "You're the higher-ranking deputy."

"I might be, but I don't have this sort of experience." She jutted her chin at him. "You do. I'm deferring to you in this situation."

"Damn it, Dayne. That ain't how this works. This is only my second day on the job."

"Okay. Let me ask you; how would you approach this?"

Joel glared at her. "I'm not comfortable with the position you're putting me in."

"We don't have time for you to sort out your feelings on the matter." Lila slapped his vested chest. "Lead. It's what you were trained to do."

Her verbal jab and the follow-up right hook did the job. Joel shifted into commando mode and began barking out orders.

Joel divided them, pairing Lila with Meyer and Kyle with Young. Joel would go it alone, doing reconnaissance outside. It only made sense.

"Stay in radio contact," he ordered. "Let's go."

Everyone split to their designated positions and moved on the old clinic. Lila and Meyer circled to the rear part of the building.

"I still don't see the sheriff's car," Meyer said.

If the department attackers had wiped out their vehicles, why wouldn't they do the same to the sheriff's car?

"I don't see any fire, so that's something," Lila mentioned.

They plowed through the mini forest growing wild around the rundown brick structure, emerging onto a well-used path. Taking care not to disturb anything, they rounded the edge of the building and stopped.

A large docking bay door was left open. Black garbage bags were piled next to it. No lights. No sounds.

"Whaddya think?" Meyer asked.

"Keep going."

At the bay door, Lila pulled up, pressing her body against the brick wall. Meyer stationed himself at her side, facing out. When he turned back to her, she motioned for him to prepare to enter.

On three, they swung around, weapons raised and flashlights piercing the darkness. More piles of trash were scattered about the bay. The stench of rotting meat made Lila want to gag.

They crept along, sweeping the beams of their lights over

the whole docking bay. It was a disaster. It looked like they had been rushing to clear out and decided to give up.

A rattling sound brought them up short. They both directed their lights on a set of wood doors with the upper half in glass. Down the center of the glass, a smear of dark red made Lila's throat constrict.

Banging came from the other side.

She and Meyer moved as one. Upon reaching the doors, she saw the crack in one. She grabbed the handle and yanked it open. A body spilled onto her boots.

"Fontaine." She flung the door wider and wedged her body between it and Fontaine. "Meyer, alert the others."

She slung the rifle behind her back and squatted down next to the undersheriff. He was bloody.

Lila grabbed Fontaine's coat and dragged him into the docking bay. "Meyer, get the EMS guy in here."

Positioned between the doors and the loading dock, Meyer barked orders into the radio while keeping a lookout.

Lila went to work assessing Fontaine's injuries. Except he kept swinging his arms about wildly, thwarting her attempts to get the coat off.

"Stop it!" she barked. "What happened?"

"Ellie," he choked out and coughed blood.

"Fuck!"

Lila finally managed to get the coat unzipped and jerked it open, then pointed her flashlight at him. His uniform top below the Kevlar was saturated. How was he coughing blood?

"I need your light," she told Meyer, setting her flashlight aside.

He aimed his beam directly on Fontaine. Lila got to work ripping away the Kevlar's Velcro straps and peeling the vest away from his shirt. Numerous holes punctured the lower half of fabric. Had to be buckshot, which meant shotgun. Fontaine's saving grace was his Kevlar—it had taken the brunt of the shot. But some of those round balls had found flesh.

He struggled with her, grappling to get a hold on her hands. "Ellie," he croaked again.

"Stop it. You're going to die if I don't get it under control." Lila restrained him and met his dilated gaze.

Her statement seemed to penetrate his addled mind and his arms went slack.

The beam from Meyer's light bounced.

"Keep it steady," she snarled.

Fontaine's throat worked furiously. His breath was becoming more wet sounding.

"Shit-shit-shit-shit. I think he got a round in his lung."

Over their desperate breathing and Fontaine's gurgling, Lila made out the sounds of pounding feet.

Fontaine reached up and grasped her arm, marking her with his blood. He tried to squeeze, but she barely registered the feel. She paused in her attempts to stem the flow of blood and locked gazes with him.

A fist of panic socked Lila hard in the chest as his eyes began to lose their gleam.

"Damn it, Rafe, don't you die on me."

Red-coated bubbles danced in the corner of his mouth.

Outside the docking bay, shouts reached them. Meyer yelled for the medic to hurry up.

Fontaine lifted his hand and managed to grasp Lila's head. She leaned closer.

"Find … Ellie …" His hand dropped from her. His eyes rolled back.

"Rafe!" Lila slapped his face. "Rafe, no!"

The clatter of the paramedic dropping his gear beside her drowned out her pleas.

"Deputy, move!" he barked.

Lila was pulled away from Fontaine. The moment she was gone, her space was filled by the trained medic. As the man worked frantically to save the undersheriff, Lila felt herself being yanked around.

"Dayne!" Joel's fierce bark shook her.

"What?" she snapped back.

"Good. I need you right here, right now," he said.

Someone could have knocked her over and she wouldn't have fought it. How did the man keep his head? It was his brother lying on the floor fighting for his life. He should be a mess.

"Listen to me," he said. "Young is going to drive them to the hospital. I have a site rep on where they took Ellie."

"How the hell do you know that already?"

Kyle materialized next to them and held out a note. Lila ripped it from his hand and stared at it. The words were written in blood. She looked from the sheet of paper to the man prone on the floor with a frantic medic working over him. Fontaine had ensured that if he'd died before they found him, they would know where to find the sheriff.

"He must have overheard the people who took the sheriff," she said. "I know where this old fountain pen factory is."

Joel gripped her shoulder. "Then we do it."

He was in full soldier mode. "Shouldn't you be with your brother?"

"I want to, Dayne, but I need to find my ex-wife and her friend. I'm trusting the right people to handle it."

The paramedic looked back at them. "Call in a helicopter. He's got to be air lifted to Iowa City."

"They can land in the parking lot," Kyle said. "Meyer, Young, help me move the cars."

"Dayne," Joel coaxed. "Get the helicopter here."

"On it," she said. "Before we leave for Fort Madison, I'm ordering backup."

"The more the merrier."

CHAPTER THIRTY-EIGHT

Day 3, Tuesday, February 27—7:45 p.m., 4 Hours Missing

"ELIZABETH."

Her name dragged Elizabeth from the dark pit.

"Ellie, get up."

That was an urgent hiss. Her head ached. Her arms hurt. Why did she feel like she was lying on something cold and wet?

"Come on, Ellie. Wake up."

That voice. It was familiar. She opened her eyes, blinking against the red glow.

"Thank God."

A figure in front of her took shape—a bloodied and broken woman was seated beside her.

"Olivia." She bolted upright only to be jerked down. "Ow."

"You're cuffed," Olivia explained. "If you can get up, be careful. My leg is next to you, and it's severely broken." She sounded winded.

Elizabeth wormed her way up the wall, careful to avoid touching Olivia. The exertion it took to get herself in a more comfortable position to take the pressure off her strained arms was draining and left her head throbbing. She rested the side of her head against the wall and regretted it at the bolt of pain.

"You have a gash on your head," Olivia said, her own head cradled in the crook of her secured arm.

Ignoring the pain, Elizabeth studied her friend. Along with her broken leg, she was supporting a blood-crusted, dirty cast on her left arm, multiple lacerations all over her face and on her right arm that was also cuffed to a steel pipe. Olivia looked weak, defeated.

"What happened? Where did you go?" Elizabeth asked gently.

Olivia gazed at her with drooping eyes. "Where I went ... that will take too long." She gasped a few times. "How I got like this ... car accident."

"Do you know where we are?" Elizabeth tried.

"No." Olivia sighed, closing her eyes. She looked ready to pass out.

God, Elizabeth recognized the signs of internal bleeding. She well knew what it felt like.

"Olivia, stay with me."

Slowly, her friend opened her eyes. She gave a tepid smile. "It's okay, Ellie. You need to worry about yourself."

"No, it's not okay. I have a concussion, I'll be fine. You're dying."

"What a crying shame."

Elizabeth snarled at the approaching male. "Ross."

He stepped into the halo of red light. "Took you long enough." He moved closer.

"Stay away." Elizabeth kicked out.

He danced back, avoiding her strike. "Pembrook should have let them end you when they took out Fontaine."

The memory assaulted her. Just before Pembrook's gunman bashed in the side of her head with a stock, they made her watch as they shot Rafe. She swallowed the grief with a fierce growl.

"I'm going to rip him limb from limb, then I'll beat you to death with his remains."

A chuckle came from behind Ross, then Pembrook joined his partner. "Perhaps I underestimated your drive, Sheriff. Here I thought my greatest threat was your deputy detective." He crouched down to her level. "You should give into your grief. He didn't survive."

Elizabeth ground her molars, but her treacherous eyes filled with tears.

"Pembrook?" Olivia lifted her head from her arm. "Steven Pembrook. Forensic anthropologist." Her eyes narrowed. "Or is it A. S. Pollard, forensic entomologist? Perhaps, maybe, Samuel Alderman? The man behind my husband's desire to be a surgeon."

Pembrook grinned. "My, she is a treasure. I see now why Dominic was enamored with you."

Elizabeth shifted, alleviating the weight on her arms. "How does Dominic figure into all of this?"

"He blackmailed my husband into doing his dirty work," Olivia said, her voice gathering strength.

"Blackmail is such an ugly word." Pembrook stood upright. "It didn't take too much pressure to convince him this was the right thing to do."

"Until he grew a conscience," Elizabeth provided.

"More like brought in outsiders," Ross growled.

Olivia gave her own dark chuckle, ending it with a gasp.

Elizabeth watched her friend gather herself and glare at Pembrook and Ross.

"You've made a multitude of mistakes in the last few days." She took a few breaths and soldiered on. "Your gravest one was pissing off Horatio Johnson."

"That Black bastard," Ross scoffed. "He'll be dealt with accordingly."

Pembrook gripped Ross's shoulder and shoved him back a step, then turned to Olivia. "I don't fear Mr. Johnson. I've seen worse men than him fall under Escobar's might." He lowered himself to look Olivia in the eye. "I know Dominic gave him the money. I also know in the few days Johnson had you in his clutches, he told you things. Like where he put the money."

"I'll tell you what I told your prick of a partner. I don't know."

Elizabeth rattled her cuffs against the pipe, drawing the men's attention to her. "So, this is what this is all about? Money?"

"Oh, it's about more than that, Sheriff." Once again, Pembrook rose to his full height. "At this juncture, there's no point in explaining any of it to you since you're not long for this world. However, there is a reason I kept you alive for the moment."

"To drag me to some Godforsaken hellhole to gloat and force me to watch my best friend die?"

"That's a mere bonus. But no. You have something of mine. The whole reason this well-oiled operation spun out of control and Dominic Thorpe went rogue on me."

"I don't have a blessed thing of yours."

"You might not have it, but you know who does. Where's the girl?"

Elizabeth had anticipated this, her gut feeling kicking in and helping her keep her expression slack. No way was she giving this sick man an inch. Elena had escaped his clutches. Her brother had paid the ultimate sacrifice to ensure his sister would live. Elizabeth would not betray them. Not on her watch.

A wicked smile tugged at her mouth. She tilted her chin up and stared right at Pembrook with a defiance born of grief and hatred. If what she knew was keeping her alive, she'd drag this out as long as her team needed to find them. He would not win this day.

"I don't know about any girl."

Elizabeth saw a flash of anger flicker over Pembrook's features. He adjusted his composure and returned her smile with a half-cocked grin.

"James, the water."

An amused grunt from Ross as he walked away made Elizabeth stiffen. She glanced at Olivia, whose head was lulling against her chest. Whatever strength she'd mustered to confront Pembrook had sapped her of the last of her reserves.

When Ross returned seconds later, he carried a bucket. Before Elizabeth had a chance to protest, he threw the contents on them. Water slammed into Elizabeth and Olivia, momentarily pulling Olivia out of her stupor.

Sputtering, Elizabeth spit water from her mouth and shook her head to clear it from her eyes.

"I'm certain you realize the position you're in, Sheriff.

The temperature is predicted to be in the teens tonight. This facility has no heat." Pembrook's grin looked evil with the watery red glow skewing Elizabeth's vision. "You're now soaked with water." He studied Olivia. "I give Dr. Remington-Thorpe only hours to live." His attention returned to Elizabeth. "You have thirty minutes to come to your senses and tell me where the girl is."

"If I don't have the answers you want?"

"Tick, tock."

Pembrook and Ross left, melding into the shadows like the evil wraiths she took them to be.

Elizabeth gave up holding herself upright and sank to the floor. In the last few hours, she had lost everything. Why did she bother to toy with this psychopath? When he ordered Rafe's death, she'd lost the last thing tethering her. She had nothing more to give.

Next to her, Olivia slumped, her body tilted away from her secured arm. She hung there unable to lay down and passed out.

"Liv, hang on," Elizabeth begged. "Please, don't leave me."

CHAPTER THIRTY-NINE

Day 3, Tuesday, February 27—9:23 p.m., 6 Hours Missing

LILA WATCHED JOEL pace as he spoke on the phone with the hospital. Around them a slew of law enforcement personnel milled about, oblivious to the man on the phone.

She looked down at her hands. Before they'd left the old clinic site, right after Fontaine was airlifted out of Juniper, she had been given hand wipes to remove his blood. Despite her best efforts, some remained. Clenching her hands into fists, she closed her eyes and then lowered her fists to her sides. The sharp metallic scent lingered in her nostrils. His pleas for her to find the sheriff echoed in her head.

A hand on her shoulder jolted her out of her reverie. She looked up at Kyle.

"You okay?" he asked, his voice pitched low and intimate.

An unfathomable urge to crawl into his arms and let him secret her away from here took hold of Lila. Everything was moving too fast. She was exhausted and running on sheer adrenaline. Her body ached. Her head was pounding. And she was the last man standing in this whole hellish horror show.

"I don't know," she said.

Kyle guided her around to face him, keeping as little of a

gap between them as possible. She inhaled the scent of him. The odor of sweat, an undertone of BO, and musk overpowered the pungent smell of blood. She relished the smell of an unwashed working man any day over blood.

"I'm not gonna lie—I'm scared right now," he said. "If we lose Ellie. And Rafe."

"We're not losing them," Lila asserted.

"Lila, we have to face reality."

She shook her head. He grasped it between his hands and held her still, tilting it up so he could look in her eyes.

"Listen to me." He bent closer. "I think you need to sit this one out."

Heat singed her cheeks. She clenched her jaw and glared at him.

"Don't get pissed at me," he pleaded. "I can't …"

It hit her. What he wanted to say but couldn't. He was more scared of losing her. They'd both suffered enough in their lifetime, maybe she more so than he, but loss was the same no matter which way they sliced it. Her anger melted.

Lila reached up and cupped her hands around the back of his neck and lowered his head until their foreheads touched. "I'm not going anywhere."

His shoulders rose and fell. "You're too stubborn for your own good."

"It keeps me alive." She gently tapped her forehead to his. "You're the one with the Viking hard head."

"Promise me you won't take any unnecessary risks."

"You should be making that promise to me, too."

"Lundquist! Dayne!" Joel's staccato voice broke through their connection.

"No unnecessary risks, please," Kyle said.

"I promise." She tightened her hold on him, refusing to let him get away.

"Ditto," he said finally.

"Let's go," Joel commanded, closer this time.

They exchanged another tap to their foreheads and broke apart. Together they joined Joel and Meyer, who were part of a larger contingent of LEOs.

With Ed's help, Lila was able to call in the Iowa State Troopers tactical force, along with the Fort Madison Police Department. The Lee County Sheriff's Office was on standby. As before, she assigned Joel to coordinate the joint efforts between all three departments. They were staged in a grassy lot next to a building material business and a block away from their target—a sprawling defunct fountain pen factory.

"How certain are you on the intel?" the troopers' commander asked Joel.

"Ninety-five percent," Joel stated bluntly. "It's the most logical position. Abandoned factory, close to the water, with a marina next door."

"We're going to need to clear out all those houses on the other side of the street," the commander pointed out.

"Already being done," the police captain said. "My crew is evacuating residents right now."

"What's the excuse?" Lila asked.

"Report of a natural gas leak in the factory," the captain reported. He laid out three layers of blueprints. "There's a lot of square footage to cover in that factory and four floors." He pointed to the prints for the older sections of the building.

"This section has a basement, but it faces the houses across the street. I don't know if your abductors would use this portion of the building."

"We check it all, Captain," Joel stated, his voice brokering no argument.

The captain dipped his head. "Your call, Deputy." His gaze shifted to Lila, held for a moment, then he resumed explaining the layout.

Once they had a solid idea of the floor plans, Joel commenced with assignments. Lila and Kyle were split up and assigned with a state trooper tactical team. Joel slated Meyer with the police officers to recon the marina, watch for any attempts for flight on the river. Those officers not going to the marina were positioned outside the factory as secondary forces. Lila appreciated Joel keeping the less experienced away from the potentially worst of the fighting.

Lila hurried along at his side as they headed for their vehicles. "What's the status on your brother?"

He looked down at her, his features marred by the swath of face paint. "He was stable when the helo landed in Iowa City. They were taking him straight to emergency surgery."

"Are you sure you don't want to be there with him?"

Joel pulled up outside the driver's side door of his borrowed truck. "Dayne, I can't do jack shit up there sitting in a waiting room. Elizabeth was taken, she could be seriously injured, and as you've so elegantly put it, I'm the best man for the task of rescuing her and Olivia." He jerked the door open. "It's what Rafe would have told me to do, not blubber over him."

"Just checking." She turned to grab the back door of the

dual cab behind Joel.

"Are you checking for me? Or for yourself?" he asked.

Lila glanced over her shoulder. "A bit of both." With that, she hopped inside the cab.

They were joined by Kyle and Meyer. In the short time it took to leave the grassy lot and creep up the street to the defunct factory, Lila had checked her weapons and ensured she had enough clips for both the rifle and her sidearm.

Teams dispersed from their vehicles at allocated points around the factory. After fist bumping each of his fellow deputies, Meyer hopped a ride down to the marina with his squad. Before he joined his group, Kyle caught Lila and snuck a kiss.

"Remember," he said and then hurried off.

Lila stared at his retreating backside until Joel swatted her shoulder and pointed for her to move.

She'd been paired with the state trooper commander and two of his guys. Everyone else had three-man teams. Lila guessed she was a fourth to have an extra set of eyes on her just in case. Fine by her. She was out of practice for this kind of thing.

Their group had been given the west dock entrance of the factory. The commander had them set up, ready to breach on Joel's command. Lila, her back to the two front men, watched their six and listened, waiting.

A loud crack echoed over the river. Lila sensed the men at her back stiffen. Two more cracks followed. She separated from the group.

"You guys hear that?" she asked.

"I swear it's gunshots," one of the troopers said.

Their radios clicked, and Meyer came over the connection. "Delta One, we have gunfire."

Before anyone could respond to Meyer's alert, more shots echoed, a lot in rapid succession.

"It's coming from the next block over," Lila said. She grabbed her mic and activated it. "Delta Three is responding." She bolted, racing across the old lot.

One of the men shouted behind her, but she didn't have time for them to figure it out. Lila tore across a grassy median, a sidewalk, then hit the paved street. Her gear bounced against her body, trying to slow her. She dug in and kicked up her pace at the echo of more gunfire.

Her path took her through a small park, then a store parking lot. At the next street, closer to the gunfight, she was joined by her team.

"We've got eyes on the shooters," the commander said.

In a tiny lot filled with rundown cars, shadowy figures were shooting back at an older building next door. From above, bright flashes of light showed return fire. Some of the lot shooters went down.

Lila veered to the commander's right. "We don't know if they're friend or foe."

Her quandary was resolved when the lot shooters swung around and began shooting at them. Instinct kicked in and she joined the men in returning fire. They kept moving until they took positions behind cars. Lila found herself pressed up against the east side of the auto shop. While the troopers were engaging with the lot shooters, Lila peeked around the corner.

There were at least fifty yards between where she stood

and the building everyone seemed focused on. Lila swung to her left and assessed her options. There was another way to the building.

"Commander!"

He was the closest man to her. He lowered himself behind the truck he used as a barrier.

"Dayne?"

She pointed at the open space to her left, then him, and jabbed a thumb into her chest.

He nodded, then shifted into a crouch. He gave her the signal he was coming. She laid down cover fire as he darted to her position. Once there, they left the spot at the corner and trotted to the north side of the shop.

Rounding the corner, they surprised another man with the same idea. The commander handled the situation. Lila ran forward, using the building's shadow to mask her progress.

At the west end, she and the commander paused. To their right was a brick structure, a garden shed or something like it. Ahead was an open area right behind the building, what was once the garden maybe. Along the building's side were multiple access points—three of them were open, and one had a body slumped in the doorway.

"What next, Deputy?" the commander asked.

"We get inside."

"Just how do you propose we do that?"

Behind the brick building a shadow shifted. Lila slapped a hand into the commander's chest. She spotted the glint of light on metal.

"Someone's behind the building," she told the commander.

And they were sitting ducks if the figure made them.

Silence blanketed the entire block. Lila held her breath, waiting for the next shot, but there was none coming.

Quietly, over the radio, came the hail. "Delta Three, report."

"Deputy Dayne," came a familiar voice from across the yard. "You're in the wrong place."

She heard the sharp intake of breath from the commander. She tapped his arm and then slipped from the protection of the auto shop.

"Horatio? What do you mean I'm in the wrong place?"

"The women ain't here," he said, coming out of the shadows.

"If they're not here, then what was this all about?"

"Evening the odds, Deputy. These men were placed here to ambush your people. You need to go back where you were."

"We came to help."

"There was no need for that. My guys had it handled."

"Guys?" Lila watched as four men emerged from the building. The taller one she took to be Adrian. "Where's Dominic?"

"Settling a score. You better go help him."

Lila's radio popped, and Joel's voice came over. "Delta Three, status, report."

"Deputy, we need to get back," the commander said.

Before she could respond, gunfire broke out at the marina.

Meyer came over the radio. "Contact at the marina.

Need back up!"

"Better hurry, Deputy," Horatio said. "We've got Escobar's men."

"Escobar?"

"Dayne!" the commander barked.

"Go!" Horatio said.

Lila ground her molars, turned on her heel, and ran for the street. The three troopers right in step with her.

"Delta Three enroute," she yelled into the radio as they hurtled the railroad tracks dividing the street from the marina. "Hang on, Meyer. I'm coming."

CHAPTER FORTY

WHEN THE SHOOTING began, it sounded more like firecracker pops to Elizabeth. She'd dozed off at some point after Pembrook left them. The *pop*, *pop*, *pop* brought her fully awake.

She hauled herself upright, stilled, and listened. The sounds increased in quantity and volume. Something was going down.

Elizabeth checked on Olivia. Despite the low lighting, she could make out Olivia's chest still rising and falling.

"Olivia."

No response. Elizabeth tried again, a little louder. The same result. A few more tries and Olivia would not come to. Elizabeth looked at her friend's mangled leg and an idea took root.

"Oh, such a bad idea."

The gunfire was joined by men's shouts. Elizabeth watched the darkened passageway, waiting to see if someone was coming. After a few moments and no one appeared, she plowed forward with her awful idea to get Olivia awake.

"Liv, I'm so sorry to do this." With her boot, she nudged Olivia's broken leg, just hard enough to make it move.

Olivia's reaction was instantaneous. She let out a garbled screech and arched her back.

"Oh God, Olivia, I'm sorry," Elizabeth babbled. "I didn't know any other way."

Gasping, Olivia rolled her head back and forth. "Wha-what?"

"Liv, look at me. Olivia."

Her voice seemed to penetrate what had to be a raging storm of anguish going through her friend. Olivia, breathing heavily and letting out stuttering cries, looked at Elizabeth. "Ellie?"

The rip of gunfire interrupted them, drawing Olivia's attention.

"What is going on?" she asked haltingly.

"I don't know, but it doesn't sound good."

Elizabeth had a fleeting moment of hope that her deputies had pulled together a crew and were coming to their rescue. But she dashed it—it wasn't possible for any of them to know where to even begin to look for her or Olivia. The only person who knew who took her was dead.

"Maybe it's that Escobar guy turning on Pembrook," Elizabeth offered.

"Maybe," Olivia whispered.

Elizabeth could see she was losing Olivia to the dark pull of unconsciousness again. "Liv, you can't pass out. I need you to stay with me."

"Let me die … on my own … terms," she panted.

"Not in a million years. We're not giving that self-important prick the satisfaction."

Olivia's head lulled to the side.

"Don't make me hurt your leg again to keep you awake," Elizabeth begged.

Olivia's eyes snapped open, and she stared at Elizabeth. "Don't … please."

The clank of metal against a hard surface echoed up the passageway. Furiously muttered words joined the sound.

Elizabeth forced her body as upright as she could, ready to face whoever was coming their way. Olivia attempted to curl closer, but with her injuries she couldn't.

Ross staggered into the pool of red light. He held his left shoulder. Something dark and wet seeped between his fingers. A pistol dangled from his left hand. He stopped at Olivia's outstretched body.

"Fuck!" he barked.

He weaved, glaring at them. "I don't give two shits what he thinks." He released his shoulder and reached down to take the gun into his hand.

"Ross," Elizabeth said.

"Shut up, bitch!" He gripped the pistol and lifted it toward Olivia.

Olivia, unable to move or avoid his aim, let out a hoarse scream.

"Ross, no!"

"I die tonight. So do you," he said.

Elizabeth screamed with Olivia as Ross steadied his aim.

The repercussive report of a weapon stopped their screams. Ross's eyes were wide as he crumpled to the floor. Olivia let out a horrific cry as his body collapsed on her broken leg.

Elizabeth gaped at the huge, bloody wound at the back of Ross's head. Another man emerged from the shadows, lowering his weapon.

"Dominic?"

He ignored her and rushed to his wife. He set his weapon aside and took hold of Ross's body and flung it away from the sobbing Olivia.

Elizabeth sank against the wall.

"Liv, shhh, it's going to be all right," Dominic assured her.

"Are you the one causing all this chaos?" Elizabeth asked him.

"No." He glanced over at her. "It's some kind of tactical team. I don't know who it is." His attention returned to his wife. "She's bad."

"No shit, Sherlock," Elizabeth snapped. "Get her out of here."

"I can't carry her. Not in my condition and not with her like this."

Dominic looked around, trying to locate something, then scrambled over to Ross's lifeless form. He searched the man's pockets and must have found what he was looking for. When he returned to Olivia, he held a small metal object that looked nothing like a cuff key. He started in on the cuff securing Olivia's bloodied arm to the pipe, having her free in seconds. After lying her arm across her abdomen, careful to avoid her cast, Dominic shifted over to Elizabeth and set to work freeing her.

"Where did you learn how to pick locks?" Elizabeth asked as he popped one cuff.

"Not a question I'll ever answer, Sheriff," he said and jimmied the lock on the other cuff.

With Elizabeth freed, he returned to Olivia's side.

"Baby, I'm so sorry for this." He cupped her battered face. "I never wanted any of this."

"He blackmailed you," she said.

Stiff and hurting in every limb and muscle, Elizabeth struggled to get her feet under her.

"It wasn't a valid reason to put you at risk," Dominic said. "My pride got the better of me."

"Because of your brother," Olivia supplied.

This stymied Elizabeth. She looked between the two, waiting for the rebuttal.

"My brother is ..." he started.

"I don't give a rat's ass," Olivia cut him off. "What's in the past is in the past. You knew about mine. There was no need to hide yours."

"Being Horatio's woman." He sighed. "I shouldn't have involved you in my life. My brother was always going to drag me into one rotten scheme after another."

"I was going to get involved anyway," Olivia sobbed.

"I'm so sorry for the hell I've put you through the last few years."

Elizabeth jerked at the scoffing laugh.

Pembrook, aiming a pistol at Dominic's back, emerged. He looked even worse than Ross had.

It was at that moment Elizabeth realized she didn't hear gunfire. She looked to the passageway Pembrook guarded. Empty.

"How touching," Pembrook mocked. "Feel like you've whitewashed your sins, Thorpe?"

Dominic remained cradling his wife's face. "There's nothing to whitewash. I'm resigned with facing my misdeeds and accepting the consequences."

Pembrook's laugh was twisted. "Don't give me that holier than thou shit. We both know you did this for the cash." He jerked. "I wouldn't," he snapped. "Keep your hand away from that gun. Get up and face me."

When there was no move from Dominic to do as he was ordered, Pembrook shifted his aim, directing it on Elizabeth. She had the fortitude not to flinch, instead staring him down.

"Move, Thorpe, or I shoot your sheriff. Be such a shame all that work you did to patch her up and keep her alive was a waste if I just pop her off right here."

"As if you had any other intention of leaving me alive," Elizabeth snarled.

"Leave her out of this," Dominic said. He bent forward and kissed Olivia. "I love you."

"Dominic, no," Olivia wept as he disengaged with her and stood.

Elizabeth looked for the gun and found it on the other side of Olivia. Too far from her reach.

Dominic rotated and faced Pembrook. "What now?"

"James was right. This turned into a cluster fuck the moment I chose this Godforsaken spot in Iowa." Pembrook's weapon returned to Dominic. "Time to cut my losses and run. I disposed of your brother, and you remedied me having to deal with Ross."

"When'd you kill my brother?"

"Why does it matter? You both got out of hand. So, where did you have that gangster prick hide the money?"

"I don't know what he did with it. That was the agreement."

"I'm getting so fucking tired of people saying they don't know," Pembrook yelled. "Tell me, Thorpe, what do you know?"

Something in the passageway caught Elizabeth's eye. She squinted at the spot, and it moved again.

"I know this doesn't end well for you," Dominic said.

A familiar form materialized from the shadowed depths of the passageway. Elizabeth had to clamp down on the urge to gasp.

"Lower your weapon," Joel said, his tone lethal.

Pembrook stiffened, then made an amused noise. "The Fontaine brother. He said you'd hunt me down."

"Lower your weapon," Joel asserted.

"Or you'll do what?" Pembrook yelled. "Shoot me in the back? Is that the type of deputy the good sheriff here wants in her office?"

The threads of fury weaved together and snapped taut at his words. This man had ordered the death of a man Elizabeth had been in love with for years. He'd been instrumental in the deaths of hundreds of innocent people. For what? Money? Power? A need to fulfill his ego?

Elizabeth looked at her ex-husband. "Do it," she ordered.

Shock filled Pembrook's face. The astonishment melted away, replaced by resignation. "I underestimated you."

The simultaneous shots reverberated off the concrete walls. There was a moment of stunned silence.

Pembrook flopped to the floor, blood beginning to drench his chest.

Dominic dropped to his knees and lingered there. Olivia's screams replaced the silence. She scrabbled around to catch Dominic's tilting body. His chest, too, was bloody.

Elizabeth's dam broke and she began sobbing. Joel reached out to her, and she grabbed his lifeline. He kept his weapon pointed at Pembrook and dragged Elizabeth close. Incoherent words spilled from her; she didn't even know what she was saying.

Joel caught her face in his free hand and forced her to look at him. "Rafe is alive."

His words penetrated her addled brain.

"How?"

"Don't worry about how. He's in surgery. But he's alive."

Like her friend, Elizabeth dissolved into uncontrollable weeping. She buried her face into Joel's neck and clung to him. She heard him tell her it was over.

At what cost?

EPILOGUE

Week 3: Tuesday, March 19, 11:25 a.m.

T HE SUN SHOULDN'T be shining. The weather shouldn't be warm with a nice breeze. They should not be standing in a graveyard in the middle of the day.

Elizabeth's stiff dress uniform helped keep her upright as she stood next to a seated Olivia. Above them, the blue awning snapped and fluttered in the breeze, drowning out the final words of interment given by the resident chaplain. Horseshoeing them from behind, the Eckardt County Sheriff's Department stood at attention.

Finished, the chaplain nodded to Olivia.

Elizabeth looked down, waiting for her friend to give the signal. Breaking from the pack behind them, Lila stepped forward and took position on Olivia's left side.

None of the attendees spoke.

Olivia stared at the gleaming brown casket. She had not shed a tear during the funeral. Olivia had claimed she was done crying. Dominic was gone, never coming back. She had no tears left.

Olivia dipped her chin and then raised her arms for Elizabeth and Lila. The two supported her as she rose from her chair. Slowly, Olivia's leg hobbled by the full-length air cast, they moved closer to the casket. Lila released her arm, and

Olivia leaned heavily into Elizabeth as she reached out to lay the bouquet of blue forget-me-nots on the casket lid.

She pressed her palm into the gleaming wood and bowed her head.

Elizabeth, maintaining her support for Olivia, closed her eyes. Every time she closed her eyes, she relived every horrifying hour of that night three weeks ago. She didn't know if she'd ever get over it.

"Ellie," Olivia whispered. "What am I going to do?" Her voice wavered.

Lila moved into place and slipped her arm around Olivia's waist.

"I don't know what to do," Olivia choked out.

"For now, don't worry about that," Elizabeth assured her. At some point, she would tell Olivia about her parents. Today was not that day.

"We've got you," Lila added.

Olivia tilted her head and rested it on Lila's.

Elizabeth looked over her shoulder at the uniformed men and woman watching them. Her gaze latched onto Rafe standing beside his brother but watching her.

She knew what he was thinking. She had been thinking it every day since they made the funeral arrangements for Dominic. They had come so close to burying him along with Dominic.

Unable to consider it a second longer, Elizabeth looked away. She couldn't bring herself to be around him longer than necessary and never alone.

Olivia lifted her head. "Okay," she said softly.

Together, Elizabeth and Lila assisted her back to her

chair. Once she was seated, the chaplain gave the funeral director the approval to lower the casket.

Listening to the crank rattle as the straps lowered the remains of a man Elizabeth had highly respected, she did her best not to dwell on how he died. There would be no twenty-one-gun salute. No "Taps." Nothing to mark the passing of a man willing to sacrifice himself for others.

Dominic might have made some terrible decisions in his life, but one thing remained true. He cared. He loved Olivia.

Elizabeth wouldn't let his sacrifice go unnoticed. As long as she had the means, she would keep his legacy alive.

LILA NOTICED HIM as the chaplain finished his words of interment. Standing next to the road.

After those who attended the funeral and interment dispersed and she'd seen to Olivia's escort, Lila crossed the graveyard.

Horatio shifted his hands from behind his body to clasp them in front. He gave her a respectful nod as she joined him. "Deputy."

"Mr. Johnson." She looked back to where Elizabeth and Kyle were assisting Olivia into a car, then returned her attention to Horatio. "Why didn't you come to be with her?"

He gazed across the graveyard, a look of longing in his eyes. "She'll never be able to look at me and not hate me."

"I guess you're right about that."

Horatio cleared his throat. "I came to pay my respects. I also came to ask you something."

Lila frowned.

"You were given a key. Did you ever learn what it belonged to?"

"No."

He reached into his blazer and withdrew an envelope. "Two weeks ago, this arrived in a larger envelope addressed to me. This was addressed for you." He held it out.

Lila stared at the pristine white envelope with her name written in neat, precise handwriting. Dominic's handwriting. She met Horatio's gaze. "Do you know what's in it?"

"It wasn't addressed to me. It's not my business."

She took it and slid a fingernail under the sealed flap. Inside was a single sheet of folded stationary. Before she removed it, she looked at Horatio once more.

"How did you know about the key?"

"Before everything went to shit, he called me. Made me swear I would take Olivia away. Things were getting hot for him and Booker, his brother, and he was certain it would end badly. He told me that in the event he died, I would receive a package. Once I had it, I was to reach out to you."

"But I thought Olivia sent you to me."

"She did. What she didn't know was, I was already aware of you." He tapped the letter. "Dominic said he had given you the key to the whole operation and something extra. I have a feeling that letter explains it all."

"What about the money? Olivia said there were millions in your possession."

"Did she now? I don't know anything about any money." He dipped his head. "Now, if you'll excuse me, I need to return home."

Lila watched him retreat to a dark-gray sedan parked along the street. "Horatio."

He paused and turned to her.

Lila glanced around and then hurried over to him. She removed the letter and shoved it into her uniform pocket. "Do you have a pen?"

He produced one. Lila scrawled out a name and a long-memorized Social Security number along with her cell. She held out the envelope and the pen.

"When you get back to Chicago, would you do me a favor?"

"For you, yes."

Lila pointed at the name. "Find her. Then call me."

Horatio folded the envelope and tucked it away with his pen. "Stay safe, Deputy."

She smiled. "Stay out of trouble, Mr. Johnson."

After Horatio slipped into the passenger seat of the sedan, she sensed a presence coming to her side. He slipped his arm around her.

"What did he want?" Kyle asked.

"To give me a letter." She pulled it out of her pocket and unfolded it.

After reading the contents, she stopped and looked up at Kyle. "Oh my God."

Deep in the morgue cooler unit was a loose steel panel. Behind that panel was a safe built into the wall. The key Lila had been given unlocked the safe. Inside the safe was all the evidence, all the information on the unfortunate souls who lost their lives for another man's greed, and possessions to return to the families. It was Dominic's life insurance policy in the event he was killed and those involved got away.

Lila stared back at the graveyard. "The dead have their requiem."

THE END

AUTHOR'S NOTE

When I started this book, I had no clue how deep down a rabbit hole I would go, or how far off my normally beaten path I would take. As a fiction author writing novels that lean heavily on police procedure and forensics, I have a lot of research to do. Some of this I've been doing long enough it comes easily. The forensics aren't so easy for me. I spent a lot of time combing through material to get things as close to accurate as possible, however, I did take creative license for some things. If it doesn't seem possible to you, it might not be, but for it to work in my novel, I made it possible.

There is a black market for organ trafficking and it's here in North America. The research I did on it noted the victims were usually left alive and only one organ taken. But I'm certain there's a ring out there harvesting all they can take and killing their victims.

I always recall a word of criticism imparted to me by a family member way back when my first novel was published. *It's too farfetched.*

Maybe so, but the entertainment world is meant to take you out of reality and entertain you. I always remind people, truth is stranger than fiction. I'm here to entertain you. So, enjoy this crazy, screwed-up world I've created in Eckardt County.

ACKNOWLEDGMENTS

First, foremost, and always, honor goes to the One who gave me this talent and drive.

There are days I can't believe I get to be an author and with such a fantastic crew at Tule. It's such a privilege to be an author for Tule. Thank you Jane, Meghan, Cyndi, Mia, and to all of the new faces who have joined the ranks at Tule. Hats off to Lee Hyat for another fantastic cover.

I will scream it to the ends of the earth: I have one of the best editors in the biz. The mark of a great editor/author relationship comes in the fact that the editor can read her author as well as Julie reads me. I'm so glad we continued working together at this level. Julie truly is the best.

My beta readers, Rachel and Jenn, are the sounding board all authors should have. I can't do any of this without either one of them. Rachel has the writer eye to catch me on those details along with the right connection for asking some of my more weird medical questions. And Jenn is my first reader. She knows how to delve into the mystery, suspense side and make sure I keep it simple. Both are my closest friends and brutally honest readers. If it won't work, or I went too far off the deep end, they get me back on track. Love ya both!

My kids have grown up, yet they're still here. When I

started this journey, they were babies. Now I have young adults out there making me proud to be their mom. I love you all.

My role as a secondary parent has been extended in regard to a gaggle of nieces and nephews who think it's awesome to have an aunt who is an author. They all keep me on my game.

Then there is my partner in this crazy thing we call life. We've been through hell and back again, and here we still stand as husband and wife. Love you, Shawn.

If you enjoyed *A Requiem For The Dead*,
you'll love the other books in the…

BENOIT AND DAYNE MYSTERY SERIES

Book 1: *The Killer in Me*

Book 2: *Hush, My Darling*

Book 3: *Straight for the Kill*

Book 4: *A Requiem For The Dead*

Available now at your favorite online retailer!

ABOUT THE AUTHOR

Winter Austin perpetually answers the question: "were you born in the winter?" with a flat "nope," but believe her, there is a story behind her name. A lifelong Midwest gal with strong ties to the agriculture world, Winter lives in Iowa with her husband and bevy of four-legged critters and a flock of fluffy velociraptors. She is the author of multiple novels.

Thank you for reading

A REQUIEM FOR THE DEAD

If you enjoyed this book, you can find more from all our great authors at TulePublishing.com, or from your favorite online retailer.

TULE
PUBLISHING

www.ingramcontent.com/pod-product-compliance
Lightning Source LLC
Chambersburg PA
CBHW022247020726
47496CB00004B/1097